HEARTS
ON
THIN
ICE

Also available by Katie Kennedy
The Presidents Decoded
The Constitution Decoded
What Goes Up
Learning to Swear in America

HEARTS ON THIN ICE

A Novel

KATIE KENNEDY

alcove
press

Published in the United States by Alcove Press, an imprint of The Quick Brown Fox & Company LLC.

Alcove Press and its logo are trademarks of The Quick Brown Fox & Company LLC.

Library of Congress Catalog-in-Publication data available upon request.

ISBN (paperback): 978-1-63910-773-5
ISBN (ebook): 978-1-63910-774-2

Cover design by Ana Hard

Printed in the United States.

www.alcovepress.com

Alcove Press
34 West 27th St., 10th Floor
New York, NY 10001

First Edition: June 2024

10 9 8 7 6 5 4 3 2 1

For my parents, John Robert McFarland and
Helen Karr McFarland, who showed me
what happily ever after looks like

CHAPTER ONE

Boston

Last March

Nick Sorensen pushed his hair out of his eyes. It had gotten shaggy
while he was in the hospital. His mother leaned forward, gave him a
fake smile, and released the hand brake on his wheelchair. Nick had
hands—he could operate the damn lever himself. But she needed to
fuss, and it was too much trouble to argue. Nothing seemed real anymore—not even his mother.

"Okay, here we go!" she said.

Across the room, his dad pushed up from the window ledge, holding Nick's discharge papers. Nick gave the room a final glance.
Through the window he could see a sliver of TD Garden, the ice arena
where he played.

Had played. The team had dropped him while he was in the hospital. One of the best forwards in the NHL, and they'd straight up
released him. They didn't think he could come back.

He shoved his hands over the wheels, propelling himself the hell out of there. The nurses applauded as he passed their station, and people in the corridors stepped to the side and clapped and took photos.

And then there were the logistics of getting him in the car and the drive to his apartment—thank god it had an elevator. He and Sammy had almost taken a place that didn't, but it had been too close to a couple of Sammy's exes, so they'd rented an apartment in a bigger building. It had a good view of Boston and no known feminine hazards.

When they got to his apartment door, his parents stood back. He had left this place laughing, with Sammy, bumping shoulders, off to meet four teammates to help with a destination proposal one of the guys had planned. They'd ended up with a crumpled fuselage in a field.

Nick turned the key, and his dad pushed the door open. He wheeled himself in and stared. It wasn't the apartment he had left.

"Um, Kaylee and Matthew came a couple of weeks ago," his mom said softly. "They needed to get Sammy's things out of here. They just . . . needed to get it done."

He nodded, blinking. So Sammy's parents had talked to his parents about it, not him. He'd stopped being in charge of his apartment when he lost control of everything else.

"They said if they got anything wrong to let them know. They asked if we wanted to be here, but we thought they should have privacy."

"And we didn't have more vacation time," his dad said. His mom shot him a poison look. Nick wasn't supposed to know how hard it had been on his parents, the call about the crash and then him being in the hospital so long. They had come immediately, stayed for a week, and then, when he'd been transferred to the rehab wing for another six weeks, they'd taken turns. He'd told them to go home, but one of them was there every day anyway, which was pointless because he wasn't talking. Mostly he looked out the window. His teammates who hadn't been on the plane had shifted through in twos and threes. They brought him contraband food and classic video game cartridges and team updates. And they left quickly, in case plane crashes were contagious.

"Nick?" It was his dad.

Nick blinked and wheeled to the refrigerator. Someone had cleaned it out. He pulled out the silverware drawer—empty. The waffle maker wasn't on the counter. Going through the kitchen like this was like losing a tooth and poking your tongue into the hole, exploring the parameters of the loss. "Sammy made waffles sometimes. He said that's how you got six-pack abs—having waffles on the inside as scaffolding." He couldn't tell it like Sammy did. It had been funny.

"None of us knew what to do," his mom said, "but they needed to get it over with." He nodded and wheeled into Sammy's room, shoving the door shut behind him. It was profoundly empty. There was more oxygen in outer space. The bed was gone, the dresser, the plant stand. His 3D puzzle of the Great Pyramid. There was a dent in a floorboard where he'd dropped a wine bottle once.

Nick opened the door and wheeled himself out, easing the leg around the doorframe. His parents stood in the living room, his mother holding her own hands. They were watching to see if he was okay, expecting him to settle back into a home with half of everything gone. He ran his thumb across the coffee table. There had been an illustrated book on ancient Egypt there when they left that night, bundled against the cold, Sammy's red scarf bright against his almost black hair. It was gone now. Sammy had given the book to Nick for his birthday, but it made sense that the Gonczys had thought it was Sammy's.

So many losses. Nick's body had become an object strangers discussed and shoved metal plates into. And for all that he loved Sammy's parents, it felt like they'd killed him a second time by removing the traces of him. Nick had thought he could still find him here, somehow. But he was gone. *I need you to not be gone.*

He had to get out of there. He wheeled sharply toward his own bedroom—nearly running over his mother's foot—but he stopped short when he caught a glimpse of Sammy's toothbrush in the bathroom, white crust on the bottom because he never rinsed well enough. Nick nodded toward it, and his father hesitated, then retrieved it and laid it across his palm. Nick closed his fingers around it, shut his eyes, and began to sob. He couldn't keep it. He couldn't throw it away.

He cried until the tears stopped on their own. His parents clung to each other. He held the toothbrush out to his dad, to let him deal with it. Then he wheeled into his bedroom and saw the white dress shirt on his bed. He'd switched shirts at the last minute when he remembered that Dragan had a bunch of white shit for his proposal—banks of white flowers interlaced with twinkle lights, all supposed to glow on the water under the moon. He would probably wear white himself, so Nick had thrown on a blue shirt at the last minute. The white one had lain here all this time, tossed casually on the bed, a mute testament to the tiny hinges of fate. If Nick had worn that shirt, would he have been ready first? Would they have taken his car? Would Sammy have boarded while he parked, instead of the other way around? Because Nick was the only survivor. When he'd taken his seat, he'd condemned the rest of them.

He grabbed viciously at the shirts hanging in his closet and only succeeded in twisting the sleeves.

"Here, honey. You want those down?" his mother said.

"I'm going to pack a suitcase. Grab a few books. Then I'm out of here."

"Do you want to come home?" his dad asked from the doorway. "We can make a bedroom on the first floor."

"Easy peasy!" his mother said brightly.

He wanted to beat the world until it howled. He settled for shaking his head. "I'm going to a hotel. I can't stay here." His parents' house wasn't home anymore. This apartment wasn't home without Sammy. He was homeless.

CHAPTER TWO

Detroit
This season

Nick had once been one of the fastest men in hockey. Now he couldn't even block the door to his apartment. When his doorbell rang, he buzzed Devin into the building foyer, then stepped into the hallway and leaned on a cane to swing his apartment door shut behind him. The point was to keep Devin from seeing inside. It didn't work.

Devin bounded up the stairs with an athlete's grace, a foil pan in his hands. "Vanessa sent a lasagna!" He beamed.

Well, shit.

"Hey, that's nice. Don't let me forget to thank her." Nick tried to take the pan while he stuck his key back in the lock, but the cane was in the way, and Devin wouldn't let go. He was being helpful, damn him.

"I got it," Devin said. Nick hesitated, then bowed to the inevitable and pushed the door open. Devin stepped in and his smile froze. "Dude."

5

"Yeah, I know." Nick took the lasagna and walked around the counter into the kitchen, his cane tapping on the tile.

"You have one chair."

Nick shrugged. "I have one ass." He swung the fridge shut and then turned, his eyes sweeping the apartment. It was a nice place—everything new and high end. He'd furnished it with one easy chair in the middle of the living room. Although to be fair, there was also a mattress on the floor in the bedroom. He patted his pants pocket to make sure he still had his keys, then ushered Devin out.

Before they left, his teammate stopped by the open bedroom door and craned his neck around the doorframe. He didn't say anything until Nick was buckled into the passenger seat of a slick black sports car. Devin pushed the start button, glanced over, and then looked away as he spoke, edging the car out into Detroit traffic. "You can't keep living like that. You know that, right?"

"Thanks for picking me up," Nick said.

Devin slid his eyes sideways but didn't say anything more.

Devin lived in a mansion in the suburbs. The house was pale stone in a vaguely French style, and tastefully landscaped. There were three other cars in the driveway, but they'd left room for Devin, the Red Wheels' captain, to pull in.

"I've got him!" Devin called as they entered through the kitchen door.

Four guys sat around an oval table off the kitchen—André Bouchard, a Black Canadian defenseman; Jakub Cermak, a small Czech left wing; Leif Bjorkland, the Swedish goalie; and Filip Simko, a US defenseman. Nick had played against all four the previous year, and he'd learned more about Detroit's system from going to practice, although he couldn't skate yet. He had a lot to learn—and a lot to unlearn. He'd played with Sammy so long that Nick always knew where Sammy was going to be. Now Nick worried that when he returned to the ice, he'd pass to where Sammy would have been. And how would he explain to the coach why he'd dumped the puck to empty ice?

The cards and chips were already out, the beers opened. "Sit down!" Jakub called. The guys shifted with nervous energy. Now that preseason had started, there was a buzz beneath everything they did, as though their skate blades touching ice completed a circuit. Anyone who thought ice couldn't conduct electricity had never been to an NHL game—that was for damn sure.

"We're ready to take your money," Jakub said cheerfully.

"You better not be talking to me," Devin said, pushing back a chair.

"No, we're gonna fleece the new guy," Jakub said. He grinned at Nick.

"The new guy plans to launch a more vigorous defense than last week," Nick said.

"The new guy's one of the best defensive forwards in the league," Devin said, putting a coaster down at the empty spot.

"And one of the worst poker players," Filip said, laughing, and then turned serious. "So you're getting rid of the cane tomorrow?"

Nick nodded. "They're gonna do a final scan and let the PT torture me for a while. But I ought to get the go-ahead to do full workouts. And they'll let me drive again."

André tapped his bottle on his lower lip. "You miss it?"

"Skating? Hell yes." He pointed at the defenseman's bottle. "Is that a local brew?"

"Yeah. It's pretty good. There's more in the garage."

Devin started to get up, but Nick waved him off. "I took out a loan against my car after last week," Nick joked over his shoulder. "So I'm ready for this game." The guys laughed.

Actually, money wasn't a problem, and they were playing very low stakes. This was a friendly game that Devin had started a few weeks back so Nick could get to know some of his new teammates before he was back on the ice. It was a thoughtful gesture that he'd returned by losing buckets of money to these guys. That hadn't been intentional, but he thought it was nice of him anyway.

Nick knew there were three stairs down to the garage, but he didn't notice the box beside the steps. His cane caught on the flap and when he stepped down it pulled him sideways and he missed a step. He sprawled down the last two steps, landing awkwardly on the box. His shoulder smashed the cardboard and his ribs bounced off the paint cans inside, knocking his teeth together.

"Oh my god," a woman said. Nick looked up from the garage floor. A tall woman with honey hair rushed to help him. She extended a hand down, but he ignored it, pushing off against the cans, which dislodged a lid and knocked the can over. A cold slick of sapphire blue spread across his shirt.

"Shit."

"Oh no," the woman said. "I am so sorry."

Nick stood without using his hands, and leaned out, trying to keep the paint from dripping onto his pants. The woman looked around frantically. No strategically placed rags. Nick sighed and pulled his shirt off, balling it to prevent the ooze from ruining anything else.

"Wow," the woman said.

He looked at the soggy mess in his hand. "Yeah. I don't think I got too much on me."

She stared at him another moment, then darted toward a workbench along the back wall. "Paper towels!" she said triumphantly. She returned with the roll over a finger and pulled two narrow sheets off for him. He dabbed at his side, which was faintly sapphire.

"Too bad our colors are red and white," he joked. She just bit her lip. "Have I got everything?" He held his arms out slightly and turned in a slow circle.

"There's a little bit on your back."

He whacked at it with a fresh paper towel, but she shook her head. "Um, you mind?" he said, holding it out to her. She flushed bright and scraped gently at his back. Was it inappropriate to ask a random woman to swab the paint off your bare torso? Of course it was. God, he was an idiot.

"Just need to get this wet!" she said, her voice strained and high. She bounded up into the kitchen and a moment later Devin and André appeared in the door.

"So, you've met Nick's abs," Devin called to the woman.

"Yep," she said, her voice still high. She hurtled back toward Nick, a look of determination on her face. "Turn." He swiveled so his back was to her, but that made him face Devin and André while she scrubbed him pink.

"You're not hurt, right?" Devin said.

"No."

"Good," André said. "Because we're definitely laughing at you, but we'd feel bad about it if you were hurt."

"Why is Nick getting a sponge bath in the garage?" Leif said, his head popping between Devin and André's.

"Okay, I think I'm clean," Nick said. "Um, thanks."

"Of course," the woman murmured. "I am so, so sorry."

"That's your paint?" he said. She nodded.

"Okay, let's fleece Nick now," one of the guys at the table called.

"Don't worry about it, Alyssa," Devin said. "He's going to be blue all evening anyway, because he's a terrible poker player."

"Hey now," Nick said amiably, reentering the house and maneuvering around chair legs and feet to his spot.

Devin grabbed the beer Nick had been going for and then retrieved a T-shirt from the back of the house while the honey-haired woman disappeared into the thicket of rooms. Nick pulled the shirt on, and

Devin gathered the cards and began to deal. Nick glanced around the house. There was a family room off the kitchen table area, and a glassed-in, three-season room that overlooked a deck and beyond it, a manicured yard. Then a bunch of rooms up front. It was a lot of house to maintain. Harder than a chair and a mattress, for sure.

Devin's wife, Vanessa, a gorgeous brunette, stood in the three-season room with the tall woman who had helped him when he'd been ambushed by her paint cans in the garage. She was pretty, and he already knew she was a good blusher. He smiled to himself. Vanessa ran her hand over a pillow, and Nick watched them until André lodged an elbow in his ribs. He grunted and picked up his cards. Play began and Nick called.

He kept an eye on the women. A moment later the blonde—Alyssa—glanced over, saw him looking, and smiled. She had warm brown eyes and a stunning smile, and he felt like he'd been caught doing something he shouldn't.

He covered by saying, "I think your wife is replacing you with a pillow."

Devin swiveled in his seat to see Vanessa caressing the accessories. The throw pillow was turquoise and shimmery and set off the other turquoise accents in the room, adding a pop of color after a kitchen with whitewashed cabinets and a family room in neutral tones and light wood furniture. "Yeah, that's the designer who redid that room. I didn't introduce you, did I? Sorry about that." Devin examined his cards and bit his lip. "It's a final walk-through or something." He rapped his knuckles on the table to pass. "They've become friends, and now I'm caught in an endless cycle of having rooms redone because they want to hang out."

"They could just have lunch," Leif said with a thick accent. "Call."

"But that wouldn't cost me as much money," Devin said.

They threw their cards down, and the Swede grinned and raked the pot in.

"Speaking of losing money," Nick said.

"Yeah, *you* can go broke even without buying furniture," Devin said, and then his eyes widened.

"No," Nick said.

"Hey, Vanessa!" Devin called.

"No."

"Could you guys come over here?"

"No!" Nick hissed.

Vanessa and the designer walked over, smiling. The designer glanced at his torso and then looked away, blushing. Nick gathered the cards in and began to shuffle with a vengeance.

"It's my deal, man," the left wing next to him said.

"It's mine now."

"Vanessa, you remember Nick."

He looked up and smiled. "Thanks for the lasagna. That was very thoughtful." The captain's wife beamed at him.

"And this is Alyssa Compton, our interior designer. Or decorator, or something," Devin said.

"The paint terrorist," Nick said, meaning to make light but regretting it when he saw the look of horror on the blonde woman's face.

"Again, I am so sorry," she said.

Nick waved a hand. "Nice to meet you. Officially." She smiled tightly. She looked as comfortable as he felt. "Sorry to interrupt your walk-through." He began dealing.

"Alyssa, Nick is in possession of the saddest apartment in all Detroit," Devin said. "He desperately needs your services."

"Oh, I'd be happy to do a consul—"

"No, thanks," Nick said. "I like it fine the way it is."

"What's wrong with it?" Leif, the goalie, asked.

"There's nothing in it," Devin said. They all looked at Nick—Vanessa, Alyssa, and five NHL players.

"I'm a minimalist." He stopped dealing and looked around the table in confusion, then sighed and beckoned for the cards back. He'd dealt out the whole deck. No one said anything. "Be a damn shame if at the end of the season I win the Selke Trophy but lose Apartment of the Year." Alyssa crossed her arms. Was he being a jerk? He just wanted them to leave him alone. He dealt again and this time did it right.

André picked up his hand, sighed, and said, "Yeah, I'm gonna need another beer."

"Don't forget the snacks on the island," Vanessa said.

"There is no chance of that," Devin said, wrapping an arm around her hips and giving her a squeeze. The other guys grunted in agreement.

Alyssa leaned across the table and handed Nick her business card. Her arm was long and lean and her hair swung as she moved. "If you ever want a consultation, I'd be happy to take a look. I can do minimalist." She gave him a dazzling smile.

"Thanks." He gave what he hoped was an indifferent smile and raised, just to have something to do.

"I could do something hockey themed if that's your thing. Put in a potato baker for you. Maybe a chicken sculpture." She shrugged and it made her hair bounce.

Nick stared at her. "Potatoes? Chickens? You want to turn my apartment into a farm?"

She laughed. "No, like old-time hockey. It was just a joke. I wouldn't really . . ."

"Yeah, you're gonna have to explain that," André said.

Her eyes lit up and she gestured as she spoke. "Well in the old days, they baked potatoes in foil in the locker room before a game, and then the players put the foil in their gloves to keep their hands warm. And they had a nice snack for later."

Nick laughed.

"It replenished their carbohydrates or something," she said defensively.

André flipped an empty chip bag inside out and stuck his hand in it. "I'm putting on the foil!" he said, waving it around. The guys cracked up. He wasn't being mean—it was just funny.

Nick lowered his head and said, "They taped foil on their hands so they could do more damage when they fought. It was an old WHA thing."

"Nope. I'm pretty sure it was potatoes," Alyssa said.

Nick's eyes sparkled. This woman was gorgeous, but she sure didn't know anything about hockey. "And the chickens?"

"It was just one chicken. Although I suppose they needed one in each town."

"I'm not following this," Leif said.

"Nobody is," Devin said.

"For the beginning of the game! So they knew which direction to go." She looked at them, waiting for them to get it. "My stepfather explained it to me. Instead of a coin toss or whatever you do now, they used to have a chicken. They'd take it to the middle of the ice at the beginning of the game and the referee would let it loose. Whichever direction it flew, that was the way the home team headed that period."

Nick laughed loud and long. He hadn't laughed that hard in months. He wasn't sure he'd laughed at all. "The chicken *flew*?"

"Yes," Alyssa said with great confidence. "And they needed the chicken wire to keep it from going into the stands and, you know, messing up people's hair." The guys howled. Jakub fell out of his seat. Vanessa dropped her head and put a hand on Alyssa's arm, opened her mouth, and then just shook her head. She and Alyssa headed out into the driveway, stepping over Jakub wiping tears from his eyes.

"Should anybody tell her the chicken wire was for stopping the puck before they had plexiglass?" Devin said.

"Definitely not," Nick said. "I mean, she was so confident." He laughed again and André waved his foil hand in his face.

They finally settled down, and the game began again. Devin lowered his head and stared at Nick from under his eyebrows. "Vanessa says she needs work. She's with some agency whose head is an old battle-ax, and she has to do so much business every month or something."

"They let a chicken loose at center ice. And it flew." Nick wiped an eye with his knuckle.

"You know a lot about this," Leif said. "The agency. Not the chicken."

Devin shook his head. "You can't imagine how much I hear about this interior design stuff. If I had a nickel for every time someone said the word 'curtain'—"

"You could give it all to me," André said, raking in the pot.

"Seriously? Damn," Devin said. He leaned back on two chair legs to snag a bag of baby carrots off the island, and ripped it open, then turned his attention back to Nick. "This girl needs business, and you desperately need to spiff your place up. You're not planning to live like that forever, are you?"

"Of course not," Nick mumbled. *Yes, I am.*

"Good."

"Next week I want to hear about your consultation," Filip said, waggling an eyebrow. "She's hot."

After that they concentrated on the game, drinking beer, laughing, and trash-talking one another loudly. When Vanessa came back in from seeing Alyssa off, she curled up with a novel on a sofa in the family room. Nick glanced up once and saw her looking at him appraisingly. She smiled faintly and went back to her book. It gave him an uneasy feeling, people watching him. And tomorrow, when he lost the cane and got back in the game, it was going to get worse.

CHAPTER THREE

Vanessa led Alyssa out into the driveway. Alyssa was thrilled that Vanessa was trying to get her a new client. She needed it—and word of mouth was the way to get business. But the brown-haired guy with the jawline—Jesus, you could slice apples with that thing—wasn't just not interested; he was standoffish. Maybe that's what happened when a guy with a cane tripped on your box. Still, she'd handed him a card with a smile and a plucky attitude. You had to keep up appearances, no matter how you felt.

She'd worn pretty black sandals and hadn't realized until she was in the Nilssons' house that one of them had started squeaking. It didn't used to squeak. How could that happen? She didn't have a replacement pair and couldn't afford one. For now, she'd discovered that if she curled her toes under, the squeaking stopped, and so she'd stomped around this gorgeous house with her left toes curled, and good grief, could she feel more awkward?

Well, yes. Because then there was that big guy with all the muscles who had no interest in a consultation. He wasn't as handsome as he thought he was.

Okay, he might be. And my god, his torso. *"I'm a minimalist."* He certainly wasn't when it came to muscles. His apartment probably had one free-form vase holding a stem of freesia on top of his expensive Scandinavian dresser. Where he kept all the T-shirts that would hug those abs. Which she wasn't thinking about. Why would she think about him? He hadn't even known about the chicken.

He'd have a white sofa. Maybe *that's* why he was so smug—he was a hockey player in his twenties living with a white sofa and hadn't stained it yet. There'd be an abstract print over it that someone else had chosen and told him it looked sophisticated. They'd have bought it to go with the sofa, and he wouldn't know the artist's name—or even realized a person had made that art. The closest he ever came to paint was landing in a box of it.

"I love it," Vanessa said, giving herself a hug for a moment. Alyssa turned her attention back to her friend. "You carried over the turquoise accents from the kitchen, but it's such a different space, and I just love it! You're a genius."

Alyssa flushed. "It was so much fun to do! Thank you for letting me play—with your credit card!"

"When we need to do a nursery, I'll be giving you a call." Alyssa's eyes widened. "No, no!" Vanessa laughed. "But soon, maybe." She looked back over her shoulder at the house. "It's just so big. I don't think we needed that much house, but it's really, really fun." They laughed. "Thank you for making it a calm place instead of an 'oh my gosh what is this room for?' place."

"Oh, it was my pleasure." Alyssa beamed. "I'm going to miss doing rooms for you. You and Devin get to work so I can design that nursery."

Vanessa laughed. "I wonder what he'd say if I kicked the guys out and dragged him upstairs."

"I don't imagine he'd complain."

"We'll work on Nick and see if we can't persuade him to get a designer—and help keep Cruella off your back."

"Yeah, but he did not seem interested. Maybe because he tripped on some of my stuff." She patted the trunk of her car to indicate it was all loaded. "Or he was embarrassed about not knowing about the baked potatoes."

"That definitely wasn't it," Vanessa said. She hesitated. "He's got a lot going on. You know which one he is, right?"

"The brown-haired guy with blue eyes and bulging muscles? Didn't notice. Hey, is he single?"

Vanessa's eyebrows shot up. "Very. Want me to—"

Alyssa flushed. "No! I meant if he's married I could talk to his wife. She'd probably be the one making decisions anyway."

"When I asked if you knew who he is, I meant the accident." Alyssa looked at her blankly. "The airplane carrying the Boston hockey players that went down in January, and there was only one survivor? He's the survivor."

Alyssa's eyes grew huge. "He's *that* guy? Oh my god. I thought he was all crunched up."

Vanessa shrugged. "He was. He's in Detroit now and ready to hit the ice again."

"Wow. Wow." Alyssa thought for a moment. "It wasn't the whole team, right?"

"No, it was six guys going to a location where one of them wanted to propose. He had some elaborate thing planned. But they never got there."

"Was Nick the guy proposing?"

Vanessa blinked at her. "Um, no. It was Dragan Novak. His girl-friend went back to Croatia. God, it's so sad."

"Nick's the guy who survived that crash," Alyssa said to herself, turning this information in her mind. It didn't match her impression of the man. Well, of his apartment with its white sofa and expensive Scandinavian dresser and the faux-sophisticated painting in the living room. Maybe she should give him a break about his *minimalism*.

"Hey, I wanted to ask you something," Vanessa said. "And no pressure. But my church has a homeless shelter for women and kids."

"That's great."

"Yeah. It's in some old Sunday School rooms that we don't need anymore because there are so few young people. We thought we'd get some good out of them, you know?"

Alyssa nodded.

"It's going well enough that we're making it permanent, and we want to spruce up the area. More than just fresh paint, but we don't know what exactly." She squinched her mouth to the side, an apology for what was about to come.

Alyssa decided to make it easier for her. "And you want a pro bono consultation?"

"No! I would pay you for the consultation. But the volunteers want to do as much of the work as they can themselves, so we probably wouldn't have you do much of the implementation. So jack up that consult fee!"

Alyssa laughed.

"Could you give us some direction, though? We want to create a bright, welcoming space, and right now it has a bad case of the dingies."

"I'd be happy to. Which church is it?"

"Trinity. It's next to that small park off of—"

"Does it have a food pantry?" Alyssa asked, gripping her bad sandal with her toes. "An outside thing?"

"Yes!" Vanessa said. "A cute white cupboard with glass doors, like a little free library, only bigger and with nonperishable food. You know it, then?"

"No," Alyssa said, flushing, and then realized how stupid that sounded. "I mean, I've driven by, but I'm not familiar . . . I don't know the area really. It's a big city."

"Sure," Vanessa said, looking puzzled. "Um, can we schedule some time for you to swing by and take a look?"

She could not. It would be matter touching antimatter. The world would explode. She could not explain this either—not to the wife of the Red Wheels' captain outside their mansion. "Oh shoot, you know what? I can't. Stacey doesn't let us do jobs like that. I'm so sorry! I would have loved to, but you know how she is."

"Sure," Vanessa said, squinting slightly. "What kind of jobs exactly?"

"I'm so sorry! It's a stupid rule. I can't afford to alienate the agency head, though."

"No, of course not. But I mean, I would pay."

"I know! Such a dumb rule." Alyssa threw her hands out in a "what can you do?" gesture, trying not to think about the disappointment in Vanessa's voice. She quickly thanked her again for her business and then walked around to her car door. With Vanessa standing right there, she couldn't curl her toes under. Vanessa would have noticed a thing like that. So she just had to let her sandal squeak.

CHAPTER FOUR

The next Tuesday Alyssa was in her small office, flipping through some upholstery samples, when the door to the agency chimed. Stacey's Interiors was a small modern building with a parking lot in front and a sign, with an intertwined "S" and "I," that was impossible to read. There was no receptionist—whoever was in took phone calls, and when a client was expected, their designer met them at the door. But when it was a drop-by, Alyssa was supposed to leave her back-corner office and make it to the lobby in a timely fashion. She'd always wanted a corner office—she'd just never thought it would have one narrow window that overlooked the trash receptacle.

She walked to the lobby, passing a consultation room, where one of the senior designers was talking with a couple of men in their fifties, and then going past Stacey Herself's office. Stacey was positioned so she could overhear anything in the lobby or consultation rooms if she wanted to. She had asked Alyssa her plan for the very first interior she had done here, and then had poked her head into the consultation room when Alyssa was there with her clients. She'd smiled, glanced at the design Alyssa was showing them, and suggested that she add an interior balcony. Which the clients loved—and was a thing Alyssa had told Stacey she was going to suggest. Stacey was not exactly *liked* in the design world, but she was respected, and this job was Alyssa's chance to make connections and build a client base so that someday she could open her own place.

When Alyssa had been in middle school, she would shut her eyes at night and imagine her someday house. She had five of them in different styles, from Victorian gingerbread to ultramodern concrete. She would choose one house to think about each night and would mentally walk through the rooms, adding furniture or changing what she'd done the last time. In her white clapboard farmhouse, she'd set pewter salt and pepper shakers on the shelf of a Hoosier cabinet in the kitchen. She'd open the glass-fronted bookcases in the columns of a craftsman bungalow and imagine the click of the hardware. She could walk through every room of her five secret houses, trail a finger over soft handmade quilts and clink a nail on the crystal in her pantry.

But then, when she'd open her eyes, she could still see stars out the car window.

This was how she was getting her own home: by designing them for other people. Someday she would have a key to her own house, despite Stacey. Until then, she'd be gritting her teeth a lot.

Alyssa hurried to the lobby, her skirt swishing as she walked. When she came around the corner, she was surprised to find Nick Sorensen, of all people, standing just inside the front door and looking deeply unhappy. He smiled when he saw her.

"Hi," they said at the same time.

"Um, I don't know if you remember me," he said. "I was at Devin and Vanessa's last week."

"Of course I do! Nick Sorensen, right?"

"Yeah. Um, I guess I need to have my apartment fixed up." *Need to? That was a strange way to put it.* "Is that something you can do?" He flushed. "I mean, I know it's something you *can* do. Um, do you have time?"

He was nervous. Why did that seem charming?

"Sure! Why don't you come with me to a consultation room and tell me about your space, and then . . ."

Stacey came around the corner. She was wearing a navy suit and heavy makeup. She smiled, but it didn't reach her eyes. Alyssa had always assumed that was because of the Botox, but a designer who'd worked there longer said it wouldn't have anyway. "What have we here?" Stacey said, looking Nick up and down. He was wearing casual pants and a cream waffle-weave Henley shirt, with the sleeves shoved up. It was getting a little cooler, day by day. Alyssa was pushing the season with her drapey skirt and cream blouse, but her fall wardrobe needed sprucing up, and she hadn't gotten to it yet.

Nick didn't shift under her gaze. "Just hiring Alyssa here," he said, nodding.

"Ah," Stacey said. "What do you do, Mr. . . .?"

"I play for the Red Wheels."

Stacey's eyes stayed the same, but her mouth made a tiny "O." Nick had money. This could be a good contract. Was Stacey going to poach him? She'd done that to one of the other designers a couple of weeks ago. An endocrinologist had come in and announced that she had a new house and wanted to work without a budget, and Stacey had swooped out of her office . . .

"Delightful. Let me take you into one of the consultation rooms, and you can explain your project to me. Shall we?" Stacey moved over and took his arm, wrapping her acrylic nails around his bicep. Alyssa's heart fell. Stacey hadn't been able to poach Vanessa because she had briefly been hospitalized when Vanessa came in—office scuttlebutt was that Stacey needed another transfusion of the souls of virgins to keep her young. Alyssa was good for a few months off of the income from Vanessa's projects, but Nick was a client who'd come in because of *her* contacts, not someone random off the street.

"No, I'm here for Alyssa," Nick said. "Thanks, though."

"Here for Alyssa." Alyssa felt a flush rise across her chest and throat. Her name sounded good in his deep, husky voice.

"Mr. . . . ? What is your name?"

Nick carefully disengaged his arm. "I'm a client of Alyssa's."

"That's not how we're structured," Stacey said, a bit of steel in her voice. "I assign projects to the different designers."

Bullshit. You poach other people's clients.

"Alyssa already has her hands full with some . . . starter projects. You need someone more experienced."

Alyssa pulled her mouth sideways and gave Nick an apologetic smile, then dropped her eyes and played with her bracelet.

"No, I'm not doing that," Nick said. "I'm not hiring an agency. I want to work with her."

"I'm afraid that's not possible," Stacey said.

"Okay." He shrugged. "You have your phone?" he asked Alyssa. She looked up, startled, then hurried to her office and came back with it, holding it out to him. Her gold glitter case looked silly in his big hand. He typed in his contact information and passed it back, brushing her fingers in the process. His hands were dry and hard and strong, and . . . he was talking.

"I'm sorry?" she said, blushing.

"I said you have my number. If you want to do a job off the books, give me a call."

"We don't do jobs off the books!" Stacey said, clearly outraged. "Then the agency doesn't get a cut!"

Nick shrugged. "I'm okay with that."

"Sir!" He'd never told her his name. "You can't come in here and steal one of my designers!"

"Looks like that's what you were doing with one of her clients," he said. He smiled at Alyssa, then mouthed, "Good luck." He turned and walked out, his shoulders almost filling the doorframe. Alyssa watched him walk out to a small red sports car and open the door.

"Well, go!" Stacey hissed. "Don't you dare lose a client."

Alyssa stared at her, then ran into the parking lot. Her sandal squeaked, and he looked over. "Um, I can work with you if you want. There is a consultation fee." She named the price, adding fifty dollars on a whim because she really did need new shoes.

He was in the driver's seat but stood back up and leaned against the car, ankles crossed, the door open. "Great. I don't want to go back in there, though. Can we go someplace else?"

"Yeah! Sure. Um, can you wait just a minute? I need my laptop."

He nodded and she ran back in for her go bag of things she'd need. She stopped for a second to put on lipstick in front of the mirror in her office. That was totally appropriate before going out with a client. It had nothing to do with the shape of his thighs when he got out of the car, or the little commas around his mouth when he smiled.

Stacey handed her a contract as she rushed past. "Make sure he signs this." Alyssa nodded absently and stuffed it in her bag, then rushed back out to his car. They got in and he drove away, paying attention to traffic first and then saying, "Have you had lunch? We could talk at a restaurant, if that works."

She glanced at the clock in his bird's-eye maple dashboard. Already eleven thirty. "Um, sure. I'll need to get in and see the space though. And I need to measure everything."

He bit the inside of his cheek. "I could send you measurements."

"I need to see the space."

He nodded and drove them for several minutes, then slowed on a tree-lined street in a nice neighborhood. "Food preferences? You vegan or anything?" She shook her head. He found a spot and pulled in directly in front of a small café. "This look okay to you? It's healthy stuff—no milkshakes or anything."

"Looks great."

The restaurant had a small arbor over the entryway, with deep purple potted clematis climbing overhead. A sandwich board advertised specials in colored chalk, and when Nick held the door open for her and she stepped inside, she saw that the entire menu was written on a gigantic chalkboard hung over the ordering counter. The place was small and crowded and had a definite hippie vibe. "Favorite spot?" she said.

"I like any place that cooks for me," he said. "But yeah. It's in the neighborhood, and it's good."

They went up to the counter and ordered. Nick got a grilled chicken, bean, and mango salad with couscous, and Alyssa went with the salad maison with a basil vinaigrette. Nick paid and guided them to a table by the wall.

"This is a fun place," Alyssa said. "A lot of energy." He nodded. The server came and poured water for them, and when he left, she tapped her glass with her fingernails. "So tell me about your project."

He looked at her for a long moment without talking, then took a drink. *Stalling? Seriously?* "I have a two-bedroom apartment and none of it is . . . decorated." He shrugged.

"Okay." He didn't say anything more. "What do you want done with the space?"

"I really don't care. Just"—he rolled his hand outward—"whatever makes it look normal and gets my coach off my back."

"Your coach doesn't like your apartment?"

"Devin didn't like my apartment and told the coach, and he gave me a choice. One option was having it fixed up, and that's what I chose. But I don't want to do it myself."

She looked at him for a long beat, and then the server was there with their order. Nick grabbed a fork and dug into his food. "You don't sound very excited about it. People usually have fun having their place redone."

"Yeah, um, sorry about that. I appreciate what you do."

"Just you don't really want it done?"

"Yeah."

They stopped talking for a moment while the waiter delivered their food. "I got chicken," Nick said. "Now we won't know which direction to go on offense at the start of a game." He smiled to take any sting out of it.

"*Anyway*," Alyssa said, "explain this to me. Why don't you want your place done? It's incredibly fun." He grabbed his water glass again. No wonder he was such a bad poker player—he absolutely had a tell. "You just want to get away with a minimal job?"

"Yep."

"Am I doing the whole apartment or just one room?"

Hope flashed in his eyes for a moment; then he bit the inside of his cheek again. "I think it has to be the whole place."

"What kind of style are you thinking?"

"Normal?"

She laughed. "Okay, I can pull some photos up after I've seen the place, and get an idea of what you like. Color, furniture, accessories— things like that."

"Can I just have you do it? Is that a thing?"

"Like on a TV show, where you don't even know what it's going to be, and then there's a big reveal?"

He squinted at her. "I don't watch those shows, but I'm going to say yes."

"No. You'll need to approve the design." He sighed and stabbed the last piece of his chicken. "If you don't enjoy talking about throw pillows, you don't have to. I mean, Vanessa and I had a ton of fun playing with swatches and swapping in different lamps, but you absolutely don't have to be that involved as a client. But the point is to make it a space that you like, and I can't do that without you."

He nodded and sat hunched a little in his seat while she continued eating. She hadn't eaten nearly as fast as he had. When she was done, she smiled and said, "Well, let's go to your apartment and get at it, shall we?" And then she realized how that sounded and flushed.

His mouth gave a little quirk, and he opened the restaurant door for her and said, "Absolutely."

CHAPTER FIVE

Alyssa sank into the seat of Nick's sports car. It was fabulous for transportation, but if he ever had to live in it, he'd be screwed. He pulled out and then glanced over at her. "I hope I didn't get you in trouble with that woman."

"At the agency?" she said. He nodded. "No, that was wonderful. I can't believe you stood up to her like that."

He gave her a curious look. "She was trying to steal a client from you, right? Did I misread that?"

"No, you're right. She's a jerk, but she's also really scary." She flushed. Maybe she shouldn't have said out loud that Stacey was a jerk, but there was something . . . solid . . . about this man. Something she trusted.

He gave a soft snort. "Sometimes you have to crash them against the boards the first time you play, and they give you a little more respect the next game."

"Hockey lessons for the interior designer," Alyssa said, smiling.

Nick pulled in behind a modest building made of white stone. It was set back from the street, and all the apartments had small balconies. The entry was faced with marble. He unlocked the door with a fob, and they walked in. He checked his mailbox—nothing. Then he turned and looked at her. And didn't say anything.

"Marble," she said, pointing to the floor, just to get past the awkward moment. "Very pretty."

"Yeah, it's slippery as hell. When I was using the cane, I was always afraid I'd go down."

"You used . . .?" *The accident.* She could see him register that she knew. "Um, when did you stop using it?"

"Just a few days ago. I'm strengthening that leg," he said, touching his left thigh. He stood there.

"So . . ." Alyssa said, cocking her head and raising an eyebrow. He was definitely stalling. What could he have in his apartment that he didn't want her to see? A closet full of whips and leather pants? Maybe a closet full of regular shirts? He *should* be embarrassed about that—it was a crime to cover those abs.

"Second floor," he said. He sighed and led the way up the stairs. He unlocked the door to the first unit, then pushed the door open with tented fingers and let her go in first.

Alyssa walked in, her bag with laptop and measuring tape over her shoulder, and stepped into the empty space. The walls were all white and completely bare. One brown recliner sat in the middle of the living room. "There's nothing here."

"I have a TV and a game system," he said indignantly, pointing toward the wall opposite the chair.

She took off her sunglasses and folded them into her purse. "How long have you lived here?"

"I moved to Detroit in April, but I was in a hotel for a couple of months because it had an accessible bathroom, and I was still in a wheelchair." His face reddened. Apparently he hadn't planned to start by discussing toilets.

She turned in a slow circle. "Wow. It's a blank canvas." She was going to have to rethink this project. "I think I'll start by measuring. Okay?"

He nodded.

The apartment spread to the left of the entry. There was space for a table immediately inside the door, and a kitchen beyond it, both against the wall to the building's hallway. The living room ran on the front of the building. She saw three doors beyond them, to the left of the public rooms—two bedrooms and a bath. The rooms were large, the windows were great, the kitchen had an up-to-date backsplash and fresh white cupboards. It was a great canvas—too bad he'd never done anything with it. *"Minimalist"?* This was just empty.

Alyssa snapped out her metal tape measure and measured each area, wall to wall, noting the dimensions in a blue faux-leather binder. Nick stood in the middle of the room, fists in his pockets. When she got to his bedroom, she took in the mattress on the floor. At least he'd pulled up his blankets. He had suits and a tuxedo hanging in the closet and piles of folded clothes and sweats stacked in trash bags on the floor. So much for the Scandinavian dresser and vase of freesia of her imagination.

She finished the measuring and double-checked that she'd gotten everything she needed. Finally she turned to him. "It's a very nice space." What else could she say? "What do you want from it?"

He looked at her helplessly. She loved that look from a client. Most everybody knew where they wanted to wind up, but they didn't know how to get there. She did, and she could take them. She savored that feeling. It made her feel like a kindly taxi driver stopping for someone in the rain.

"So a typical plan would be to put a table here," she said, indicating the space off the kitchen. "A sofa and probably two chairs here." She waved her hand toward the living room. "Maybe two sofas, or the second one could be a loveseat. It's big enough for that. In the bedroom a dresser, bed, and probably a desk." She glanced around. "Where do you do household paperwork? Like paying bills?"

"I mostly do that online."

"Okay. But where do you process mail?"

"We're at the end of the route, so it doesn't come till I'm gone for games or practice. I pick it up when I get home and dump it on the end of the counter." He nodded toward the kitchen. "Then I mostly throw it away in the morning."

So he'd known his mailbox was empty when he checked it as they came in. He'd been stalling. Interesting.

"Okay, I'm going to give you a space to do that. It can be in your bedroom, or there's room in the living room for a desk. Or we can make the second bedroom a home office."

He flushed. "I want to leave that bedroom alone."

She blinked at him. "*Alone* alone?" He nodded. "It's completely empty."

"Yeah."

"We could make it a combined guest bedroom and office, so it would work for you when you don't have guests, and if you do, you can let them have the run of the place."

He shook his head. "Let's just leave it alone."

"Okay." The client was the boss. Even when he was being stupid. "Any thoughts on the balcony?" She stepped over and slid the door open. The balcony was eight feet by five feet. Plenty big enough for him to come out with a date, sip wine, watch the sunset . . . "I forgot to ask. Which way does your apartment face?"

"East."

"Well, I guess you can watch the sunrise from out here."

"I've done that a few times."

She was surprised. "You got up and watched the sunrise? Where did you sit?"

He smiled ruefully. "I just sat on the balcony floor."

"Huh. Do you have a vision for the space? Do you want to be able to entertain here, or have a chaise lounge so you can read?"

"I guess it would be nice to read out here." She must have looked as surprised as she felt because he said, "I know how to read."

She smiled. "Um, I'm going to show you some photos of rooms, and you tell me what you like and what you don't, okay?"

"Sure." She caught the slight sigh.

Alyssa sank down against the living room wall and sat with her legs pulled sideways. It was a bad day to have worn a skirt, but how would she have guessed the day would go like this when she'd dressed that morning? She booted up while he lowered himself beside her. She was suddenly aware of his bulk, of the ropey muscles in his forearms as he pushed his sleeves up again, of the bunching of his thighs as he sat down. "Does that . . . hurt?" she asked. She knew she shouldn't say anything, but she did anyway. It was a thing she did.

"My leg you mean?" She nodded. "No. I'm doing full workouts, so now my whole body hurts." He grinned and wow, it was a good grin.

"Um." For a moment she had no idea what she was doing in this empty apartment beside this muscular guy with a day's scruff on his jawline.

And then his eyes flew open, and he stood and ran at the kitchen counter that separated the kitchen and living room. He threw his right hand down flat on it and vaulted over, landing in front of the refrigerator. "I forgot the blueberries!" he called. He opened his refrigerator, and for a moment she caught a glimpse of a couple dozen glass containers filled with fruits on the middle shelf and chopped vegetables on the bottom shelf. He pulled a bowl of blueberries out, swung the fridge door shut, and walked back toward her. He set the blueberries between their knees. "In case you're hungry."

"We just had lunch."

"That never stops me." He grinned again and took a handful of berries, then held his fist over his mouth and dribbled them onto his tongue.

"Note to self: do not put top cabinets over that counter," she said. "Do you always go into the kitchen that way?"

"Hmm? Oh, just if I'm in a hurry." He shrugged.

"Well, your leg must be doing pretty well."

"It is. But I made sure I landed on the right one." He nodded toward her laptop. "You have pictures for me to look at?" A graceful way to say he was done talking about the injury.

Alyssa pulled up three photos of living rooms—one contemporary neutrals, one black leather and galvanized steel tables, and an old English manor house look with dark wood and Staffordshire dogs on the mantle. She was pretty sure he wouldn't like the last one, but you never knew.

He shrugged. "They're all fine."

She stared at him. "They're very different. Which one looks most like what you want?"

He shifted on the floor beside her. "I'd really rather have you choose."

"Okay. Let's look at three more." She pulled up the interior of a New England saltbox that was filled with Shaker furniture and primitive quilts, a comfort-focused room filled with a sectional with embedded drink holders, and a breezy beachfront room with pillows covered in a lobster print, a bleached wood floor, and a white slipcover on the sofa. It would be a hard look to pull off in Detroit, but she didn't know what else to do. There was absolutely nothing in this place to give her a key to his taste—or even his personality.

"Nice," he said.

"Which one?"

"All of them?"

She lowered her head and stared up at him from under her brows. "Don't make me crush you against the boards."

He smiled. "There you go."

She flipped the laptop shut. "You said earlier that your coach gave you a choice. Getting your place fixed up or something else? What was the something else?"

He bit the inside of his cheek, then said, "I have a big mouth."

"I'm trying to get a handle on this project. To figure out what will make you happy. Help me out here."

"I don't care what it looks like," he said. She thought about picking up her laptop and braining him with it, but considering the bulk of his shoulder beside her and the hardness of his arm when he'd bumped her as he sat back down with the blueberries, she was pretty sure he could stop her. So she just gave him a long stare. He sighed. "Devin squealed, the rat, and Coach said I have to get it decent and normal or go to counseling." Her eyes flew wide. "So please make it decent and normal so they'll all leave me alone."

"They want you to get counseling because you haven't fixed up your apartment?"

"No, they want me to get counseling because I lost my five best friends in an airplane crash. They think this"—he waved his hand vaguely at the empty space—"is unhealthy. So I have to fix one thing or the other."

She was silent for a moment. "I'm sorry. I shouldn't have pressed you."

"You're doing your job. It's . . . an unusual situation."

"Yeah. So here's the thing—I know absolutely nothing about you, and the only thing your apartment tells me is that you eat exceptionally well." He looked at her, puzzled, and she said, "I got a glimpse inside your refrigerator. You cut up vegetables when you get back from the grocery store, right?"

"I eat dinner really late because of game time, and if I don't have leftovers, I'm too tired to make anything. Also I'm a terrible cook." He grinned again, and there were those commas around his mouth. "This way I can just eat straight out of the containers in the refrigerator."

"You don't eat out?"

"On the road, sure, but not as often here. Maybe I will some once I get to know the guys better." He shrugged.

He's new. He doesn't have good friends yet. Could I possibly poke any more sore spots? God, I'm a jerk.

"Okay, I'm thinking maybe black leather sofas, a framed jersey, a display case for trophies." Did he have trophies? She couldn't ask—what if he didn't? She'd already brought up his leg injury, his friends' deaths, and the fact that he didn't have anybody to eat with. She was becoming the mean girl from junior high. "A comfortable space for you to lounge in, with extra seating, a place to eat, and a center for household paperwork."

"That sounds great. Thanks."

"Do you like that sort of design? Sort of sporty? Because if I show you the design and you don't like it, I can redo it, but it will cost you more."

He hesitated for a moment, then said, "That'll be fine."

Alyssa couldn't think of anything else to say so she took a handful of blueberries and looked around the space again. "How do you feel about houseplants?"

"I almost bought one at the grocery store. But I'll have road trips and it would probably die. I'd feel bad." He flushed.

She nodded and handed him the contract, but she was thinking about his phrasing. He hadn't made a black thumb joke or a comment about his bad luck with plants. He said he didn't want to kill it.

She was going to have to put a fake philodendron on top of his trophy case, and that struck her as terribly sad.

Nick signed and handed the contract back; Alyssa stuck it in her bag, then thanked him for his time. Her eyes swept over the apartment once more before she left. For a man who had absolutely no place to hide anything, it felt like he was hiding plenty.

CHAPTER SIX

Alyssa was at home in her apartment, a sunny space with pearl-gray walls and baseboards she'd painted a glossy white to cover what must have been decades of scuff marks. She was flopped on a charcoal linen sofa, propped up by two textured white pillows. A cheap framed print of Monet's *Nymphéas*, 1916–1919, hung over the sofa, the water lilies floating on a lake of lavender that echoed the purple accents on her white bookcase—an asymmetrical vase and a pair of glass candlesticks. It was a cool, sophisticated space, and she loved it. And she had enough money socked away to keep it for several more months, so that was something.

She sighed and turned back toward her laptop. The design for Nick's apartment was going well. The living room had been fairly easy—big, comfortable furniture, broad tables that could take feet being propped on them, or drinks without coasters. He didn't look like a coaster kind of guy. But it seemed lacking somehow, and she knew what it was—there wasn't anything of *him* in the space. She had some hockey memorabilia and a print of Bobby Orr horizontal over the ice after his 1970 Stanley Cup winning goal. Her stepdad had helped her figure out what to choose there.

But the space felt . . . generic. Too sports bar.

When she'd been measuring the rooms, she'd opened his kitchen cabinets—he had two place settings of Corelle ware. So she'd chosen a dish pattern—round and white. Traditional and serviceable, but so boring. But if she went with square black ones or an Asian-inspired watercolor design—well, what evidence was there that he'd like that? And she wasn't going with a floral. Despite his passivity in the face of an apartment redo, she planned to wow him—to win him over to the side of well-designed interior spaces. She just wasn't sure how.

She looked up his contact info now and texted him. *Nick? This is Alyssa. Could I drop by this afternoon with some samples for you to look at?* She was going to pick up a few single plates so he could feel the weight of them, see them in his hand. And she could gauge his reaction in person—better, in this case, than just sending links. If she tried that, she was almost positive she'd get a *"They're all fine"* return text—and that he wouldn't have opened any of the links.

Her phone rang and she smiled—he'd called! Then she saw the number, shook her head, and answered.

"Alyssa, hear me out," Janet said. It was her traditional greeting.

"It's a wedding, isn't it?"

Alyssa heard her old friend sigh through the line. "It's always a wedding. They're the worst. I have all the table decorations to do yet, and there was a delivery mix-up, and I just . . . need some help."

"Where are you?" Alyssa asked.

"Doing it on-site. St. John's Lutheran. The parish center, behind the church."

"When is the wedding?"

"The reception starts at six PM."

"Today?"

"Heeelp meee."

Alyssa laughed. She had worked at a party shop in high school, starting when she was fifteen, when they moved out of the car, and their lives started getting back on track. She sold napkins and blew up balloons and stocked the shelves with blue and pink plastic storks. Sometimes she helped the customers actually plan themes for their parties, and ensured they had everything they needed. She loved it. It was also where she'd met Janet, who'd worked there longer and had keys to the store. One night, after hours, Janet had broken out the helium tank and they'd huffed it, quoting movie scenes in squeaky voices and giggling hysterically—until on a whim Alyssa did some googling and found out huffing helium could be dangerous.

When the owner of that party shop added event planning as a genuine sideline—not just recommending color schemes or finding coordinating products—Janet made sure that Alyssa got experience planning parties too. They were only four years apart in age, but it had seemed like a lot at the time. Janet always treated her as an equal, though, and Alyssa would forever be grateful.

A year after Alyssa went off to college, Janet bought the business. It turned out that running the place was a lot different from punching the clock, and Janet had called on Alyssa more than once to help out in a pinch. Alyssa was happy to do it, for old times' sake.

"I'm supposed to meet a Persian rug rep this afternoon, just to see their new line," Alyssa said. "I can reschedule that with no problem. You need me to bring anything?"

"Your superior party planning skills," Janet replied breezily.

Alyssa blew air out. She'd left the party planning business and had no intention of going back. During the summers in college she'd worked a job at a small design firm. It wasn't anything fancy and the older woman who ran it acknowledged Alyssa's point that it needed a better sign and some sort of advertising—they were getting by on repeat clients and had little discoverability. But the owner was winding down and simply hadn't cared. When Alyssa graduated, she'd applied all over town, and the one place where she got an interview was one of the best—Stacey's Interiors.

"I'll just be tying raffia around mason jars or whatever you're doing. I won't be *planning* anything."

"Thank yooouuu! Please break several traffic laws on the way here." Janet made a kiss sound and hung up. Alyssa looked at the phone and shook her head, then called and rescheduled with the carpet sales rep.

The trip to St. John's took longer than she'd expected, in part because she stopped by a sub shop and picked up a sandwich to eat in the car. When she got there, she hurried into the parish center, where she could see several stacked boxes—undoubtedly supplies Janet was using for the reception decor. Not a good look a few hours before the reception. She hurried in. "Janet, I'm here."

Her friend turned in her seat at a long folding table. "Oh thank god. I am overwhelmed." She stood and gave Alyssa a quick hug.

"Why are you here alone?"

"Roberta got drunk again. We're being honest, right? She threw up in the bathroom and went home. So now the bathroom smells, and I have ten thousand billion water lilies to deal with."

"Water lilies? I love water lilies. Did you get them from Emma?"

"Yeah, she came through for me. She had to jump through some hoops to get them too."

"We three need a girls' night out soon. You're the best friends ever."

"We are!" Janet said. "Speaking of which, start by propping open the bathroom door so it airs out."

Alyssa gave her a fake dead-eye stare, then made a genuine face when she opened the door and the vomit odor hit her. "At least she didn't make a mess," she said as she pulled up a chair and opened a box to peek inside.

"Oh, she did. Cleaning that up was my top priority."

"I can see that. And ugh—sorry you had to deal with it. Why do you keep her anyway?"

"Because my bestie and favorite party planner got a new job as an interior designer. How's that going, anyway?"

Alyssa shook her head. "Tell me what to do before we start talking."

"Good point. So this couple met when they were both walking in a park. The dog of one of the brides got loose and charged the other bride, who fell into the pond she was walking past."

"Oh my gosh," Alyssa said.

"She surfaced with a lily pad on her head, and instead of apologizing, the first woman laughed. And then a frog jumped off the wet one's shoulder and she screamed, and the first woman laughed harder."

Alyssa gaped. "This resulted in a *wedding*?"

"It did!" Janet said. "A water lily–themed wedding. So the caterer is setting up the tables and cloths, but I need the centerpieces ready to slap down as soon as the tables are set. We have these square mirrors, and these low flat bowls to sit on top. Put three of the pink-with-yellow water lilies in each, and three tea light candles floating between."

"We'll need to fill them with water now to keep the flowers fresh . . ." Alyssa said.

". . . and then move them to the tables already full of water. Yes! Isn't life a delight? But yeah, preventing drooping is top priority."

Alyssa's phone buzzed but she ignored it. "What else is there?" Alyssa said. "The caterer is decorating the cake?"

"Yes, but there is plenty for you to do, my talented friend! Why don't you throw the centerpieces together, and then—"

"How many?"

"Thirty!" Janet said.

"*Thirty?* Why are these people so popular?"

"I know, right? Stupid popular people. Oh god, they're good-looking too. Wait till you see them."

"Well, this shouldn't take too long. It's mostly cutting the stems."

"And then you can do the decorations for the head table, the buffet table, and the cake table, while I string up the arch over the entryway."

"No. There is *not* an archway."

"Indeed! And all fresh flowers and ribbons and shit wired on."

"Gonna be hard to wire the shit," Alyssa mused, forefinger pressed to her lips.

"I cannot currently sass you because I need help so badly, so don't say things that require sass from me."

Alyssa flipped open another box, found what she was looking for, and began laying mirror squares out on the table. "That is precisely why I can indulge in witty rejoinders." She grinned at her friend.

Alyssa stacked the mirror squares, thinking it would be easiest to place them on the tables separately rather than trying to carry them with bowls full of water on top of them once the caterers had the tables ready. She got the bowls out and went into the parish hall kitchen to poke around for a pitcher to fill them. Her phone buzzed again. She blew a stray strand of blond hair out of her face and checked it.

Nick, forty minutes ago: *Sure. Drop by when you want. I'll be here till 4.*

Nick, just now: *Are you coming by?*

Crap crap crap.

Alyssa texted back: *Oh so sorry! A friend is having an emergency. Can we reschedule?*

She saw the three little dots scrolling, indicating that he was writing back. "What are you doing?" Janet called. "These water lilies aren't going to shove themselves in bowls!"

Nick: *I'm sorry to hear that.*

Nick: *We're leaving tomorrow for a ten-day road trip. Maybe after that?*

Nick: *Hope your friend's okay.* 🙁

"He used a sad face!" Alyssa called. "I love a man who's not afraid of an emoji."

"Who did? And does he know how to pour water in a bowl? Get him over here."

"Oh, a client." She smiled at the phone, rereading his messages.

Janet straightened from her position by the white lattice archway over the door where the new couple would enter the reception hall. "Your face doesn't say *client*. Your face says *hot guy*."

Alyssa flushed. "No, he's a client."

"You realize your circulatory system has weighed in, right? Gooey expression and pink cheeks do not equal 'client.'"

Those aren't the only parts that think he's handsome.

Alyssa texted back. *My friend is an event planner! That's what I used to do.* Her coworker got—Alyssa hesitated—*sick, and we're trying to get everything finished before the wedding reception tonight.*

Alyssa: *Sorry I gave the wrong impression.*

She saw the three little dots.

Nick: *Whew. Will the wedding be saved?*

Alyssa: *It will be! I'm shoving water lilies into bowls as we speak.*

Nick: *Careful. You're gonna piss off Monet.*

Alyssa stared at the screen. He didn't seem like an art guy. Then again, Monet's water-lily paintings weren't exactly obscure.

Alyssa: *I'll keep an eye out for Frenchmen in berets.*

Nick: *Just watch for dead Frenchmen in black berets. That's what he wore in his self-portrait. Dead guys in blue berets are probably fine.*

She stared at the screen. He couldn't have looked the painting up that fast. She ran a quick search on Claude Monet's self-portrait. Black beret. *I'll be darned.* She bit her lip, took a deep breath, and texted again.

Alyssa: *Long shot, and no pressure AT ALL, but if you want to see some samples before your road trip, you're welcome to drop by here.* She hit "Send," then wanted to stuff herself into one of the centerpiece bowls. As if he were desperate to fight traffic to see dish patterns. Because of course he was—the guy who had no opinion whatsoever what his completely empty apartment should look like.

Her phone buzzed.

Nick: *Sure. Where are you?*

Nick: *Will I be safe from the scary wedding reception?*

She smiled. *St. John's Lutheran Parish Center. Flee if you see any black berets.*

Nick: *I'll be there in 20.*

Alyssa smiled, laid her phone down on the table, and turned to see Janet staring at her. "What? Oh, by the way, the client is going to stop by to look at some samples." Her eyes flew wide. "The samples, which I completely forgot to pick up after you sent up the bat signal." She'd been going to stop at a store on the way to the carpet consultation. Which meant she'd just lured Nick Sorensen to a random Lutheran church on the promise of looking at dishes that did not exist. She sat down and began scrolling madly on her phone, checking the inventory of a favorite store.

"Alyssa, I am seriously panicking here," Janet said. "Please do some work."

She looked up, her expression guilty. "I'm sorry. This is an important client, and I kind of messed up."

Janet smirked. "Aw, look at you smile."

"I hate you," Alyssa said. "But I will still put candles in your bowls."

Nick got there exactly when predicted, which seemed a little fast for the distance involved. His car nosed into a parking spot at the far end of the line, and he stepped out—in a charcoal-gray suit, white shirt, and black and blue tie. He opened the door to the parish center and stepped in, smiling at Alyssa. "Hey."

Janet stood by the arbor with her mouth open, a bucket of water lilies beside her, a roll of florist's wire forgotten in her hand.

"Hi!" Alyssa said. Squeak. *Dammit.* "Um, sorry about . . ." She waved a hand vaguely at the room. "Oh, this is my friend Janet." Nick raised a hand. "Janet, this is Nick Sorensen."

"Dang. I know," Janet said. Nick grinned. "Don't you clean up nice."

"Um, come on over," Alyssa said. "I just wanted to get an idea of your taste in tableware. I was having trouble choosing something you'd like."

They pulled chairs up to one of the round guest tables, still without its cloth, and Alyssa produced her phone. She hoped he didn't know she should be more prepared—that this presentation of samples should be more formal. "So what shape plates would you like?" she said, scrolling to a screen that showed different outlines.

"Round."

An answer? Really? Predictable, but an answer. "Okay! That's easy. And what color?" She braced herself.

"Black."

She looked at him. "Black?"

He grinned. "Like a puck."

"Are . . . is that really what you want?"

He shrugged. "I don't care. I just thought that would be funny." She dropped her head into her hand and looked sideways at him. "Is it possible I'm not as funny as I think?" That brought a small smile from her.

"Hey, Nick," Janet called. "Do you actually give a crap about your dishes?"

"Nope."

"Then could you grab that pitcher and fill those shallow bowls about two-thirds full?"

"Janet!" Alyssa said.

"I'm sorry, but I'm having a crisis here, and he looks strong enough to lift a pitcher."

Nick stood and walked over to the table, picked up the pitcher, and shambled into the kitchen. The women exchanged a wide-eyed look. "Nick Sorensen?" Janet mouthed.

"Yep," Alyssa mouthed back.

"He likes you."

"He doesn't." But she smiled. When Nick returned, she walked over and tried to take the pitcher from him, but he didn't let it go. The result was that she had wrapped her hand over his. "You're obviously going somewhere," she said. "We can't let you get wet."

He looked at her for a moment, confused, then glanced at his suit and flushed. "Oh, I put this on because you said it was a wedding reception. I didn't want to embarrass you if there were other people around. I mean, I was wearing sweats and no socks."

Behind Nick, Janet raised her eyebrows significantly, then wiggled them wildly until Alyssa acknowledged her with an irritated shooing motion by her thigh. Nick turned. "These bowls?"

"Those are the ones!" Janet beamed. "I finally got some good help."

"Hey!" Alyssa said.

They worked for half an hour, Nick and Alyssa putting the centerpieces together, then working on the decorations for the head table. Nick cut the water lily stems to the length Alyssa showed him while she lined the vases with aspidistra leaves. "Is there a reason you're being so helpful?" she said.

"It distracts you from dishes," he said.

"Oh! About that, I was thinking . . ."

He moaned softly.

"Hey, what are you crazy kids doing over there?" Janet called. "This is a wedding, not a honeymoon." Alyssa flushed furiously. Nick smirked. "Actually, I need your help over here." Janet was on a step-stool beside the arch. She had the water lilies and some lily of the valley wired in, and was holding a huge roll of pink tulle ribbon. Nick looked at Alyssa and shrugged, and they walked over. Janet stepped back and grabbed her phone.

"Can you guys stand in there for a second? I need to see how high to put the bow."

"The bow?" Alyssa said. What difference would . . .

Nick obediently stepped into the archway. "Just pretend to be the newlyweds," Janet said. She looked around the phone and smiled. "This helps so much!" She clicked a photo of them standing under the arch of flowers.

Janet lowered the phone and her lips twisted to the side. "I think it may cut off the groom's head, though." Alyssa's eyes snapped over to her. There was no "groom" in this wedding. What was her friend pulling? Janet smiled sweetly. "It would help so much if you—I hope this isn't asking too much—but I need to know if the bow height will work when they kiss."

Alyssa stared at her. Beside her Nick looked between them and then turned slightly toward her. She was going to kill Janet. She was going to stab her through the heart with a water lily stem. It might take a while, but she had the will to see the job through.

"Is that okay?" Nick whispered, his lips by her ear. She thought she might melt, puddle on the floor, and stain his Italian leather shoes.

"Um, I don't want to . . . impose. You really don't have to. Um, if you don't want." She risked a glance up at him. His ridiculously handsome jaw hovered dangerously close, and his eyes were looking at her, a touch of amusement in them, along with a touch of something else. Longing? And then he slipped an arm around her, put his hand on her lower back, and bent to kiss her.

He pulled her to him, arching her ever so slightly backward. His arm was hard, and the chest he pulled her into was a slab of muscle. But his lips were soft and the kiss was gentle. Her mouth moved against his, wanting more than this chaste brush against her lips. Her whole *body* wanted more. She put her hand on his back, steadying herself as he melted her core.

And then he released her and looked up at Janet. "Was that good?"

Oh God, yes. That was very, very good, Alyssa thought.

"Yes, that helped *so much*. Thank you!" Janet said.

Nick looked down at Alyssa and flushed slightly. "Well. Looking at dishes was more fun than I'd I expected." He gave her his rakish grin.

"Wait till we choose end tables," she said, then flushed. Holy crap, why had she said that? Janet snorted and Nick laughed, lifted her hand in his large, strong one, and gave it a tiny squeeze. "I can't wait." He lifted one eyebrow, then stepped out of the archway and said, "I better be off. Any plates are fine. Hope the reception goes well." He walked off to his sports car and lifted a hand to Alyssa, who was watching him through the parish center window as he got in, and drove away.

Alyssa wheeled on her friend. "You had to check the *bow height*? That doesn't even make sense. That's not *a thing*!"

Janet shrugged. "Yeah, but he doesn't know that. And look, I have two pictures of you kissing Nick Sorensen." She turned her phone so Alyssa could see the screen.

"We're standing under a floral arch, he's wearing a tailored suit, and I'm in skinny jeans and tennis shoes! It looks like I wore skinny jeans to my wedding!"

Janet gave her a wolf grin. "If you finish your work, I will send you these pictures and not post them on the interweb claiming that you got married in inappropriate attire."

"You're blackmailing me!"

"I'm not sure threatening to post a photo of you kissing Nick Sorensen qualifies as blackmail. First, he is hot. Second, wow is he hot." Janet put her phone down and grabbed the roll of tulle ribbon again. "I'll send these to you later, but I'm going to keep a copy and photoshop myself into your spot. And blow it up to poster size and tape it to my bedroom wall."

Alyssa snorted and turned back to the water lilies. She'd been humming and smiling for five minutes before she realized that she was humming and smiling. And that Janet was watching her with a look of smug amusement.

CHAPTER SEVEN

Nick traveled with the team on the road trip. His leg was stronger—
it had come along quickly—and he'd lifted weights and kept the rest
of his body in shape during rehab. He wasn't sure what day he'd play
again—the coach was keeping his thoughts to himself as he watched
Nick's progress—but it felt good to be on the ice again.

Boarding the plane as they left Detroit was a different story. Everyone very carefully didn't look at him as they filed on. He hung back,
trying to be the last guy on, and they let him do it. They were all hyper-
aware of him—very accommodating. He was appreciative and irritated.

The last time he'd gotten on a plane, it had crashed in a field, at
night, and he had been in absolute darkness for an hour before the first
responders found them. He'd shouted to the other guys but no one had
answered. And then he'd screamed for maybe half an hour. By the
time the fire trucks rolled in, he'd stopped making noise except for the
ragged breaths he drew in as he clutched his ruined leg. He'd never lost
consciousness and it was a damn shame. He didn't want these
memories.

When he'd signed with Detroit, his dad had driven him to the new city so he wouldn't have to get on a plane. It was dumb and took two days and he loved his dad for it.

Now he lingered by the cockpit, fiddling with a bag while everyone else got settled. He'd told Devin the day before that he'd like to be the last guy to choose a seat. Devin had quietly spread the word. The last time he'd chosen a spot on an airplane, it was the only seat someone could survive in—at least, it was the only seat someone *had* survived in. Which meant that when he'd chosen his seat and sat down, he'd condemned everyone else to death.

Other people wouldn't see it quite that way, he knew. But they hadn't been there.

So once his teammates were settled, he chose his spot—on the left, halfway back. Not where he'd been on the last flight, but maybe this was his new place. Takeoff was uneventful except for the guys carefully not paying attention to him, and the team trainer moving to sit across the aisle from him. For no particular reason, obviously. Did they think he might freak out and need to be sedated mid-flight?

Jesus. What if he *did*?

He kept himself busy playing a game on his phone. It was a stupid game. Ridiculously cheerful gnomes ran around with pickaxes cutting gold and gems out of tunnel walls. They jumped up and down every time they finished a vein—and squealed. He had to play with the sound off because of the squealing and because it was an embarrassing game to play. It was probably made for ten-year-olds.

His friend Luka had introduced him to it and had played it with the sound up, fist pumping when his avatar, the gnome in the green hat, amassed enough gold to advance to the next level. That gnome had looked like Luka too—they both had a mess of yellow hair. Nick had bought him a bright green hat as a joke, and the idiot had worn it—proudly. There was nothing that could embarrass Luka.

Since his death, Nick played as the green-hatted gnome, helping him chisel gems and dodge the occasional ghost whooshing past in the tunnels. No matter how much gold he amassed, though, he never won. Not really. Luka never came back, so the ghosts won anyway.

Just before the plane started its descent, Devin and André leaned forward from their seats behind Nick. Devin put a hand on his shoulder. The pilot announced that they should buckle up. Nick was already strapped in—he'd stayed that way the whole flight. "Hey, you know any good restaurants in St. Louis?" Devin said. "I want to make sure we eat someplace good while we're in town."

Nick swiveled to look at him. "There's a lot of good restaurants in St. Louis."

André had a hand on his other shoulder now, and Nick turned the other way. "Are we talking ambiance or the quality of the food?" André said. "Because I am a man of discernment and require both."

"You will literally eat a cold hot dog," Devin said.

"True," André said. "But we need something elegant this week, to start preseason. Some place with fancy-ass garnishes."

The plane touched down. The brakes locked with a squeal, and it decelerated sharply.

Nick swiveled to look at them both, the faintest of smiles in the crook of his mouth. "The team obviously made all the arrangements already. Like it always does. But thanks for the distraction, guys." André lightly bounced his fist off Nick's head, and Devin gave his shoulder a soft smack.

When the plane had taxied to a stop, the other guys began fiddling with bags and phones and pretending to tie shoes. Letting him get the hell off there first. Thoughtful enough to do it; thoughtful enough to pretend they weren't. He took advantage of it and shot down the steps to the tarmac, touching one finger to his forehead as he passed the pilot. The man nodded to him.

Detroit had been at the first brush of fall—time to hang a jacket by the door. But St. Louis was still in late summer, and the sun glared off the tarmac and the glass in the terminal. When they walked into the building, Coach caught up with him right as the smell of the terminal hit him—plastic and carpet and bodies and faint food smells, and underneath it a sharp hit of aviation fuel. "Nick, I was thinking, if you have a good practice tonight, I might start you Wednesday in Boston."

He looked up sharply at that.

"Just keep you out this first game, then turn you loose. The timing would be right for your leg, I think. But what do you think about returning to the ice there?"

Nick took a second. What *did* he think? "They bet against me," he finally said. "That's what it comes down to. The GM didn't think I could come back."

"Which is how we got you." Coach looked at him closely. "You want revenge? Or you want to wait another couple of days?"

Nick stopped walking and turned to face his new coach. "I want revenge."

CHAPTER EIGHT

The Red Wheels dropped the game in St. Louis, but they played well. Nick was listed as a healthy scratch and watched from the stands. The second flight—the one to Boston—was easier. He still boarded last. It was odd seeing the city rise to meet him—it had been his home for several years, and he'd hoped to stay there for his whole career, unrealistic as that was. It was a city he loved and where he'd had good friends. Granted, most of them were now dead.

Game time was seven PM. He was at the arena hours earlier to warm up. In the visitors' dressing room he looked up, eyes searching for the spoked "B" logo before he even realized it. The ceiling was undecorated. The room was damn cold, too. It was right by the ice and back when he'd been part of the Boston team he'd heard visiting teams bitch about it, but now he got it. He spent a little extra time stretching out to counteract the effect of the chill—and then a little longer skating to warm up. He didn't want to get hurt his first game back. It hurt enough, just being on this ice. He knew he couldn't glance to his right and see Sammy slap a puck at him for warm-up passing drills, but he looked anyway.

Damn it, this was hard. He skated back to the bench for water, and the locker room manager pointed—shit, he'd gone to the wrong bench. The Detroit coach saw his mistake and came by and asked, "How you feeling?"

"Great." It was true, regarding his leg. While it would take two or three more weeks to get his conditioning fully back, he was ready to go. He might need shorter shifts for a few games, but his blades were ready to hit the ice. But it was a damn lie regarding his heart. The Boston team had cut him not just because of the crumpled leg and other more minor injuries, but because the psychological injury was severe too. He'd spent an hour in a plane filled with dead guys, waiting to see if it would catch fire and unable to drag himself out if it did. And he remembered all of it. The team had had to decide if they thought he could claw his way back—and had guessed that he couldn't.

He was going to play incredibly well, bring the Stanley Cup to Detroit by sheer force of will—and make his old team's management kick themselves for underestimating him, for dropping him while he was still in the hospital.

In the locker room, as the coach read the starting lineup for the night, the guys gave their right thighs two sharp smacks after each name. Their pads made the blows reverberate. It reminded Nick of an old Viking ritual—like beating on your shield. When the coach said, "Sorensen," the guys grinned as they smacked their thighs, and several guys gave full-throated cheers. Nick ducked his head slightly, but he grinned.

They skated out onto the ice and stood at the far end, in front of their goal. The fans applauded when he came out, and he raised a hand briefly. Colored lasers shot around the arena, and the announcer introduced the visiting team—Detroit. When he said, "Nick Soooo-rensen!" Nick pushed off and glided out to join his teammates at center ice. The crowd erupted, leaping to their feet, stomping, clapping wildly, and cheering. Nick lifted a hand again. It went on and on, and Devin chucked him in the shoulder. The Red Wheels began to tap their sticks on the ice, a sign of solidarity, and the home team joined them. His eyes pricked at the show of support for his long, painful comeback. He turned in a circle, hand raised, and the applause grew deafening.

And then the Boston line broke as its players skated forward, not waiting for their names to be called, and embraced him, thumping his back and smacking his helmet. These men had been his teammates—until a quarter of the team died. It was a lovefest at center ice for a full minute, and he was blinking back tears, thinking of Sammy, Tyler, Eric, Luka, and Dragan, and desperately wanting not to cry in front of TV cameras. He needed to think about something else. Now.

Did he need to clean his refrigerator? No. He'd like to get a dog. But he couldn't because of road trips, so no dog. That didn't help. Crap, he really was going to cry. What could he think of? Vomit? Cleaning gutters? And then he imagined Alyssa standing under the half-finished arbor at that church hall, with her hair falling in soft waves. And that kiss. It distracted him, and just in time. He wasn't crying. Thank god.

The Boston players skated back to their line, and the announcer called their names, and the fans cheered again, but not as loud or as long as they had for him. Not by a long shot. The noise and applause had been a welcome-home gift from the fans, and he appreciated it. Even though this was no longer his home and he was set on destroying their team to get back at the general manager.

It was a close game, scoreless until late in the second period, when Nick got a breakaway and skated the length of the ice, hitting a hard wrister. The puck sailed over the goalie's glove, the goal horn sounded, and the red light flashed. *Yes!* He skated sharply around, blades hissing, and pumped his arm as he glided on one blade. No reason not to have a little celebration there. His teammates came over and pommeled him.

The lines changed then and he vaulted over the boards to the bench, sat, and grabbed a water bottle. Behind him the coach set a hand on his shoulder and bent to talk to him. "Nice shot. You okay with being done for the night?" He nodded, still breathing hard. He'd let his stick say what he wanted to the general manager sitting in his box high above the ice.

Detroit won the game 2–1, and they brought Nick out as the star of the game. There was another ovation. And then he showered and came out of the locker room and saw Evangeline Jorgenson. Eric's wife. A cannonball hit his stomach. She was a beautiful woman—a tall, willowy blonde, elegant and well dressed. She reminded him of Alyssa, the decorator, with her inherent sense of style. Evangeline was holding a maybe four-month-old baby. He walked over to her, their eyes locked, and he felt the familiar sense of vertigo, of falling, falling.

"Hey," he said, putting a hand on her upper arm. "Is this . . .?"

She nodded and gave a weak smile. "I thought you might like to meet him. Eric Jr."

He crouched down and looked in the baby's chubby face. Impossibly clear blue eyes stared back at him. His mouth was drawn up in a tiny pink bow, ready to laugh or cry. Eric Jr. clearly wasn't sure what to make of the encounter. Nick wasn't either. He put a hand on the baby's head. "His hair's so soft," he said, and Evangeline nodded. "Are you doing okay?"

What a stupid question. Your husband died. You had your baby alone. You're a new mother and a widow. So hey, how's it going?

"My mom's helping."

"Do you need anything?" Another dumb question. Eric had been a veteran with a much better contract than Nick's. Nick was a young star, just reaching the serious pay levels. Still.

"No. We're good." She blinked. "I just thought you might like to meet him."

"Can I hold him?" She nodded and Nick reached out and took the baby in his strong hands. Eric Jr. looked up at him, and his face crumpled in slow motion and then he wailed.

"Hold him closer," Evangeline said, and Nick nestled him against his chest.

"Your daddy loved you," he whispered. "He was so excited about you coming." Evangeline began to cry, but he had to tell the baby, had to make sure he knew. He put a strong arm around his friend's widow, pulling her close, and bounced the baby against his chest with the other arm while they both cried and people walked past them in the hall, and somebody stopped to take a couple of pictures. He'd like to hip check the guy, but he couldn't take his eyes off baby Eric. He rubbed the top of the baby's head with his cheek. So soft.

And then Evangeline pulled back and held her arms out, and he reluctantly handed Eric Jr. back to his mother, running a finger over the back of his neck where the fat creased. "He's beautiful," he said, his voice husky.

She nodded. "Are you doing okay, Nick?"

"Me? Sure." She looked at him. He swallowed. "I shouldn't have survived."

She squeezed his bicep. "They would have wanted you to."

He nodded and looked away. "Yeah."

They glanced at each other quickly, as much as they could stand, because their eyes said so much and it was a conversation neither of them could handle. Her husband was dead, and she'd give anything to have him back. Nick would trade places with him, but he couldn't.

But I could have on the plane. There was a time when I could have traded places with him, and it would have saved his life. His baby would have had a father.

Nick leaned in and gave Evangeline a quick kiss on the cheek before they turned and walked in opposite directions down the hall. Neither looked back.

CHAPTER NINE

Alyssa filled the tub she used for washing sweaters with hot water and fragrant salts and carried it carefully to her small dining room. She was wearing rolled-up sweatpants and had her hair in a high ponytail, and she sat at the table, which was scattered with sketchbooks and fabric and wood stain samples. She lowered her feet into the tub and sighed with pleasure. She had once thought this was a luxury only for older women. Then she'd tried it.

She picked up a colored pencil and tapped it against her chin. The design for Nick Sorensen's apartment was almost done. The living room was a cool blue with big dark furniture. She added a little industrial swank in his open dining room with a steel table with rivets showing. It was masculine but playful in a way. The lamps in the living room carried over the industrial steel look.

The kitchen was a streamlined, modern space. She was going to get him a better coffeemaker than the twenty-dollar box-store brand he had now. And what was with that? She sort of understood not bothering to decorate his apartment. Weird, but okay. But if you were going to buy a coffeemaker, why wouldn't you get a good one? The guy had money.

She'd chosen sleek, modern flatware. The plates were round and white, but he was going to get square dessert plates. The stemware was chunky glass. She could remember the feel of his hand on her back when he'd pulled her in for a kiss—he'd have no trouble wrapping those strong fingers around the glasses.

She was going to paint his bedroom a midnight blue with grommet-top curtains on a steel pole and blackout shades underneath. Most of the Red Wheels' games started in the evening, and by the time he showered and drove home, it was probably pretty late. He might sleep in in the morning and would appreciate a dark bedroom.

As for the art, she was going to put a hockey stick up on the wall, and the Bobby Orr print. That was probably enough hockey. She had generically masculine duck prints to go in his bedroom. She didn't like them—they seemed like something you'd find in a law office or a bank, but he needed something, and she couldn't take a chance on a Rothko reproduction. She'd found some cute, framed vegetable prints at one of her favorite stores that would go in the kitchen. She was going to put a neutral landscape over his sofa. Then it got tricky.

Alyssa believed there should be a human face in every room—a photograph of a loved one, a reproduction Roman bust, a Modigliani print—something with eyes, whether it was two- or three-dimensional. Rooms without them were lonely, and you didn't know why—it didn't rise to the conscious level. If there were ever a guy in need of art with faces, it was Nick Sorensen. But she couldn't tell him that—she could just see him roll his eyes. The thing was, on the floor beside his mattress, he had a small framed photo of people who were obviously his parents, and that was it. No team photos, no friends, no vacation selfies. His living space was sterile. It was *desolate*.

This refusal to reveal anything of himself was what earned him the ducks. He had no one to blame but himself.

She had checked with Vanessa, and the Red Wheels were getting back from their road trip today—they were probably back now. She had gotten in the habit of checking the sports news and earlier that day had called her stepdad to ask if Detroit was off to a good start. Her mom answered and sounded relieved when Alyssa asked for Bill.

Her mother, Linda, hadn't always been so stiff. When she'd had to sell their house after her husband left, she'd had a giant garage sale. She'd bought price stickers and had told Alyssa and her brother, Ryan, to put one on everything. Alyssa stuck one on her dollhouse last, and she put it on the bottom, hoping no one would know it was for sale. That hadn't worked out.

When a neighbor walked over to the sale and turned one of Linda's mother's china plates in her hand and asked why they were selling everything, Linda had told her. She had debts. She was losing the house. And the neighbor had said, "Well, you really need to unload these, then," and had given Linda a lowball offer. Alyssa had watched as her mother smiled brittlely and boxed the china for the woman. Then she had left Alyssa in charge while she went in the house.

When she came back out, her mascara was gone and she was . . . older. It was like she had duct-taped herself back together, and now she could never pull the tape off without falling to pieces. Of course she was stiff—she was taped together.

Alyssa's stepdad, Bill, came on the line, and when Alyssa asked about the Red Wheels, there was silence at the other end. Then he said, "I've waited for this day."

"Ha ha," Alyssa said. "Nick Sorensen is doing pretty well, isn't he?"

"His plus–minus rating is good," Bill said. "His shifts are short right now, so his TOI isn't very high, but when—"

"Enough, enough!" Alyssa said. "I'm not actually a fan."

Her stepfather was silent for a moment, then said, "Someday I will sit, brew in hand, flanked by my children, discussing Leif Bjorkland's save percentage, and you will listen to me with bated breath."

She laughed. "Maybe you can be flanked by Ryan and a cardboard cutout also of Ryan."

"I love your brother," her stepdad said, "but he's already a hockey fan. You're the one I have to work on."

"Yeah, yeah." She might not be interested in hockey, but she was becoming interested in Nick Sorensen. Purely for professional reasons. In order to give him a more functional design.

Alyssa pulled her feet out of the little tub and let them drip back into it, then wrapped them in a fuzzy lavender towel. She would text Nick the next day and ask to meet him at his apartment to show him her sketches and plans. She didn't expect much reaction out of him, but maybe he could muster a *"Looks comfortable"* for the furniture. Something.

Without thinking through why she was doing it, she typed his name into her browser's search bar and scanned the results that came up. A box on the right of her screen contained a brief biography: birthday, height, contract amount—dang, that coffeemaker did *not* make sense—draft pick, current and former team affiliations, and a montage of photos. One of them was a tiny picture of a crumpled plane. She clicked and a story opened—six friends taking what was meant to be an evening trip. Six dead—five passengers and the pilot—and one survivor. There were thumbnail photos of all the guys, plus the pilot. It had been a mechanical failure, the article said—nobody's fault. The pilot had done everything he could, played it out a long time—which meant they'd known they were going to crash for several minutes.

What would that have been like?

She clicked her back arrow, stared at the Red Wheels' publicity shot of Nick—a handsome young man with an easy smile. Then she scrolled further and clicked on a site that offered photos posted by fans. Many were blurry restaurant photos taken by people who didn't want to be seen snapping his picture. Some were street shots. He was using a cane in some of the photos and was pale and in a wheelchair in a few of them, his left leg extended straight in front of him.

But others were fun photoshopped images and memes. Someone had used a professional photo of Nick taken straight on as he headed down the ice, a fierce look in his blue eyes. On it, they had superimposed the words *"Me heading for the last piece of cake the way Nick Sorensen heads for the net."* And there was a five-second video of him standing in a suit, waiting by a bus, sunglasses suspended in his left hand. He swung them slowly back and forth and looked like James Bond. Someone had posted, *"You're never going to be as cool doing anything as Nick Sorensen is waiting for a bus."* He had such an effortless elegance—a sense of style in his clothes and the way he held himself. How could he have let his home be so . . . nothing?

She was ready to close the laptop, when she saw three photos that had been uploaded in the past week, according to their time stamp. They showed Nick in a suit, his hair wet, one arm around a gorgeous woman and the other holding a baby. They looked completely comfortable together, and the way they were looking at each other—there was real familiarity there. Old friends? His sister? She ran an emergency search: *Nick Sorensen* AND *sibling*. He was an only child. Maybe he was married, and the woman his wife lived in a different city, and they were keeping it quiet? Maybe it wasn't quiet, and Alyssa was the only one who didn't know. After all, she hadn't known about the plus–minus thing. But his online bio said he was single, so this was probably his Boston mistress. He traveled all the time—a guy that good-looking? And rich? He'd have one in every city. She'd felt the muscle in his chest, and that was a thing a person could want to lean against. Probably everyone in every city did. Of *course* he wasn't available.

And there was no reason at all why that should bother her, so obviously it didn't. It's just that she had a backup plan to make the second bedroom a very generic guest bedroom if she could get him to approve it, but if it should be a child's room—well he should have told her that. And then she realized why he didn't have any photos in his home—he had a network of mistresses and couldn't risk forgetting to switch out their pictures. What if Margot from Los Angeles flew in and saw a photo of Angelique from New York on his bedside table? The only way to avoid a mess-up was to pretend he couldn't be bothered to decorate at all.

If she was right, he would let her do this design to placate his team and Devin, and then quietly cancel their agreement. He'd pay her for the work she'd done so far, but not let her actually buy the damn duck prints. Because that could upset Margot from Los Angeles.

She looked again at the photo, at the look of deep understanding between Nick and this tall, beautiful woman, of the way he cradled the baby—protective, with his head tilted onto the baby's silky crown. This wasn't a random encounter with a fan. This was a woman he loved, a baby he cared for. That surely was his. And that was perfectly fine. What did she care? She did not care. "I do not care," she said out loud, to make it more official.

Then she added a third duck print to his bedroom, because screw him.

CHAPTER TEN

The next morning Alyssa showered and put on a peach blouse that did wonders for her skin and a pair of swishy pants that, Janet told her, made her butt look fantastic. She added a couple of thin gold necklaces, and when she put on her makeup and the mascara flaked, she redid her whole eye—and this time her lashes didn't clump. She was having a good hair day too. Sometimes the universe smiled on you.

She texted Nick at 10:07 AM. That wasn't so early that he was likely to be sleeping, and the ":07" meant she hadn't set a timer to remind her. She'd spent ten minutes deciding what would be the perfect time to text to indicate that he was *not* on her mind. She was pleased with the choice.

Alyssa: *Hi! I have your design done. Let me know when it works for me to come over and show you.*

He didn't respond immediately. He was probably practicing sports puck, not having an orgy or expanding his network of mistresses to smaller cities like Kalamazoo and Toledo.

She was at her office, desk spread with samples of printed flannel fabrics—ducks and bunnies. She was working on a nursery for a young couple on a limited budget who found out halfway through their pregnancy that they were having twins. That meant the design had to change—two cribs, and now no room for the reading nook she had planned—but also that their budget was tighter. She loved working for clients like this, where she had to get creative. They had low expectations and were grateful for any help, but she wanted it to be beautiful.

She had the impression the man's mother was an issue too. The design would bolster a young woman's confidence as she dealt with her first child—children!—in the face of an overbearing mother-in-law. Designing interiors might not seem important to some people, but it could set the stage for relationships. That young mom might find the courage to set boundaries—if only Alyssa could decide if there should be two rockers in the room so both babies could be soothed at the same time. And even if there wasn't a designated reading area, there had to be space for picture books . . .

Her phone buzzed. Nick: *I'm at the rink, just about to hop in the shower.*
Don't visualize him naked. Don't visualize him naked. Oh, you visualized it.

Nick: *I'll be home in about forty minutes. Do you want to come over then?*
Alyssa: *Sure! I look forward to showing you the design.*
Nick: *Maybe give me 50 minutes. I reeaally need to shower.* 😌

Alyssa laughed, put her phone down, and began to gather up the things she needed to take to his apartment. Then she grabbed her phone. Should she send a final text? She never knew when she was playing a conversation out too long. Once it degenerated into happy faces and thumbs-up and LOLs—she didn't want to be the one to send one too many. But he'd changed the time, and that should be acknowledged, surely? So she sent another text.

Alyssa: *lol*

There. Let him withstand that level of wit and creativity.

Fifty minutes later Alyssa cruised his neighborhood, snagged a parking spot, and slung her go bag over her shoulder. She walked up to the door, rang, and he buzzed her in. He stood at the top of the steps as she came in, wearing sweatpants and a three-quarter sleeve baseball shirt. He was barefoot and his hair was still damp. "You need help with the bag?"

"No, I got it. Thanks."

He pushed the door open with his toe and let her in. The space still startled her in its blazing white emptiness. How could he live like this? She would have tacked gum wrappers to the wall just to break the monotony of it. "How have you been?"

"Good," he said. "I'm playing again."

"That's great! Actually I heard that from my stepdad."

He laughed. "He's a Red Wheels fan?"

"Oh, the worst."

He raised an eyebrow. "By which you mean 'the best'?"

"Yes. Yes, that is precisely what I meant." He grinned. Dang. She really hadn't meant to insult his profession. But he was standing close and he smelled of the shower, and her mind had already taken its little road trip there. "So," she said breezily, "normally I would set up my laptop on your dining room table and talk you through it." They both looked at the empty space beside his kitchen that was meant to be an eating space. "In this case, are you okay with sitting on the floor?"

"Sure." He started to slide down the wall, then stopped midway in what she thought of as the exercise position from hell. With his massively muscular thighs he apparently didn't even notice. "You can sit in the chair if you want. It might be more comfortable."

"No, that's fine."

"Actually I feel bad. I probably should have bought a second chair." He strode over to the brown recliner in the middle of the room, lifted it as if it were a folding chair, and carried it into the dining space, lowering it carefully. "There." She looked at it, then flicked her eyes up at him. "Oh! You probably need a counter." He picked it up again, making the sleeves of his baseball shirt bulge, and set it down by the passthrough counter to the kitchen. He stood back and looked pleased with himself. "There! Problem solved."

"Um, thank you." She walked forward and set her bag on his kitchen counter. No crumbs, at least. She pulled out her laptop and booted up, then laid swatch samples on the counter. She stood awkwardly by the chair.

"Sit!" he said. "Hey, do you want a drink?"

"Um, water would be nice."

He opened the cupboard, took out the single clean glass, and poured water from a pitcher he kept in the refrigerator, giving her a clear look at his stacked glass containers of cut fruits and vegetables.

"I feel bad about my diet every time I see your refrigerator," she said.

He handed her the glass and grinned, then pulled a dirty one out of his sink and washed it quickly. "You like junk food?"

"I'm pretty good, really—but not *that* good."

"Yeah, the nutritionist loves me." He poured himself a glass of water. "My injury was bad enough that I wasn't sure I could come back. There wasn't anything about it that was for sure a career ender, but to play at the level I have to play at? I mean, it wasn't a given. I didn't feel like I had any margin for error."

"One cupcake and that could be it?"

"Yep. Felled by the Cupcake of Doom."

She laughed and tapped her keyboard a couple of times, then looked up at him. "You'll have to be where you can see this. Do you want . . ." She trailed off. Was he going to just stand there?

The answer was yes. Nick came around the kitchen counter and stood next to her, still smelling of a shower. "So how does this work exactly?"

"I show you the design. If there are things you don't like, we change them. We talk it through as long as you want, and when you're happy, you sign off on it. Then I can start implementing it for you." He took a sip of water. "Or if you hate the whole thing, I can start over. But you'll need to tell me what doesn't work, and why. Ready?" She smiled up at him.

"Game on."

His abdomen was right by her head. It was extremely distracting, and also it looked very hard, like you could poke it and it wouldn't give at all. His shirt skimmed over it as he shifted his weight. Was there a socially acceptable way to poke someone's stomach to see if it was as muscley as it looked? Probably not. Stupid social conventions.

"So here's the living room," she said, and brought up a screen showing the design. It looked like a colored-pencil sketch but was so much easier to change. "It reads as a blue space—masculine, neutral but with some color. The furniture is large and comfortable, the kind of thing you can flop on. You can't really hurt it." She risked a glance up at him. He was looking at the screen with a completely inscrutable expression. How could he be so bad at poker?

She went on, using her cursor to highlight things as she talked about them—the industrial chic lamps, the steel dining room table. "The kitchen has a couple of stylized vegetable prints—not cheesy—to give you some color on the wall. I wasn't sure if those worked for you, but you need something there. We can switch out the artwork if there's something you'd rather have. I was thinking last night maybe you'd prefer photographs."

"Photographs?" It was the first thing he'd said since she's started talking him through the plans.

"Black and whites of the city, the ice rink. Paris? A forest? Anything like that would work really well with this space. It was just sort of hard to . . . get a bead on you." He didn't say anything. "Anyway, we'll put some sort of art there. You can see the kitchen light fixture has exposed wiring. That's part of the industrial look, but it's perfectly safe." She paused, giving him the chance to say something. He took a drink of his water instead.

"Here's the bedroom. It's a really dark space, so if you wake up and still have an hour to sleep, you can roll back over. The walls are darker here, and there are room-darkening shades behind the curtains. Those grommet-tops echo the metal accents found in the rest of the space, and they're really easy to slide on the pole." She risked a glance at him, then went on. "There are two versions of this bed. It's king sized because you're a big guy . . ." She flushed slightly, very aware of the middle of his body so close to her face. "I've shown it here with a riveted steel headboard like what you saw in the dining room table, but . . ." She clicked over. "There's also this version with a slightly padded headboard covered in fabric. We can play with what fabric to use, but I'm showing it here in gray flannel." Nothing from him. "It softens the space a little and could make it seem more bedroomy. Just depends on how you want it to look."

He didn't say anything, so she moved on to his bathroom, which echoed the cool blue tones and metal accents of the rest of the space. She finally sat back.

"So. First impressions?" she said.

He chewed for a moment on the inside of his cheek, then took a drink. That was his tell when something was wrong. She was sure of it. It was probably also his tell when he was thirsty. "This is . . . great," he said, hesitating a nanosecond before the last word. *Not great. Damn damn damn.* "It would be a big change."

She cocked her head up at him. "Well, it would make the space usable. An actual living space. You have enough seating to entertain," she said, clicking back to the living room with its generous sofas and two arm chairs. "You have a dresser in your bedroom so you won't have to keep your clothes in garbage bags."

He nodded. He was still chewing the inside of his cheek.

"What's the thing you like least about the living room, say?"

He studied the screen for a moment, a slightly pained expression on his face. "This is great," he said again. "It's a very nice-looking space. I'll probably want to think about it for a couple of days, if that's okay. Let me pay you now for the design work, though."

He was going to cancel the project. Crap crap crap. He was going to cancel. "One thing I forgot to ask you," she said, desperate. "Do you have any kids?"

He stared at her, startled. "No. Um . . .?"

"I just thought if you had a child somewhere . . ." *Boston. The baby in Boston.* ". . . you might want the guest bedroom to function as a child's space."

"Oh. No. No kids." He gave her a funny look, then grabbed his wallet from the far end of the counter, where he seemed to keep it with his phone and keys, and extracted a credit card. "Can I pay you here, or should I call the office where you work, or . . .?" He stood in his desolate apartment, handsome and muscley and pinched around the eyes, holding a credit card. Was her design that bad?

"I can run it here," she said. "But Nick, there isn't anything that can't be changed. Or if you want to go one room at a time, we can do that too." *I don't want to lose this commission.*

"No, it's great," he said with no enthusiasm and handed her the card. He was going to cancel after she left. He would pay her in full and wait a couple of days to look like he was thinking about it, and then come up with some excuse not to go forward. She was sure of it.

She pasted on a smile, took his credit card, and shoved it into the machine a little harder than was actually necessary.

Half an hour later Alyssa was back in her office, realizing she'd forgotten to pick up any lunch, and not sure if she was hungry anyway. The front door buzzed—someone was coming in. Nick? Did he want to talk about the design? Had he figured out what he didn't like? She jumped up and ran to the front to catch him, almost colliding with Stacey in the hall. Stacey raised a cool, drawn-on eyebrow at her and said, "Expecting someone?"

"Um, no," Alyssa said. "Did you want to get this?" The agency owner usually wanted her to deal with foot traffic.

Stacey peered around the corner and then walked out, all smiles. "So nice to see you!" she said to the well-dressed elderly woman in the lobby. "Meredith Harriman? From the county board?" The woman smiled, and Stacey ushered her past Alyssa and into a consultation room. "I'll take care of Mrs. Harriman," she said, "since I assigned you to the Sorensen account." She smiled sweetly.

Assigned? Nick had had to walk out to get her as his designer. *Bet he regrets that now.* And it looked like Stacey was going to lighten her client load as payback. Right now all Alyssa had was the young expectant couple; a newly-divorced man who wanted her to buy some starter furniture because he didn't have time; and Nick Sorensen, who was supposed to want an entire apartment redone, but clearly didn't want anything at all.

If he was going to cancel, the least he could do was to be less handsome. And not smell like shampoo and make her think of bubbles running off his shoulders in the shower, water sheeting across his back . . . It was incredibly rude to be that good-looking while simultaneously not liking her design.

Alyssa was wrong about one thing. He didn't take two days. Her phone beeped in the late afternoon.

Nick: *Hey, I was thinking about the apt, and this isn't really a good time to go forward with it. Hockey and everything. But thanks for all the work you did! It was great.*

Clearly. She didn't bother to text him back.

CHAPTER ELEVEN

The regular season started the first Saturday in October. Nick played well and relished the burn in his thighs and lungs as the game wore on. He scored on a power play early in the third period, and the hometown crowd stomped and shouted as lasers shot across the arena. The preseason had been great, but this was official—all the pain and work of rehab had been worth it. He was back. After the game he had his jersey off but was still in his pads when a reporter approached him in the locker room. "Nick, you're only twenty-two goals behind Arne Swanson on the all-time goal list now. Think you'll get him this season?"

Nick stared at the guy as he felt the familiar vertigo, the falling, falling. He sat on the stool in front of his locker.

"Nick?" the reporter said.

Leif, the Swedish goalkeeper, turned to look. "Nick? You okay?"

Nick nodded. "Um, I don't know," he muttered to the reporter, and then he headed off on his skates to the bathroom. He stuck his head under a spigot and ran water over his face and hair. Twenty-two behind Swanson?

Once the reporters were gone and he'd showered, Devin cornered him. "What was that about?"

Nick played dumb and shimmied into his shirt, then buckled his belt.

"You went pretty white," Devin said.

"It's the Norwegian blood. We're a pale people."

"Tell me."

Nick exhaled sharply and turned to face him. "Sammy Gonczy and I had a bet going on who would pass Arne Swanson first. A half gallon of butter pecan ice cream was riding on it."

"Oh, man. I'm sorry."

"My stats are changing and his aren't. I'm going to pass Swanson and then go on to get the next guy on the list. And Sammy will always stay exactly where he is."

Devin was quiet for a moment. "It bothers you to see your stats change?"

"We were tied," Nick said. "Can you believe that? He was as likely to get there first as I was. More, maybe. It's unfair as hell."

"Yeah." Devin was quiet for a moment, and Nick moved to step past him. "How's the apartment coming?"

"I canceled it, okay?"

Devin took that in. "Coach know that?"

Nick took a step forward. Aggressive. In Devin's space. Devin didn't react, just looked at him calmly. There was a reason he was the captain. "My *home* is none of his business."

"Looks to me like you don't have a home," Devin said, then turned and walked out of the locker room.

Nick made it through three days of practice before Coach Pedersen called to him after a scrimmage. "Sorensen. Over here." The coach nodded toward the penalty box, and Nick cocked his head. Really? But he opened the door and sat on the bench, surrounded by high plexiglass to keep fans from doing more than shouting at a player serving a penalty. Pedersen stepped in and let the door swing shut behind him.

"Was I naughty?" Nick said.

"Yeah. Heard you decided to keep living with nothing." Nick's mouth pulled tight. "We had a deal."

Nick shrugged. "It's my place."

"It's not normal."

"Jake Hilstrap has seven girlfriends. Tyler Maki collects caterpillars. *Caterpillars*, Coach. I'm not any weirder than that."

"Neither of those things affect the team."

"It will if Jake's girlfriends find out about each other."

The coach lowered his gaze and looked at Nick for a long time. "When we signed, you we knew we taking a chance. You had a serious physical injury."

"All better," Nick said, standing. The coach didn't move.

"And the psychological injury. I'm mad as hell at us for not requiring you to go to counseling."

"I wouldn't have gone."

"So you said. That's why we should have made you go. We probably still will. For now, you get your living space fixed up. That's an order."

"Not in my contract."

"It is."

"Bullshit."

"You can't do anything that would be detrimental to the team."

"I have a good mattress! I'm not going to get a stiff neck."

"This is obviously about the plane crash. I haven't worked out how exactly, but it doesn't matter. You're messed up somehow, and you need to get it fixed before you crash during the playoffs." Nick stared at him. "Sorry. Poor choice of words. But the pressure's going to get worse, and I don't know if you're going to be able to handle it."

Nick took a long step over and got in the coach's face. "I fell fifteen thousand feet out of the sky in a metal tube"—he threw his arm toward the arena ceiling—"that slammed into a field at night." He bit the words. "Everybody else died, and I was alone out there for an hour before they found me. You understand that? I spent five weeks in the hospital and months rehabbing my effing leg, and I'm *back*. So excuse me for not giving a damn about your feelings about my goddamn silverware."

The coach looked at him soberly, not flinching. "I just made a decision. You get your apartment vaguely normal. I don't care if you leave dishes in the sink or you buy an ugly sofa. Just get somewhere in the normal range. And we're going to find you a counselor, and you're going to go."

"The hell I will."

"It's a health issue, Nick. I need your head facing forward by the playoffs." He gave Nick an appraising look. "And frankly, it could take a few months."

"What's a counselor going to do? Make me talk about the crash? About my best friends dying?" He was gesturing wildly in the small enclosure, and his hand bounced off the plexiglass. "Guess what? I don't want to talk about it."

"But you obviously need to."

Nick leaned in, his eyes hard. "I can talk for an hour. I can talk for a week, and you know what? *They'll still be dead*." He wiped his nose on the back of his hand and maneuvered toward the gate. "How does it help anything if they're still dead?" He grabbed the gate and jerked it open, clipping the coach in the thigh, and skated the few feet to the tunnel that led to the locker room.

Two days and a loss to Edmonton later, Nick was finishing breakfast when he got a text.

Coach Pedersen: *You have a counseling appt tomorrow at 10 a.m. The trainer's driving you.*

Coach Pedersen: *I have Moose McFarland on call if necessary.*

Nick smiled faintly. Moose was a goon, a journeyman teams picked up for a year at a time and who wasn't a skilled player. He went on the ice to intimidate other guys. He didn't play for Detroit, but the coach's meaning was clear—they'd stuff him in the car if they had to. Fine. Apparently he was going to a counselor—but that didn't mean he was going to talk.

His phone rang. Nick tapped it on. "Yeah, I got your text. Screw you."

There was silence for a moment, then a woman's voice said, "I didn't send a text. But screw you too." He whipped the phone around to stare at the screen. Alyssa, the decorator. *Shit.*

"Alyssa?"

"Yep."

"Oh geez, I am so sorry. I thought you were my coach."

"You talk that way to your coach?"

"Um. Well, long story. I'm really sorry."

"I'm in front of your building. I have a question I want to ask you, and I want an answer."

"Yeah, okay. Of course. I'm sorry." He walked to his apartment door and buzzed the main door open, then ran down the steps anyway and pushed it open. That seemed better—more apologetic. She was wearing a blue skirt and silver jewelry, and her hair was doing that thing where it sort of curled over her shoulders and made him want to touch it. "I apologize," he said as she brushed past him. She had her work tote over her shoulder, and her sunglasses were still on. She walked up the steps to his apartment without talking and stood waiting for him to open the door. He pushed it with his foot, letting her walk in first.

Alyssa stood in his apartment and glanced around. "You didn't get somebody else?"

It took him a moment to understand what she meant. "A different decorator? No! Of course not."

"But you hated my design." He didn't say anything. It was true. He'd hated it. She pursed her lips and took a breath as if gathering her courage. Then she pointed a blush pink nail toward his kitchen. "Explain your coffeepot." She lowered her bag and crossed her arms over her chest.

He looked at her for a moment, then slowly said, "I pour water in through the top, and I add—"

She rolled her eyes and said, "It's a cheap piece of crap."

"My coffeemaker has offended you?"

"Yes." He smiled faintly and waited. She really was pretty—tall and elegant. "You have a lot of money and plenty of counter space. Yet when you went out to buy a coffeemaker, you got a bad one. Who gets a bad coffeemaker when they could get a good one?"

He blinked at her. "Me?"

"It makes no *sense*. I can see maybe you didn't get around to dealing with your place. I mean it's weird, but okay. But you got around to buying a coffeemaker and chose that monstrosity?"

"Monstrosity seems a little harsh."

"Mon*stros*ity."

Nick smiled. "There's a cup left. You want it?" Alyssa exhaled with a little huff. He grinned. "So you want to know why I defied social conventions and purchased a household appliance that doesn't meet your expectations?"

"Yes." She stood there waiting.

"Do you really want to know, or did you just want to yell at me for a while?"

Alyssa thought for a moment. "Both."

"I'll tell you if you'll take the job again." She stared at him. "Coach says I have to get the apartment done. If I have to deal with it, I'd rather have you do it. If you're willing."

"Is that why you were yelling at him on the phone?"

"No, he's doing other stuff to me too."

She pulled her mouth again in that way she had. It made him look at her lips, which was a problem, since he'd already kissed them and therefore knew what they felt like and how easy it was to pull her against him.

"You know, some people enjoy having their space done."

Nick walked into the kitchen, grabbed his second coffee cup, and poured the rest of the coffee. He stood looking into the cup for a moment. "Might be some grounds in there," he said, then shrugged and set it on the counter as close to her as he could get it.

"I'm a coffee snob," she said.

"I can get something decent delivered if you want."

"No. But thank you."

Jesus, she was still waiting. She actually expected an answer. He raked his hair back and then left his hand on his head, elbow up, saw her sneak a look at his abdomen where his shirt had ridden up, and tried to control his smirk. He might be about to have a difficult conversation with a casual acquaintance, but he did have great abs. He dropped his hand, took a sip of his own coffee, and made a face. Then he said, "I seem to be having trouble going on. After the crash."

Her face lost its pugnacious expression and instantly looked stricken. That didn't make this easier.

"I had great friends. They were good people. And they're not getting any coffee."

"You're drinking bad coffee on purpose? So you won't enjoy it too much?"

"Yep. If I were a better man, I would do without completely. But I'm not."

"Nick." She didn't go on.

Oh shit shit shit—she was starting to cry. He stepped forward and put his hand on her upper arm. "I am so sorry."

She shook her head. "I shouldn't have been mad about your coffeemaker. I shouldn't have asked."

"No, it's good. Apparently I'm supposed to *talk about things*. This actually gives me some material the next time I have to explain myself. I'll just work my way through the household appliances."

"You have *one*," she said, sniffing.

"You underestimate me. I also have a clock in the bathroom." She smiled. "I probably need a potato baker too, so I can keep my hands warm during games." He smirked at her, then realized his hand was still on her arm and he dropped it. "So are you willing to do the apartment? You can take out your nemesis." He jerked his head toward the kitchen.

"Yes, but you have to tell me what you didn't like about the first design. Otherwise, how will I do something you like? Also I might have a slight problem with perfectionism."

He took a sip of coffee. "It looks like a plane crash." She stared at him. "Blue interiors, metal accents, rivets, exposed wiring—that's what it looks like."

"Oh my god." She pressed her fingers against her mouth and squeezed her eyes shut.

He shrugged.

"Oh, Nick. I am so sorry. I didn't mean . . ."

He let her talk for a while, then said, "I'll pay for your time, obviously, but I'd like it different."

She sat on the floor with her back to the outside wall and said quietly, "What do you want it to look like?"

"Not blue. My old apartment was blue, for one thing, and I don't want it to look too much the same. I think that would be harder."

"Okay."

He sat beside her, his thighs drawn up. He was barefoot. "I lived with Sammy Gonczy. He was going to get his own place—it was just time. But we'd roomed together before we were in the NHL too. I lived with him for a long time." He curled his toes under. "When we moved into that place—the last apartment we had—I asked him what color he wanted the living room. And he said blue, just to shut me up. Because he didn't care, see? And I said no, that's not how you pick the color you're going to live with." He flicked his eyes toward her. "Color's important to me."

Alyssa glanced around his stark white space. Desolate. "How do *you* choose the color?"

"I go to the museum, wander the galleries, and see what's calling to me right then."

She blinked. "Are you serious?"

"Yeah." He turned to look at her. "Why? You think that's dumb?"

"No!" She put a hand on his forearm, then quickly removed it. "I think it's great. I'm just surprised."

"I almost have a double degree in art and art history. Did I tell you that?"

She stared at him for a moment, then back at his walls. "No. You did not."

"So I spent parts of three days in the museum, just swimming in the colors, and finally Henry Brokman's *Meta* hit me over the head. You know it?"

She shook her head.

"Here. Hold on." He jumped up and ran into his bedroom, then came back a moment later with his laptop and booted it up. The keys glowed with a red light below the keyboard. He tapped and brought the painting up, then pointed. "That shade, right there—on the water. Where the sun backs off the wave and the color deepens, just a little? That's what I painted the living room."

He took a deep breath and looked around as though he could see it. "So I'm painting with a roller, right? I have half of it done when Sammy comes home with his girlfriend and says, "See? Blue." He barked a laugh and turned to look at Alyssa. Her eyes were wet. "I made you sad. I knew talking was a bad idea."

"No, it's really helpful," Alyssa said. She hesitated. "Is there any chance I could see what your old apartment looked like? Do you have a photo?"

He thought for a moment. "Somebody did an article on us. She came out to our place. Would that work?" He tapped the keyboard as he talked. A moment later he had an article from a Boston-area entertainment magazine up. "Um, it has us in it. You just have to ignore that." He tapped one more time and then angled his laptop so she could see it better.

Alyssa sucked in her breath. There was Nick with a striking young man with almost black hair, their arms thrown over each other's shoulders, smiling at the camera. Behind them was a beautiful living room with gray-blue walls, bookcases full of what looked like art and history books, solid but elegant furniture with wooden trim and turned legs. It had a European country feel, more French than anything, warmed with touches of yellow. Framed prints and original canvases hung on the walls and leaned on the bookcases, and sculptures of varying sizes littered the room, including a two-foot tall bust of Pericles wearing a cap with a hockey logo.

"Who chose the art?" she said, finally pulling her eyes away to look at him. "You?" He nodded. "It's a beautiful space." She tapped the touchpad, and the article flipped to the next page.

Nick made a strangled noise low in his throat. It sounded like he was choking. Alyssa glanced up at him, alarmed. He pulled his shirt up over his face and hunched forward, his shoulders shaking as the tears came.

CHAPTER TWELVE

Alyssa sat frozen, unsure of what to do. She looked back at the screen. The second page of the article about the two young hockey stars was mostly text, but at the top there was a picture of Nick and the guy who must be Sammy in their kitchen, a bright space with white cabinets. This photo was different from the other more posed one. It was a candid shot—they were looking at each other and laughing, heads thrown back, sun splashed on their faces. They were sharing a secret, and the camera had caught it. She looked a moment longer, memorizing it. They were obviously best friends. Plenty of people never had a friend like that.

"I'm sorry if I shouldn't have clicked forward." He must have known that photo was on the next page—but he definitely hadn't been ready for it.

He stood, his shirt over his head, and shrugged his arms out as he walked to the bathroom. She heard the water running, and a moment later he walked out, bare chested, wiping water off his face with the shirt. He stepped wordlessly into his bedroom and emerged with an eggplant-colored T-shirt. He pulled it on and sat beside her again without making eye contact.

"Hey," she said. "I am so sorry."

He shook his head slightly. "Anyway, she didn't take pictures of our bedrooms."

"Okay." She was quiet for a moment, unsure whether she should flip back to the previous screen.

"That's one of my favorite pictures," Nick mumbled. He glanced sideways at her, fleetingly, but he had a faint smile. "See the grapes? Because we thought we'd be fancy-ass city boys and put grapes in a bowl." She nodded. "He'd just bounced one off my eyeball."

She exhaled in surprise. "That's terrible!"

"Right? The little bastard."

"Do you . . . want a similar space here? Not the color, but the vibe?"

He locked eyes with her and didn't look away. "I don't know what I want. Making a decision means choosing to step away, you know? I can't take that step." He raked a hand through his hair. "It's probably better if you just do it." He stood.

"No." She stood up too. "You have to go to the museum with me and choose a color."

"I'm really not going to do that."

"Then go to the museum and eat something from the snack bar in a surly manner while I choose the color."

He paused. "I guess I could do that."

"Are any of the things in your old place available? Because you had some great stuff."

"Everything's in storage there. One of the guys—not one of the dead ones . . ." She winced. "He put things in storage for me after I left. I was in a wheelchair when it was being packed up, and I couldn't deal with it." He rubbed his knuckle across his nose. "I don't have any kitchen stuff. That was Sammy's. He liked to cook, and I hate cooking." He stubbed his toes along the floorboards, making a sound like an eraser. "His parents cleaned his stuff out while I was in the hospital. I came back to a place I didn't recognize."

"Nick."

"They got a few things wrong."

"They took some of your stuff?"

"A couple of things. I don't care. I mean, we lived together so long, they might as well have been his." He smiled faintly. "And they left a framed picture of me that he'd hung in the living room to embarrass me."

"Why would that—"

"Because I was three and standing next to a trophy that was literally taller than I was. I had my head cocked toward it, and man was I grinning. Sammy saw that photo at my parents' once and conspired with my mom to get a copy made. Then he hung it near our front door, right? So almost anybody who stopped by would see it."

"It sounds adorable!" Alyssa laughed, her eyes sparkling.

"I was *definitely* adorable." He gave her a cheesy grin. "But he thought it would look like I'd done it, and he thought it was weird to hang up a picture of yourself." He dumped his coffee down the kitchen drain. "This really is crap. You were right about that."

She tapped her forehead.

"Anyway, every girl he brought home thought I was incredibly cute, and it totally backfired on him." He laughed, then his expression grew serious. "His parents left it. I guess they thought I'd hung it too." He sighed, then walked over to pick up his laptop.

"Nick?" Alyssa asked, gently. "Do you want me to get some things out of storage so you have a few familiar items here?"

He looked at her for a long moment, then shrugged. "I don't know."

"I mean, we can stick with the duck prints in your bedroom if you want."

"Don't you dare." He grinned. "I really hated the duck prints."

She laughed. "They were a punishment."

His mouth dropped open. "Seriously?"

She nodded. "I was kind of mad at you." She bit her lip. "I didn't understand. I'm sorry."

"You should be! You gave me effing ugly duck prints. They were seriously a punishment?"

"Oh yeah." She smiled wickedly.

"That was a fowl thing to do," he said. Then: "You heard the 'w,' right?"

"Sadly, yes."

"Excellent." He beamed.

"What time should I pick you up tomorrow? We have a museum to tour."

CHAPTER THIRTEEN

Alyssa met with the expectant couple at eight the next morning. They loved her design and were thrilled that she'd tucked a little bookcase under the slant of the eve. Because of the ceiling line, she'd gone with a circus motif—the architecture itself suggested a tent. Adding circus animals and striped curtains completed the look. They left by nine, holding hands, and she was able to pick Nick up at nine thirty, as promised.

She double-parked in front of his building and scanned the street quickly, wondering if she could get away with just texting to let him know she was here so she wouldn't have to find a parking space. Before she could even open her texting app, he came bounding down the steps, wearing a cream Irish fisherman's sweater under his jacket. He pulled the passenger door open. "Hey!" he said, settling himself into the seat and buckling up. At once, the car felt different—alive and energetic.

"Hi," she said, and knew her smile was too big. "Are you ready?"

"You bet! Hope you don't mind me just coming down. My coffeemaker didn't want to see you."

"Is it sulking because of the other day?"

"Yeah. You hurt its feelings."

She laughed, then concentrated as she edged into traffic. "So tell me about yourself," Nick said. "What are your qualifications to be my designer? Specifically, are you a Red Wheels fan?"

She glanced over, amused. "Is that the main requirement?"

"Pretty much."

"Well, my stepdad and brother are."

"Good start. Your mom?"

"She doesn't like sweating and visible effort, so no sports. She doesn't mind if it's on, though. So that's something?"

"Hmm. We're gonna have to work on your mom."

Good luck with that. Alyssa parked at the Detroit Institute of Arts, and they walked up the long, shallow steps to the Woodward Avenue entrance. The museum was white, with three tall arches for entry. Nick took a deep breath. "The anticipation is great, isn't it?" he said, turning to her. He pulled the door open for her, they walked in, and he paid for them. They lingered in the lobby, breathing in the smell of a public space. He stood beside her, tall and hard-bodied, but he wasn't what she had anticipated. She hadn't thought he was this layered, but there was a lot to this man.

"I love it here," she murmured.

He smiled at her, then stuck his hands in his front pockets and rocked back on his heels. "I guess I could walk around with you instead of just sitting at the snack bar. But since I'm here against my will, you take the lead."

"Against your will?"

"I said no, and you made me come anyway. You basically kidnapped me."

Her eyebrows shot up at that. "I am known for my brutality. I mean, right now I'm taking a guy with an art degree through an art museum." She patted his shoulder. "You hang in there, cupcake."

Nick grinned. "Ouch."

Alyssa led him into the Native American art gallery on the first floor. They walked slowly, stopping in front of several exhibits, chatting occasionally about an artifact. Alyssa held a small notebook loosely by her side, not writing anything down at first so that Nick would get used to it and feel less stalked. Eventually she started jotting things down—objects he'd stopped to admire, fragments of his conversation.

They moved through the gallery. "Look at that eye," he said, nodding toward a bust. "That's three thousand years old and it's still better than I can do."

"You're a sculptor?" Alyssa asked.

He shook his head. "I painted, but . . ." He shrugged.

"But not eyes?"

He laughed. "No, I can paint eyes. They're hard. Teeth are too. The brushstroke is especially important with teeth."

"Is that so?" She rocked back on her heels to look at him. They were standing closer than she'd realized, just a breath between their arms, even though the gallery was nearly deserted at mid-morning on a weekday. Their proximity wasn't intentional—they'd both been drawn in to look at the head of a young Greek woman who'd lived and died millennia ago. But Alyssa was suddenly aware of the bulk of him, the heat from his body in this cool space. That she had to tip her head up to look at him. "What makes you like a sculpture?" *Tell me what to put in your space.*

"I like movement in paintings, but I kind of want sculpture to balance that."

She looked at the young woman's marble face. "To bring a sense of serenity."

He turned to face her. "Yes. That exactly. And a . . . timelessness."

"You like modern painting but more classical sculpture?"

"Yes!" He walked on. "It's nice to have someone to go to the museum with."

"Sammy didn't go with you?" she asked. She felt awkward saying his name, as though it was too personal somehow.

"Oh no, not his thing."

"What was he like?"

Nick looked at her and then was quiet so long she thought he wasn't going to answer. Finally he said, "He was fun. Most of the trouble we got into was his doing."

"He was the Minister of Hijinks?"

"Exactly. Like Dragan believed in paranormal stuff—all sorts of crazy shit. That's the guy who was going to propose. When our plane went down."

She nodded. "Unusual name."

"He was Croatian. We made lots of 'Dragan breath' comments, because we're culturally sensitive."

She laughed.

"So one day we're at his place, and Sammy uses his bathroom and gets this idea, right? He noticed that the bathroom vented up onto the roof. When we got home, Sammy pointed out that meant it also vented *down* from the roof." Alyssa gave him squint eyes, not sure where this was going.

"Sammy played the flute in school. He was never that into it, but he still had the flute. And we told Luka that we'd both heard a ghost in Dragan's bathroom." Nick shook his head. "Luka was so gullible. He just believed the best of everyone, you know? Never saw ulterior motives. So I told Dragan I wanted to watch a game at his house because Sammy wanted our apartment for a date. That seemed realistic."

"Sure," Alyssa said.

"But instead, Sammy and I went together, and I parked behind the neighbor's trees. I threw a ladder up against Dragan's house, and

Sammy climbed onto the roof. Then I hid the ladder in the bushes. If Dragan had looked out right then, we'd have been busted, but he didn't. Then I walked back to the car and drove up. Luka arrived right when I did—I told him to come over too. When we went in, Sammy was sitting up there by the vent pipe with his flute, grinning like a cheerful gargoyle."

They stopped by a collection of figurines in a case. Alyssa only glanced at them. She wanted to hear the end of the story.

"After about half an hour, Sammy began to play a little. First just a note or two, then real spooky woo-woo stuff. Luka heard it first, and once he told Dragan, he just flipped. I mean, he knew Luka wouldn't prank him. He just didn't have it in him. So Dragan went in the bathroom and came out just white." Nick ran his hand past his face, illustrating. "He was talking about calling a priest. I was trying not to laugh because the two of them were getting each other cranked tighter and tighter. And then it started to rain."

"Oh no! Poor Sammy."

"Eh, Sammy had it coming. Of course, I did too, but I was snug inside."

"How did you get him down?" Alyssa asked.

"Oh, I didn't! I left him sitting up there while I watched the rest of the game."

"You're horrible!"

"Yep. And after a while he started playing 'Up on the Rooftop,' but Luka and Dragan were too busy running searches on exorcisms to notice. When the game was over, I drove off . . ." Alyssa gasped. "Dragan was standing there waving. What was I supposed to do? I came back around with the ladder a few minutes later. Sammy tried to be mad, but he was laughing too hard at my imitation of Luka and Dragan. And it was all worthwhile because Dragan told everybody his bathroom was haunted. He started showering at his girlfriend's—like his morning shower. And he'd run errands just so he could pee somewhere else." He shook his head at the memory.

"Was Dragan mad when he found out?"

"No, he laughed his ass off. He was still plotting his revenge when . . . you know." They walked on. "What about you?" he said, bringing the conversation back to art. "You never said what you look for in a work." His phone buzzed and he ignored it.

She thought about it as they entered the Egyptian room. "You're going to laugh."

"I wouldn't laugh at a fellow artist."

"I'm not an artist. I'm a decorator."

"That's obviously the same thing. Space is your canvas. Duh." He bumped her with his shoulder, very gently.

She blushed. "I like things that are . . . pretty."

He smiled faintly. "Nothing wrong with the pursuit of beauty." He kept looking at her. Her face was hot, and she wished he'd look away, and also she wanted him never to take his eyes from hers. Finally he said, "I don't want anything Egyptian in the apartment."

She blinked. "Okay. Any reason?"

"It reminds me of Scooby-Doo."

She gave him a look of mock outrage. "You have something against Scooby-Doo?"

He grinned. "Not really. But I think we're more likely to find our color inspiration somewhere else."

They worked through the African gallery. He stopped at a number of places, putting his hands in his pockets and tilting his head. Alyssa surreptitiously jotted down the exhibits so she could find commonalities—even come back later if she needed to. His phone buzzed, then again and again. It was on vibrate but it went off five times, six, seven in quick succession. He grabbed for it with fumble-free hands—an athlete's hands—and as a guard gave him a dirty look, he tapped it off. Then he checked the screen and blanched. "Excuse me," he said. "I need to make a call."

He stepped out into the promenade and tapped to reply, then held the phone to his ear. In the lofty space the sound echoed, and Alyssa didn't have to sidle too close to the exhibit's exit in order to eavesdrop. "I'm sorry," he was saying. "No, I . . . no. I didn't . . . I get that. I understand. No. Damn it, fine me whatever you want, it was an accident." She moved to the edge of the exit so she could see him. He was standing with his back to her, thirty yards away, bent slightly forward as though that gave him more privacy. "I'm *saying*," he said, voice clipped, "I completely forgot." He was silent for a moment. "I'm at the art museum." Silence. "No, I'm not kidding."

Nick turned and saw her. He motioned her over, and she hurried to him, her flats clicking on the floor. "I'm in trouble," he whispered. "I was supposed to be somewhere. Can you say hi to the team trainer for a second?"

She raised her eyebrows and stared at his phone. He mouthed, "Please?" She took the phone. "Hello?"

There was silence for a moment, then a man's voice said, "Miss, can you tell me where you are right now?"

"I'm at the Detroit Institute of Arts." He was silent for a moment, then said, "Could you please put Nick back on?" She wordlessly handed him the phone. He murmured another apology and got off.

"So that went well," he said, raking his hand through his hair. "Sorry. We were . . . going somewhere."

"If you need to go . . ."

He shook his head. "Too late." He ran his hand over his jaw, making a soft scraping noise. "Coach is making me see a therapist. I told him I'm getting the mattress off the floor, but that wasn't good enough for him." He looked at her ruefully. "I was supposed to go there this morning."

"Oh, I am so sorry!" Alyssa said. "I didn't realize—"

"Not your fault," Nick said quickly. "I'll pay for it later. Let's just enjoy ourselves now."

She gave him a sympathetic look and said, "Let's hit the European painting exhibit, then."

They walked into the gallery, and Nick stalked through the first room, fists in his pocket, the muscles in his back tense. His jaw was fixed. That thing needed a plastic guard like the one on the wickedly sharp chef's knife she kept in a kitchen drawer. Six landscapes in, he began to relax a little, stopping here and there to point out line work he thought was particularly good, or to ask what she thought about the way the sun burst through a cloud in a field in Provence two centuries ago.

He stopped once in front of a J.M.W. Turner. "Do you like it?" He stepped back to get out of her peripheral vision and let her concentrate on the painting. It was a soft swirl of mist over the sea— everything mixed and edgeless and a little . . . dull. Would she sound like a provincial hick if she said that? Yes, yes she would.

"Not a lot," she finally admitted. "I appreciate the technique involved . . ."

He waved his hand dismissively, as if to say she didn't need to apologize for her feelings. "What don't you like about it?"

"Well . . ." She hesitated, biting her lip, and he stepped back toward her, which did not actually help her concentrate on sorting it out. "There's nothing . . . appealing about it."

"It's not pretty?" He smiled faintly.

"No, it's not." He nodded. "That's what you think too?"

"No, I like lots of things that aren't pretty—I mean, Michelangelo is more about power, right? Physicality. And who doesn't love Michelangelo? Turner is too indistinct for me. I need the lines. Nothing makes sense without them." He shrugged and they moved on.

He paused several times. She tried to let him dictate their flow through the gallery. His stops and starts told her things—the way he rocked back on his heels and tilted his head, the way his eye lingered on the sun filtering through a tree in an English meadow. She didn't want her own rhythms to interrupt what she was learning. She stopped only once for herself, in front of a floral painting with lush pink peonies, and white roses tucked in among them. She could almost smell the heavy fragrance. She tried to memorize the bouquet so she could revisit it in her mind later. It was a way she had of giving herself a tiny secret vacation—to sit in a meeting with Stacey Herself but see a windswept seashore or a path through a meadow carpeted with yellow flowers.

When they exited the gallery, they walked silently to the stairs and then descended. The architecture was magnificent. The space had a loftiness that lifted the spirits. They were halfway down when Nick said contritely, "I'm sorry I couldn't give you any color direction." He twisted up the corner of his mouth, trying to smile. "I wasn't trying to be difficult."

"Oh, it's no problem," Alyssa said. *I've got you, sucker. You may not know what color you were rolling in, but I do.*

CHAPTER FOURTEEN

Alyssa had so much to get done that afternoon. The city wanted the lobby of the waste management facility redone, and of course Stacey had assigned that to her. The lobby was to be clean and flow well and have durable furniture and look sharp, but also not look like taxpayer money was spent on it. Do a good job! But not too good. That was the message. When Stacey had given her the project, she had smiled sweetly and said, "It'll be another line on your résumé!" As if she wanted "waste management" in her client list. And there was a final walk-through with the newly divorced guy who'd wanted someone to buy him a sofa, and . . .

"You have time to grab lunch?" Nick said, nodding toward the food court.

"Sure!" she said, then wondered if it sounded too bright.

They walked down to Kresge Court and got sandwiches. The dining area was dotted with seating arrangements of different sorts—varied furniture and sizes. Nick led them over to a sofa and set his plate down with a clink. Alyssa hesitated. Sitting beside him seemed inappropriate—despite that whole kissing-for-the-sake-of-the-bow-height thing—so she sat in the chair opposite, put her plate down, and swiveled her legs sideways.

"That's not good for your knees," Nick said, nodding toward her lady-folded legs.

"It's likely to shorten my career?"

"Yep."

"Maybe they'll keep me for my locker-room decorating skills."

He grinned and took a bite of his sandwich. They ate in silence for a moment, then Nick asked, "Why do you work for that woman?"

"Stacey?"

He nodded.

"She's . . . well respected."

"Not for her personality."

"No. But it's hard to start out on your own. I'm trying to build a client base, get some experience so I can say I have some, and then start my own firm." She sighed. "It's going to take a while."

"Wait. You're *practicing* on me?"

She grinned. "Sure am."

"Huh." He wiped his mouth and folded his napkin by his plate. "What if you don't get exactly the right . . . I'm gonna say dining room table? I'll be devastated."

"Yeah, I could tell."

Something crossed his face. He took a sip of water. "Um, I've been thinking about the apartment, though." He fidgeted with the napkin. She stayed quiet and waited. "The bedroom, um . . ." He trailed off. Oh god, did he want a sex swing on the ceiling? What could possibly embarrass him and make him hedge like this? "You know how you made the bedroom dark in that first design?" She nodded. "I want it light."

She took this in. "I thought you might have late games and want to sleep in some mornings."

"Yeah, that's true. But light is better."

"Okay. Like a pale color on the wall? Or do you mean you want more delicate furniture, or . . .?"

He took another sip of water, rolled his lips, and blew air out tightly, and finally looked up at her. "If I wake up in the night, I need to know right away that I'm in a bedroom." She blinked at him, not understanding. "Like immediately—not after I turn a light on."

"Okay."

"I need to know I'm not in wreckage. I can't always tell at night. If I've been sleeping."

"Oh my god, Nick." What an idiot she was—giving him a dark blue bedroom. "Of course. Something homey and comforting?"

"It can have a cartoon bedspread for all I care, but I want to know that I'm in a bed. To see vague outlines of bedroom-shaped things."

"Yet you'd pitch a tantrum if I gave you a Scooby-Doo bedspread," she said, tapping her lips, trying to lighten the conversation.

He laughed. "No, Scooby's okay. Before I was just covering my crush on Daphne. She's pretty hot." He waggled an eyebrow. "She was my dream woman in third grade."

She started to laugh, but it turned strangled when she caught sight of the young man across the courtyard. He was heading their way but hadn't spotted them yet. How in the actual hell?

Alyssa slumped down, trying to let Nick's tall frame block her. Ryan was looking around—definitely searching for someone. For her. He stepped into the Ancient Middle East room and Alyssa thought, *We should go now!* and looked at her half-eaten sandwich. Nick had soup with his sandwich, and the bowl was still almost full. He didn't seem like the kind of guy who'd walk away from his lunch. Actually, she wasn't sure any guy would do that. How could she get him out of here before Ryan saw her? Because there was absolutely no possibility that he was here to enjoy some paintings.

He was bad news. He was her nemesis. He was her brother.

"Did you like the Gentileschi?" Nick said. She blinked at him. "Aw, come on, everybody likes Gentileschi."

Ryan stepped out of the gallery and turned in a slow circle, headed toward Kresge Court—no, no—and brightened as he saw her.

Nick looked at her seriously. "I'm sorry. I didn't mean to tell you what you should like." She stared at him, confused. "You look upset. It's fine if you didn't like it. I just wanted to hear your thoughts about—"

"No, it's not that," she said, and then Ryan was behind Nick, beaming at her.

"Alyssa!" She wanted to die. He was going to embarrass her. He had never not embarrassed her. She'd be lucky if he didn't dance naked on the steps before he left. "Hey, I'm glad I found you."

"I'm having a private consultation, Ryan."

Nick twisted to look back at her brother standing behind him.

"Yeah, I just need a couple of minutes," Ryan said, stepping around to plop on the sofa beside Nick.

"This is *inappropriate*," she hissed. It was her greatest insult.

He shrugged. "I'm in trouble."

"When are you not in trouble?" she snapped.

Nick's eyes widened fractionally, and he shifted on the sofa, turning so he could see Ryan better.

"Ouch, Lyssie. But seriously, I need help."

"Aren't you supposed to be at work?" Alyssa said. Was he going to ask to borrow money again? His custodial job didn't pay much, but he also could manage his budget a lot better.

"I took a lunch hour. Possibly a long one."

"Ryan!"

"You're her . . . brother?" Nick said, finally putting the use of the nickname with the similar features. Ryan was tall, handsome, and utterly irresponsible.

"Yeah," Ryan said, looking at him for the first time. "Shit. Shit. You're Nick Sorensen."

Nick smiled. "Nice to meet you." He stuck out his hand. Ryan grasped it and pumped it and didn't let it go. "You're . . .?"

"Ryan Compton. Alyssa's my big sister." Ryan beamed. Nick extricated his hand. "So are you guys an item or something? You dating my sister?"

She would have to find a secluded place to bury the body. Maybe she could put a false wall in some project, because she was definitely going to kill him.

"She's doing my apartment for me," Nick said.

"Wow." Ryan brightened even more. "I bet you have a cool place."

Nick glanced up at Alyssa, amused. She was too frustrated to share the laughter in his eyes. "You like ducks?" he said.

"Ducks? Sure!" Ryan said. Nick's mouth quirked.

"How did you find me?" Alyssa demanded.

"That mummy with lipstick at your office told me where you were."

"Stacey? You talked to *Stacey*?"

"She said to tell you that your poop project won't wait. I don't know what that was supposed to mean."

Alyssa reddened. She took a moment to be sure she kept her composure. "What do you need, Ryan? I'm at work. And you should be."

"That's the problem," he said. "They want me to paint a mural on the cafeteria wall."

"So do it." She ripped a bite out of her sandwich and chewed it savagely.

"I sort of can't."

She finished chewing, swallowed, and then said, "Why is that, Ryan?"

He ran his hand through his hair. "I can't draw."

"So why do they want you to do a mural?"

"I might have told them I could when they hired me." She opened her mouth, and he rushed on. "Lyss, I needed this job. They asked about it at the interview, and I thought sure, I'll just supervise the art students. They're going to color it in anyway. I'll just tell them my vision and let them hash it out."

She balled up her napkin in her hand. If she squeezed it any harder, it would turn into a diamond. "So why don't you?"

"They want it outlined by the end of school tomorrow so the art club can start. Apparently it needs to be finished before some chess tournament."

"Ryan, I have to work. I can't go draw a mural on the cafeteria wall."

"Please." He looked desperate. But it was another situation he'd gotten himself into. Like hanging out with drug dealers because he was so damn amiable and got along with everyone. And then he got busted. If he hadn't done time, he could have gotten a better job. He was smart but aimless. This mural was his problem, and he needed to solve it. Ryan dropped to his knees and folded his hands in front of her, beseeching. A few people around them stirred, looking over. Someone pulled out a camera, thinking it was a proposal.

"God, Ryan, get up," Alyssa hissed.

"What's the mural?" Nick asked.

"That's the thing!" Ryan said. "It doesn't matter. Just something related to the school."

"What's your mascot?"

"The Tigers."

"Ah. Because Michigan is known as the home of jungle animals." Nick glanced at Alyssa, and she tried to look as menacing as possible. "Your sister kind of scares me."

"Welcome to the club."

Nick grinned. "I have an hour this afternoon if you want to show me the wall. If you want some help. I need to know the size, if it's cinderblock—"

"It is."

Nick made a sound in his throat. "Doesn't matter what you do if it's on cinderblock. It's not really going to look good."

"I just need not to get fired." Ryan studied Nick. "Do you . . . do you draw?"

Nick clapped him on the shoulder. "Yep."

"He's supposed to have the art students do it," Alyssa said.

Nick shrugged. "I'm an art student."

"You have a degree. That doesn't count."

"Nope. Never finished. I had one project left in one course."

"Why'd you stop?" Ryan said.

Nick shrugged. Not something he discussed with random little brothers, apparently. "If you want, I can take a look at the project today. Pretty sure I can help you outline a tiger."

"You are the best! Literally the best," Ryan said. "I love you, man." He reached over and hugged Nick, who smacked him once on the back. As he moved back, Ryan's knee clipped Nick's plate and knocked his soup bowl over.

"God, Ryan!" Alyssa said.

Ryan glanced down, saw that the soup hadn't splashed on Nick's legs, and stood. "So now's good?"

"Sure," Nick said, rescuing his soggy sandwich. He grabbed a napkin and wrapped it. "Can I eat this in your car?"

"You can do anything you want in my car, man," Ryan said. "Nick Sorensen! Holy crap!"

Nick turned to Alyssa. "I'm going to go save a tigerless school. Thanks for taking me around this morning. I enjoyed looking with you." She nodded, swiping furiously at his tray with a ball of napkins. "I got that." He picked the tray up and returned it, stopping to lift a hand to her in farewell. Then Nick's tall, athletic form moved off beside her brother's familiar outline. This was a disaster.

"I liked the Gentileschi," she whispered.

CHAPTER FIFTEEN

Nick asked Ryan to slow down three times. Finally he said, "If you crash and ruin my leg again, an entire NHL team is going to fuck you up." Ryan hesitated for a moment, the sun bouncing off his aviators, then eased off the accelerator.

"So you know how to draw tigers? This isn't some joke my sister set up?"

"How could she have set this up? She clearly had no idea you were going to show up at the museum today."

Ryan was silent, drumming short fingernails on the steering wheel of a battered metallic blue muscle car.

"Besides, it wouldn't really be funny," Nick continued. "She has a better sense of humor than that, doesn't she?"

"Yeah. Well, no." They both thought that was funny and cracked up.

Ryan turned at a bank of rust and gold chrysanthemums by a brick sign announcing they were entering the high school's compound. He parked behind the school, and they got out. "You have to jiggle the handle a little," he said, and Nick dutifully jerked the passenger handle until the door would shut.

Ryan led them up to the back door of the school. It was locked. He glanced at his watch, said, "Shit," and jerked his head around to the front. "So in San Jose when Stevens tried to check you into the boards, but you just squirted out of the way, how did you do that?"

Nick grinned. "I just accelerated."

"There's an awesome clip of him hitting the plexiglass instead of you. His face sort of slides down it."

"I've seen that," Nick said. "I probably enjoy it more than he does."

Ryan barked a laugh as they went up the steps to the main entrance. A security guard nodded to him and stopped Nick. "What's your business here?" he said—pleasant enough, but not a guy who was planning to fall for something.

"He's with me," Ryan said. "Some building and grounds stuff."

The guard looked at Nick for a long time, then motioned to him to move his arms out so the guard could see his waist. Nick complied, giving Ryan a wry smile. The guard waved them through the metal detector. Ryan walked through. Nick hesitated, then stepped through, and the thing gave a low angry buzz like a bulldog on the other side of a fence.

"Step back through," the guard said, all business now. Nick walked back through.

"It's my leg," he said. "Got a lot of metal in it."

"Can you take your jacket off?" Nick took his jacket off and let the guard examine it, then spread out while the guy patted him down. "You have any weapons on you?" he asked.

Nick was shaking his head when Ryan said, "This is Nick Sorensen." The guard looked at them blankly. "Of the Red Wheels! Come on, man. You have to recognize him."

"I'm a football guy," the guard said, stepping back to look at Nick. "Let's see your ID."

Nick produced it while Ryan tapped his phone. He showed a team picture to the guard. "Huh," the guy said. "A Red Wheels player, huh? You guys gonna win the Cup this year?"

"A little defense would help," Nick said, taking his jacket and following Ryan down the hall to the cafeteria. It was a large rectangle, windows overlooking a courtyard on one side, open to a hallway on one short end, with the kitchen and student lineup area on one long side. The remaining short cinderblock wall was blank. "Our canvas," Ryan said, throwing his arm out.

Nick rocked back and studied it. A few straggling students across the room took his photograph and giggled. "You have something in mind?"

"No," Ryan said.

"You just kicked the can down the road? When you were interviewed?"

Ryan shrugged. "I did time, man. A year for a piddly drug charge, but it's on my record. I was lucky this school was willing to give me a job as a janitor."

"Hard to get a job with a record," Nick said. He cocked his head. "A tiger, then?"

Ryan gave him a thumbs-up. He got paper and a stubby pencil when Nick asked for them, and stood back while Nick sketched the wall in proportion, and then a tiger viewed from the side. He hadn't sketched anything since . . . well, since the crash. He just hadn't wanted to.

He flipped the sketchbook to show Ryan, who pronounced, "That is awesome, man!"

Nick's mouth twisted as he evaluated it. "Lacks menace. It's more like an anatomical drawing."

"Are you kidding me?"

"What if its head is turned toward us and it's roaring?" He flipped the page and resketched the tiger.

"Dude. Nailed it!" Ryan said, leaning over his shoulder. A couple of kids sidled up to them, guy-giggling.

"Hey," Nick said. "Are you in the art club?"

"*No,*" one of them said. "We're hockey players."

"You realize you can do both," Nick said flatly.

"Art club is for losers," the bigger boy said.

Nick dropped his head and raised an eyebrow. "Really?" He turned to Ryan and said affably, "Turns out I'm a loser. Must be why I got nudged out for the Selke Award a couple of years ago."

The boys' eyes bulged.

"Wait. You're Nick Sorensen," the bigger one said.

"People keep telling me that," Nick said. He stood back and angled the paper. "What do you think?" The boys and Ryan crowded around. Ryan slapped him on the back. "If you have a marker or some chalk, I could do the outline right now," Nick said. "Then the art club can paint it tomorrow." He slid his eyes sideways at the students.

"We could maybe join . . ." the smaller one said. "To help Nick out."

Nick put a hand on each of their shoulders. "That would be great, but it's Ryan's project." The guys took selfies with Nick, asked for hockey tips, and moved on. Ryan scrambled after a chalk marker and sat on a lunch table while Nick sketched the tiger in. "So how does Alyssa keep up with everything?" Nick asked, his arm arcing to make the tiger's back with one bold stroke. "She's got a demanding job, the boyfriend, the friend she helps with party planning . . ." He kept his eyes on the wall, waiting for Ryan's response as the tiger began to emerge.

"She's dating somebody?" Ryan said. "I didn't know that." He shrugged. "She's super woman. Better than the rest of us and happy to remind you."

Nick finally glanced over and gave Ryan a rueful smile. He wasn't getting involved in family dynamics—he'd gotten the information he wanted. Alyssa wasn't dating anyone. And he'd helped Alyssa's brother—she'd for sure be grateful for that. Always smart to bank a little goodwill.

Twenty minutes later the big cat's lines were on the cafeteria wall, right down to the claws, and Ryan had ushered him back to the parking lot. "You saved my ass, man. Thank you so much."

"Happy to help," Nick said. "I kind of enjoyed sketching something out again."

And he was aware of how much he'd liked touring the museum with Alyssa that morning. Twice he'd risked putting his hand on the small of her back to guide her, and both times he'd felt a flicker of feeling he didn't allow himself.

Enjoying life was off-limits now. He'd have to watch that.

CHAPTER SIXTEEN

Alyssa ordered the furniture for Nick's space—living room, dining area, and bedroom. She'd left his spare bedroom alone as he'd instructed, but she wasn't happy about it. If he ever gave her the go-ahead, she knew just what to do with it.

He had a road trip coming up and would be gone for three days, so she was going to paint his walls during that time. All of the furniture could be delivered next week, partly because she'd chosen a number of antique pieces from local stores and partly because of dumb luck.

Which might not be so lucky because it meant the project wouldn't go on forever.

Alyssa poked around online and in shops in town, finally found the right bedding, and took Nick's bedroom wall color from it. She was going with a soft butter-yellow that accented the yellow-and-blue antique star quilt she would fold over the bottom of his bed. The bedspread itself would be plain—a balance between homey and masculine. The bed frame was made from wood that glowed with the warmth only an antique could bring, and his bedside table was large and solid. She was giving him a table lamp with two lights—a traditional task light in case he read in bed, with an ivory-look inlay around the base that emitted a soft light and made the switch for the task light easy to find. He could turn it off if he wanted, but it would function as a miniature night-light, right there at hand. The kind a six foot two guy with a rock-hard body could use without looking like he had a night-light.

She found a desk with clean lines, made of salvaged wood, that had the top modified so it could tilt up if he wanted to use it as a drawing table. She'd bought an easel for the desktop that would hold a small painting, but he could move it and put his own canvas on it if he wanted to paint. It wouldn't hold a large canvas, but that was his own fault for being too dense to see that he should use his second bedroom as a studio. Maybe she'd hang a duck on its door as punishment.

Or a tiger. She'd texted with him briefly about a table but hadn't heard how things went with Ryan. She presumed it had been a disaster. Anticipatory mortification was her specialty, but in fairness this was Ryan. He had absolutely no sense of decorum. She'd texted her brother the previous day and asked how it had gone, and had gotten a thumbs-up emoji. She followed up, asking for details, and he sent a photo of a tiger painted on a cafeteria wall. It was remarkable—Nick had captured the cat's energy as well as its lines. She was impressed, but she didn't want to see the mural. She wanted to know how badly Ryan had embarrassed her. But how did you ask that?

She checked in on the sewer department job and was back at the office when her phone buzzed with an incoming text.

Vanessa: *Hey, I have great news! I called your agency and asked if I could hire you for a consultation on the homeless shelter.*

Vanessa: *Stacey said yes! She was nice about it too.*

Alyssa stared at her phone. *Frick.*

Alyssa: *You talked to Stacey??*

Vanessa: *Yes! Can we set up a time to meet? I'll send directions.*

That won't be necessary.

Alyssa: *Great. I'm swamped right now. Is it possible to push it to next week?*

Vanessa: *Sure. Will be in touch!*

Vanessa ended with a string of emojis, starting with heart-eyes and ending with the red-dressed dancer. Most of the flowers were in between. Alyssa stared at her phone for almost a minute, then at the ceiling. She didn't want to bring Nick into this, but she trusted him. She finally gave in and texted.

Alyssa: *Just curious. Do you happen to have any time today?*

Alyssa: *It's not important! Just if you do.*

Nick responded immediately.

Nick: *I'm at a coffeeshop in Midtown. Practice will be long today because apparently we're supposed to hold onto the puck.*

Nick: *If you need to meet, earlier's better.*

Alyssa: *How long will you be at the coffeeshop?*

Nick: *Until I'm caffeinated. I'm a big guy, so if you leave now, you can catch me.*

Nick: *Joe's Grounds*

Alyssa pulled up the address on her phone and slipped out of the agency, sliding the marker by her name to indicate that she was out of the building. She didn't know the coffeeshop, but it was easy to find. It had a red and white all-caps sign, and when she opened the door, instead of a chime it played birds chirping wildly. She stared at the door, then slid her eyes over to Nick, sitting in a corner nursing a coffee. He had a second cup waiting opposite him, so she skipped ordering and sat down.

"This place seems . . . rudimentary," she said, then took a sip. "You noticed how I take my coffee when we were at the museum?"

He nodded. "This place may be rudimentary, but it beats my coffeemaker." He grinned.

She laughed. "Arizona could beat your coffeemaker." He raised his eyebrows, and she rubbed her nails on her shoulder. "That's right— Ryan fed me some hockey information."

"Hey, did he show you the tiger we did?"

"He did!" She took another sip. *I'm picking up his habit: sip to delay.* "Um, I actually wanted to ask you about that. Did that all . . . go okay?"

"Sure." They drank coffee in silence, looking at each other over the top of their cups. "There's something else going on here, but I don't know what it is. Pretend I'm dumb and just explain it."

"No! I . . ." She sighed and scored the cup with her fingernail. "So, Ryan sometimes . . . He has a history of . . . How do I say this?"

"He can't hold a line on cinderblock?" He raised an eyebrow. "You can hit me with the brutal truth."

"The brutal truth is that he embarrasses people. He just doesn't . . . think."

"And you're afraid that us running naked through the halls shouting 'Down with the principal!' would somehow be a problem?"

She smiled ruefully. "See, he would actually do that." She took a deep breath. "I just want to know how much he embarrassed me."

"You're serious." He took that in. "Well, he drove too fast, but that was my only complaint." He shrugged.

"Huh. Okay." She blew on her coffee. They sat in companionable silence.

"I'm a little disappointed in Ryan," Nick finally said. "He must have great prank capacity if you came all the way down here just to find out what happened at the school. And yet he was well-behaved."

"Can we walk with these?" Alyssa asked.

He shot her a curious look but said, "Sure," and they grabbed their cups and headed out. It was a sunny, crisp day, and several businesses had yellow and rust mums in planters out front, as if they'd coordinated for a few storefronts and then given up.

"I find myself in an embarrassing situation and I don't know what to do." He stayed silent, waiting. "Vanessa wants me to work on a charity project with her."

"Oh." Clearly this wasn't where he'd thought she was going. "Oh! And she wants you to donate your time, but you can't afford to?"

"Not exactly." She exhaled and trailed a finger over the last yellow mum as they passed. "At the museum you asked about my favorite painting."

"Monet's water lilies," he recalled.

She nodded. "I discovered them when I was in junior high. It was . . . a bad time. Ryan and I used to go to the public library after school every day. They had this Monet book that I'd slowly thumb through until our mom came to pick us up."

"Yeah?"

"One day I went in, and it wasn't on the shelf. The art books didn't get checked out that much, so I kind of panicked. And this old librarian—well, she seemed old then; she had long white hair and blue cat-eye glasses—she came over and said the book I always looked at had been withdrawn from the collection because it hadn't been checked out in so long."

"Hey, why didn't you ever check it out?" Nick asked. "Why not just take it home?"

"We didn't have library cards right then. We, uh, didn't meet the residence requirement." She moved aside as a kid on a bike went past. "I was always afraid the librarian would run us out of the library."

"Why? Did Ryan act up or something?"

"No, he mostly played games on a computer. I was worried that she'd figure out that . . ." Her voice trailed off. "Anyway, she held the book out and said there wasn't space to store it until the next book sale, so did I want to take it off their hands?"

Nick smiled. "Hey, that was lucky!"

Alyssa shook her head. "She stole the book for me. She withdrew it from the collection so she could give it to me."

"Ohh. Those librarians are shifty."

"Right?" She smiled back. "It's my most treasured possession."

They paused at a corner, waiting for traffic to pass. "Why did it mean so much? That book?"

She slid a toe over the curb, caressing its curve. "It was so beautiful, and things weren't beautiful at home."

"Is that when your parents got divorced? Were they fighting?"

"No, they actually never got divorced." His eyebrows shot up. "My dad had gambling debts he couldn't pay, so he left. A couple of years later, he died. Mom had tried to serve him to demand child support, but she couldn't find him."

"Ouch."

"Anyway," she said breezily, "money was tight, and our living situation wasn't ideal."

"Not a lot of art on the walls?"

"No." She paused. "But there was a steering wheel."

"Alyssa." He reached out and rubbed her arm. "You lived in a car?"

She leaned into him and rested her forehead on his shoulder. She spoke into his jacket. "During middle school. When kids tend to be at their most sensitive."

"Aw, geez." He gave her a one-arm hug, then dropped his arm as she shifted to look up at him.

"I try to avoid telling people."

He gave her an appraising look. "You know there's nothing wrong with that, right? Having lived through hard times."

"There was a *lot* wrong with it," she snapped, then whispered, "Sorry."

He waved his fingers, dismissing any insult. "I didn't mean it was okay that it happened. Just that there's no shame there."

"Except that there is," she said. "I'm always afraid someone will find out." The light turned green but just for the turn lanes. They still had to wait on the corner.

He looked at her. "Why?"

She stared at him. "Why?"

"Yeah. Why?"

"Because . . ." she spluttered. "When things went bad, people took advantage of us. Mom had to sell a lot of things for less than they were worth because people knew she needed the money. She felt like she shouldn't have let them know." She shrugged helplessly. "I was just always ashamed." She swiped at her eyes.

He reached out and touched her pinky with his. "I feel a profound sense of shame just for being alive," he whispered. "So there's zero judgment here." Alyssa slipped her hand into his, just for a moment, and gave it a squeeze. The light finally turned green, and they crossed the street.

Nick brought the conversation back to Vanessa's request for design help. "So you don't want to do a charity project because it reminds you of bad times?" he asked.

"No, because it's for a church that helped us." He looked confused. "It has a food pantry in its parking lot. It's painted white and filled with nonperishable food. They planted herbs around it, and there's a little pair of scissors on a string and baggies so you can snip some basil or dill and take it home. Which is a fantastic idea for people who aren't living in a car."

"And you used to get cans of . . . something . . . there?" He clearly had no idea what was wrong, but he was trying.

"Mom parked overnight in a park across the street. She'd take us to school in the morning and then drive to her job." She glanced up at him. "She didn't want us using the food pantry because someone might see us, and she was still pretending everything was fine. And she said we had enough money for food, which we didn't, really."

"I'm sorry."

Alyssa shook that off. "Mom worked as a waitress and she was always exhausted. When she fell asleep, I'd slip out and check the pantry for food that Ryan and I could sneak eat in the back seat. Pop-Tarts were the best, but I had to open them outside because they crinkled."

He gave her a sad smile. There was a bench there, and he sat and pulled her down beside him.

"But Ryan left crumbs all over. I would carefully pick them off the seat and floor, but I could never get *him* clean. In the morning Mom would find those clingy fruit-filling crumbs on his mouth or under his fingernails."

"She checked your *fingernails*?"

"Mom has a deep commitment to not being embarrassed." She sighed. "Anyway, she told me to stop taking food from the pantry, and I said I would, but instead I just waited until Ryan fell asleep too, and I'd sneak out and eat them myself and not share." A fat tear hurtled down her cheek and hung off her chin. He lifted it off with his forefinger.

She looked at him searchingly. "Am I telling you too much?"

"Hell no. I like knowing what makes you tick."

She gave him a shy smile. "Janet and our florist friend Emma know. I try not to tell other people."

"Why not?" He looked genuinely curious.

She stood up straighter and inhaled audibly. "It's just not relevant to anything," she said breezily. "Going forward, I mean. It has nothing to do with my life now."

"Jesus," Nick said. "Now I know what I sound like when I refuse to talk about the crash."

She gave him an almost apologetic look. "That's why I thought you might understand," she whispered. "Because you're pretending everything's fine."

He cleared his throat and Alyssa hurried on.

"Anyway, at that food pantry one night, a creepy guy stepped out from behind the herbs they'd planted—they get tall. I turned back for the car, but I was afraid to scream because Mom would be so mad. But Ryan hurtled out of the car in Spider-Man pajama pants that hit him mid-calf. He charged the guy and just bounced off him—he was only nine. But it startled the guy enough to give me a chance to grab Ryan, and we made it back to the car."

"Your mom didn't wake up?"

"She did, but we just said we'd let a bug out. It explained the doors closing."

Nick put his hand over hers for a second, then folded his hands around his cup, as though to keep them there.

"The worst part wasn't the guy—it was that Ryan knew I was going without him. He'd been watching to make sure I was safe. He knew." She opened her eyes wide, hoping the tears would evaporate off her eyeballs before they fell, but she didn't have any luck there either. "I was a terrible sister."

He unwrapped the napkin from around his coffee cup, shook it out, and gently patted her face. Then he rubbed under her eyes, cleaning up the mascara. "It's waterproof," she mumbled.

"It's really not," he said, smiling gently. He folded the handkerchief again and they sat in silence, watching people walk past. "You were a kid. You did the best you could under the circumstances. And feeding him wasn't your responsibility."

"Maybe not. But sharing with him was."

An elderly woman with thick ankles approached and looked pointedly at the bench. They rose, and Nick took Alyssa's arm, threading it through the crook of his elbow. He raised his eyebrows and looked at it and she nodded. *Okay.* They headed back the way they had come.

"Were we going anywhere?" Alyssa asked, throwing her empty coffee cup in a trash can buzzed by one energetic fly.

"Nope. But I want to hear how this ended."

"So I joined a club that met before school. They served breakfast."

"Ah."

"And I'd take an extra biscuit to keep in my bag and give to Ryan after school, before Mom picked us up. But Krystelle Rohrbach saw me, and later when she saw our car just parked—you know, nobody getting in or out—she told everyone I was living in it."

"Krystelle Rohrbach was a little shit." He made mock-strangle hands.

She gave a half laugh, acknowledging the sentiment, then shrugged. "It was a juicy scoop, and we were in eighth grade. I told her it was French camping, the way they did on the Île de Navet."

Nick pulled his head back and squinted at her. "That means 'turnip.'"

"Yes, but none of us knew that, and it sounded fancy. Anyway, it shut them up until French class, when someone asked Madame about 'French camping.'" Nick grimaced, but Alyssa smiled softly. "She backed up my story, then quietly got us help."

"Yay for Madame!"

She gave him a sober look. "She ratted us out to social services. And then Mom made us switch schools to get away from her."

"The hell? She helped you."

"That doesn't make up for the knowing."

He raked his hand through his hair and tossed his cup in a trash bin on the street. "So you don't want to do this thing for Vanessa because it brings back bad memories?"

"No . . . well, not exactly. It's more that Vanessa's a friend now. I don't want it to change the relationship."

He squinted at her. "Vanessa wouldn't—"

"I can't take that chance!" Her voice was rising, and she could hear it but couldn't stop it. "You have to keep appearances up, or people will use it against you."

He raised his eyebrows. "Is that something your mother said?"

They were back at Joe's Grounds. Alyssa shrugged heavily. "She was right, though. One time, she had a date and the guy didn't know about us, and of course he couldn't pick her up. She said she'd meet him at the restaurant. And we were supposed to stay down."

"For like three hours?"

"Ryan had to pee and went in in his pajamas, walked right up to her, and asked to use the potty. She was mortified."

Nick raised a brow. "You know, all this bad stuff Ryan did to get a reputation doesn't sound that bad to me."

"Yeah." She sighed heavily. "The guy fled. But the next day she told a friend at the restaurant about it, and Bill overheard. My future stepdad."

"He was a customer?"

"Yeah. And he thought it was funny and asked her out. We got McDonald's and went to a Disney movie—it was a family date." She smiled at the memory. "He asked if we wanted something from the snack bar, and Mom said we didn't, but I said we wanted popcorn and Ryan said he wanted candy. Bill bought us both, and then a popcorn for him and Mom to share. He said later he wanted an excuse to bump her hand." She gave him a wan smile. "It wasn't the food so much as the . . . care." She looked at him, and there were tears in her eyes. "Ryan hadn't had something special in a long time. It was the candy— but also the *choice*."

"Bill sounds like a stand-up guy."

"Yep. I used to wonder what he saw in Mom. I know that's terrible." She looked up at him, then gave a little shrug. "His first wife left him. I think he realized Mom was a woman who would never walk out." She blew air out, then whispered, "I don't want to go to that church—I'm afraid someone will recognize me. They put us up in a hotel for a couple of nights back then while social services straightened things out."

When Nick spoke again, he seemed to be choosing his words carefully. "And you're afraid to go back because of two nights fifteen years ago?"

"Not quite fifteen." She sniffed.

He grunted. "Okay, it's official. You're not as messed up as me, but you're a strong runner-up." He bumped her shoulder gently, and she gave him the stink eye, but then smiled. "Why don't you give Vanessa a chance to be a Bill, not the other guy? You know, the first one." Her face twisted, but she didn't say anything. "Okay. Well, they could get somebody else to do it. Alright if I talk to Vanessa?"

She gave him a small nod. "That's why I told you all this. Can you finesse it? Slide it by her without making it awkward?"

"Sure." He pulled out his phone and scrolled down his contacts list to place the call. "Vanessa? Nick. Listen, Alyssa needs to not do that church job and doesn't want to talk about it. That good?" He listened for a moment. "Thanks." He clicked off.

She stared at him. "That was *finesse*?"

"Hockey players are known for their subtlety," he said, shrugging.

CHAPTER SEVENTEEN

Alyssa was in her office, rooting in the closet for the painting equipment she stored there, when she smelled Stacey's perfume. She turned, paint roller in hand.

"How's everything going?" Stacey said.

"Fine." Alyssa could hear the suspicion in her own voice.

Stacey didn't smile. "Wonderful! How close are you to being done with Nick Sorensen's place?"

"Um, maybe three weeks? The basic design decisions are made, but I still need to put everything in place." She gave the roller a little twirl.

"Well, when you're done, I want to use it in a commercial."

Alyssa gaped. "You mean show his apartment? I don't think he'd like that." She was sure he wouldn't. It seemed like an invasion of privacy for someone as well-known as he was. He didn't need fans criticizing his throw pillows.

"He doesn't have a choice. The contract specifies we can use the finished project in promotions."

Alyssa shook her head. "I don't use that contract. You know that. I think the client should make an informed decision after they see their space."

Stacey's eyes didn't move—too much Botox—but her lips spasmed like a lizard whose tail had been run over on the highway. Probably it was a smile. "Well, that's the contract Nick signed."

Oh, shit. Stacey had shoved the contract into her hands as she ran out to catch Nick at his car the day he first came in. *Shit shit shit.*

"Stacey, you *know* that's not the contract I use." She sounded shrill. She hated sounding shrill. When she'd come on board here, she'd negotiated to use a slightly altered contract—one that was nearly identical to Stacey's boilerplate but that included a few minor terms that Alyssa felt were more fair to her clients—instead of taking a signing bonus. At the time, being able to use the slightly altered contract had seemed like a symbolic victory. Alyssa took a breath to calm herself.

"You really should look more carefully before you have a client sign things," Stacey said. "I handed you the contract *I* use. Anyway, do a good job because his apartment is going to be all over our digital marketing. He's a hunk—a lot of ladies are going to be happy to see his bedroom, even if it's only online."

Frick.

Stacey turned and went back to her own office. Stunned, Alyssa gathered up the rest of her painting supplies and loaded up her trunk.

She called her mother from the paint store while the jiggle machine shook up her gallons of paint.

"Alyssa?" her mother said. "Is it urgent? I'm ironing the table-cloths. My women's group is having tea here this afternoon."

"No, it's not important." She hesitated and her mother didn't fill the silence. "I just had a bad morning at work."

"Well, work harder next time."

"It wasn't that I didn't work hard." She heard the defensive note in her voice. "I just made a mistake and . . . it feels bad."

"Well, just don't pull the tinsel, and you'll be okay." Her mother laughed lightly. "And wear navy for the next couple of days—it's never wrong. Don't say anything inappropriate, and you'll be fine."

"Okay, Mom. I'm gonna run." She ended the call.

Once she had the paint cans loaded in her car, she texted Janet and Emma.

Alyssa: *My life is a wreck. Have lunch with me? Right now?*

Emma: *I'm in the middle of a carnation delivery.*

Alyssa: *A. Wreck. Enough that I called my mother.*

Emma: *Wow. Was she . . . helpful?*

Alyssa: *She didn't take the time to find out what was wrong, but she did suggest that it's my fault.*

Emma: 🙄

Janet: *I'm free. Did your life wreck on the hunky shoals of those big shoulder muscles I met?*

Janet: *Muscle Shoals. I crack myself up.*

Alyssa: 😵

Alyssa: *Sort of. Details at Gilda's in fifteen?*

Janet: *I hope there are pictures.*

Emma: *Nobody told me there were muscles involved. I'll be there.*

Aw. Friends were great.

Gilda's was a '50s-style diner with chrome-edged stools and waitresses in poodle skirts. They also had a juke box that took tokens, and Gilda kept a bucket of them right beside it. When Alyssa had asked her about it once, Gilda had said, "Listen, honey, music makes the world a better place. Why wouldn't I help make the world better if I could?" She walked away, calling over her shoulder, "Chrome makes the world a better place too. And Elvis's butt. Oh, lordy." Gilda was a trip.

Alyssa got there first, snagged a booth, and looked over the shake menu. All the food was named for singers or bands, and she never remembered what was what. Janet and Emma walked in seconds apart, greeted Gilda behind the counter, and slid into the booth opposite her. Janet was wearing faded jeans and a political T-shirt from a few election cycles ago. Emma had a short, spiky cut that she could pull off because of her bone structure. She wore her signature high heels, skinny jeans, and a red blouse with white polka dots. Alyssa could talk fashion with Emma. Janet, not so much.

"Spill," Janet said, but Gilda herself walked over just then. She was a Black woman who was probably . . . eighty? Then again she'd looked eighty for twenty years now. Today she was in a pale blue poodle skirt and carried an order pad.

"I'll have the Buddy Holly and a large Ella Fitzgerald," Alyssa said.

"You make good life choices," Gilda said, scribbling on the pad.

"Is any of your food a *bad* life choice?" Emma asked.

"Nope," Gilda said.

They finished ordering, and Gilda brought their shakes right out. Their burgers followed quickly.

"It's Stacey again," Alyssa said finally. She brought Emma up to speed on the Sorensen job and explained how her boss wanted to use his home in a TV commercial. "And I know she's just doing it to punish him for standing up to her, and me for . . . I guess going along with it."

"You don't use her contract, though," Emma said. "You told me once you thought there were problems with it."

"I don't think it's fair to the client in several places. But she handed it to me when I was rushing after him when he first came in, and I used it without noticing." She hung her head. "I hate myself."

"She's a snake," Emma hissed. "Let's sneak into her closet and pry the rhinestones off her designer purses."

Alyssa reached across the table and squeezed Emma's hand. "You guys are the best."

"What did your mom say?" Janet asked.

"She told me to wear navy, which I'll admit is good advice. She also told me not to pull the tinsel."

Janet and Emma looked at each other. "Um . . ." Emma said.

"The year after she married my stepdad, she threw a party for the Stuck-Up Ladies of Charity."

"Catchy name," Janet said.

Emma waved her hand dismissively. She didn't remember the group's actual name. "It was at our house in December. She set up lots of small tables so she could tuck more people in, but that meant making extra table decorations, and she was doing the food herself, and . . . She wanted to prove that she belonged, and, well, she was really stressed. She felt very *evaluated* by these women. And I understood how important it was that everything be perfect."

"And a piece of tinsel ruined it?" Emma said. "Doesn't sound like tinsel."

"All the ladies were seated and served and had just started eating. I had been paraded around in a red velvet dress. Then I was supposed to stay in my room. But of course I peeked. So when the cat walked toward the living room with a piece of tinsel stuck to her butt, I grabbed at it so she wouldn't walk out like that. It would make things *not perfect*."

"And she jumped in the Christmas tree?" Janet guessed.

"Nope. I grabbed at her and she ran, but I got a hold of the tinsel. Turns out it wasn't on her butt, it was *in* it." Emma gasped. "And I was left standing at the edge of the room, holding a piece of tinsel covered in cat poop, which I had just pulled out of the cat's butt. Some of the women saw, and started whispering to each other."

"Oh my god," Emma said, pressing her fingertips to her lips. Janet slowly sank sideways until she rested against Emma's shoulder.

"Mom grabbed my shoulder with a 'you have embarrassed me' look and marched me back to my room. She said, 'Alyssa, that was so *inappropriate*.' And then she left me holding the tinsel."

"Should I ask what you did with it?" Janet said.

Alyssa shrugged. "I stood there holding it, then I finally sneaked into the bathroom and flushed it."

"Is it funny now?" Janet asked.

Alyssa raised an eyebrow at her. "You've met my mom. What do you think?"

"Aw, honey," Janet said, and squeezed her hand. "So what are you going to do about Stacey? I hope it involves arterial splatter. Just a reminder that I have drop cloths."

"I'm going to finish Nick's apartment as fast as I can and try to make it a space he can enjoy. If he doesn't mind having it featured, no problem."

"And if he does?" Janet said.

"I drink twelve Little Richards and stick my head under a pillow."

"Always good to have a plan," Janet said. "You know I wish you'd come back to the party planning business."

"Yes, but no," Alyssa said.

They hugged goodbye on the sidewalk. Janet and Emma demanded that she keep them updated, and Emma told her to stop by the flower shop she managed because the mums were magnificent this year.

Full of fat, sugar, and friendship, Alyssa drove to Nick's, parked, and lugged her box of paint supplies up to his apartment, then made two more trips for the paint cans. She thought about him tripping on the cans in Vanessa and Devin's garage and smiled faintly. She'd decorated him before his apartment.

She set the last can down and turned in a slow circle. The space felt empty, and not just because of that one lonely brown chair in the living room. She'd been here without him a couple of other times—she had a key—but she felt that she had betrayed him with the contract issue. Accidentally, sure. But from the way her dad and brother talked about him, she knew he was a big deal to hockey people—and Detroit was Hockey Town. Just moving with him through the art museum, she'd seen people recognize him and whisper to their companions—and that was a museum crowd. He was a guy who was going to want privacy, and she'd accidentally robbed him of that right. At some point she would have to face him. All six foot two, hard-muscled, ridiculously handsome Nick, looking at her with disappointment. Maybe anger.

He had been so kind when they'd met at Joe's Grounds and walked with their coffee. She'd told him about living in the car, the scary man at the food pantry—my god, she'd told him about the Pop-Tarts. And he'd really listened. She didn't just lust after his handsome, muscley body—although hell yes, she'd liked kissing him under the arch. And she would absolutely help Janet with more receptions if she could make that happen again. But Alyssa really *liked* Nick. She felt safe with him, and she hadn't returned that safety. She'd messed up.

Alyssa covered the floor in the living room and tugged his game system away from the wall. She should have asked him to do it before he left. Might as well have gotten some work out of those bulging don't-like-her-anymore arms. Stupid judgy biceps.

She cut in around the floor, ceiling, and doorways of the living room, then did a first coat on the kitchen. She normally hired a professional painter, but Nick hadn't wanted someone else in the apartment while he was gone, and anyway, she enjoyed painting. It was late by then and she was hungry, so she ran out for Chinese takeout. She was going to be up all night—she needed to get as much of this done as she could so that she could put the second coat on tomorrow and get the place aired out before he got back. If she was done painting when his road trip ended, she wouldn't have to see him very much.

She cleaned her paintbrush in his bathtub, laid it on the edge of the sink to dry, and stepped out onto the balcony to get some of the paint stink out of her nose. She had all the windows open and hadn't been chilly while she was inside, but now she grabbed a clean drop cloth and wrapped up in it, using her purse as a pillow.

She'd just take a catnap on Nick's balcony, and then she was going to paint his bedroom. She yawned and fell asleep watching night settle over Detroit's skyline.

When she woke an hour later and went to slide the glass door open, it was locked.

CHAPTER EIGHTEEN

Oh no. Had the door automatically locked behind her? Or was he home early?

Which would be worse?

Alyssa peered through the door and saw nothing different—her painting equipment was still lying around, drop cloths on the floor and draped over the one sad overstuffed chair. She couldn't see into the bedrooms or bathroom, but there was no suitcase visible. Could a man really move through the world and leave so few traces?

No, he couldn't. His keys were on the kitchen counter. *Crap.*

Alyssa would have to knock and knock now, because it was late, and he would be tired from traveling. Or call him, and then explain she was standing two feet away. She didn't want to catch him in his pajamas. What if he didn't wear any? Maybe she *should* wait. . . .

She hooked her bag over her shoulder, gathered the drop cloth, and took a deep breath. And then Nick walked out of the bathroom, a white towel around his waist, his hair damp. There was a rivulet running down the middle of his chest, one drop careening through the

Katie Kennedy

valley in his chest muscles. Did he just walk around like this, half naked, with his balcony blinds open? And if so, where could she park to watch?

She rapped on the glass and he turned, his eyes popping wide, and then a broad grin spread over his face. He walked over. "Hi."

"You seem to have locked the door," Alyssa said through the glass.

"You seem to have been lurking on my balcony. Lurker."

"May I come in?"

He tilted his head and considered this, one hand still gripping the towel at his waist. He tortured her another moment, then flicked the lever on the frame and slid the door open. Alyssa stepped through, carefully averting her eyes from the towel. It was a fairly big towel, which was disappointing. She'd have to replace it with smaller ones when she did his bathroom, in case she found that parking spot.

"Ah, thank you." She sidled past him into the living room. "I seem to have misunderstood when you were getting back." He shrugged and all sorts of good things happened with his naked chest and ripply arms. She needed to talk about something because otherwise she was going to drool. Although if he whipped off the towel to wipe it up, that would be a win. "Um, Stacey wanted to know if you'd be willing to have your place featured in an online ad. When it's done."

He blinked. "Is that your boss? The . . . unpleasant one?"

"That's her."

He shook his head. "Nope." Her stomach twisted. "I don't really like being recognized. I mean, I love the game, but I don't want everybody in Detroit judging my coffeemaker."

"May it rest in peace," she said, not at all surprised by his answer. It wasn't as if he wanted to show off his place the way Vanessa might have. "I'll clear out and let you get to bed."

But before she could take a step, he said, "You painted my living room green."

She took a deep breath. "At the museum you stopped at landscapes—summer and spring ones. And you talked about the plants, about botanical shapes, about painting leaves in the foreground versus the background, about ink work in veins. You said you missed a courtyard garden at your old apartment building, where you could eat outside in dappled green light."

Nick rubbed his forehead, blushing. "Jesus, I'm a chatterbox."

She laughed. "We were there for three hours. But 'dappled green light,' Nick. It will be a summer meadow kind of space—a connection to nature." She looked at him, worried. "Is that okay?"

"Will I get a cow? I think I'd enjoy a cow."

He was standing a foot away from her, still gripping the towel. He smelled like some spicy man-body wash for his man body, and it was distracting, and damn him, he'd gone and woken up her girl parts— which had been asleep for so long she'd started calling them Rip Van Winkle. And now that they were awake, they wanted to stay awake. And claw that towel off. Did the man *never* lose his grip? Stupid athlete hands. Would it kill him to be less coordinated?

"No cow." She sounded slightly breathless. Because of the paint fumes, clearly. The front of his towel shifted.

"I'm going to get dressed." He went into the bedroom and shut the door. "So there's a gallon of paint in here," he called. "Were you going to paint it tonight?"

"I thought I'd do the first coat. But obviously I won't now. It's fine."

"Is your boss pressuring you?" She hesitated. He popped out of his bedroom, shirtless, sockless, wearing a pair of sweatpants that accented his muscular butt. "Are you under time pressure?"

No. I'm under marketing campaign pressure. Also you have veins wrapped around your arms and these strange round muscles disappearing under your waistband, and as a professional decorator I would not change a thing. "Um . . ."

He went back in the bedroom and rummaged through a garbage bag. "Socks!" He sat on the mattress on the floor and pulled his socks on, one long smooth pull each, and she wondered what else his competent, strong fingers could do. Oh, Rip Van Winkle was *not* going back to sleep. "I'm going to run an errand. You go ahead and do whatever you want to," he said.

She could feel herself flush and prayed he didn't notice.

He walked into his shoes while pulling a baseball shirt over his head, grabbed his keys, and started out. "Anything you need?"

Oh god, yes. "I'm good."

He nodded and left.

Alyssa walked into his bathroom and took one deep breath, then acknowledged to herself that she was a total perv, went in his bedroom, smelled his pillow, and considered turning herself in to the police. She wouldn't have chosen to paint when he was going to be home, but didn't think she should leave before he got back. Alyssa decided to cut in around the ceiling and baseboard of the far wall. It would give her a head start. He wasn't likely to bump into the wet paint, and the cleanup would be fast when he got back with his takeout or giant box of condoms. Whatever he was picking up.

She set up the drop cloths and pried open the paint lid. The stir stick brought up a soft butter color, smooth and glossy. She was pleased with it and knew it would dry to just the shade she wanted.

She got around the top and bottom of the wall on three sides. She held the handle of the brush against her nose as she stared at the fourth wall, debating whether to pull the mattress out, when the lock scraped. Well, that solved that dilemma. Besides, he'd probably push it back into the paint.

"I could use a little help," Nick called from the door, and she raced into the living room. He was juggling his keys and four bags, and she rushed forward to grab a bag, when she realized his big hands were holding them just fine. He set the bags down on the kitchen counter. "So I got some stuff." He had a goofy expression on his face. His mouth was serious, but his eyes were up to something.

"Okay?"

"If you're going to be working all night, we need party supplies."

"We . . . what?"

"Beer. Ice cream." He extracted items as he announced them and displayed them proudly before setting them on the counter. "Matching T-shirts." They were orange, with jack-o-lantern faces on the front.

"Oh my god."

"Classy, right? Yours might be too big. I had to guess. Oh, and a disco ball, obviously." He pulled out a black base topped with a sphere imbedded with different colored lenses. "Let me set this bad boy up." He plugged it into an outlet in the living room. Alyssa hadn't put the outlet covers back on and had to stop herself from shouting not to electrocute himself. He played a very fast and unpredictable game at an elite level; he could probably handle an outlet. Nick flicked the switch, and the light inside the sphere snapped on. The ball began to rotate with a soft grinding noise, and bright circles of colored light splashed across the drying walls.

"Huh," he said. "I think this would look better on white walls. Would you mind repainting?"

She gave him a mock glower and he laughed. "What's in the other bag?"

"Oh, just things I needed. We were on the road for a few days. Guess you knew that." Nick stuffed the bag in the refrigerator, then walked over and handed her a T-shirt. He pulled his shirt off, tugged the cheap grocery-store shirt on, and grinned. "Do I look like a pumpkin?" She tried to form a coherent sentence, or even a coherent thought, then gave in to laughter. "So a particularly handsome pumpkin, right? That's what your laughter indicates?"

"Definitely. A very handsome pumpkin." She took her shirt and pulled it on over the one she was already wearing. "You're the best-looking of the gourds for sure."

He hoisted himself onto the kitchen counter, popped open a chilled beer, and offered it to her. She pointed at the frosty ice cream containers beside him. "Ah. Peach or chocolate?" he asked.

"Okay, I want both."

"Yeah?" He rummaged in his cupboard, scooped an enormous amount of ice cream into a bowl for her, and stuck a spoon in, down straight. "Energy to keep going all night," he said.

Shut up, Rip Van Winkle.

"This is amazing, Nick. It's like a slumber party starter kit."

"I know how to braid hair," he said.

She laughed. "You get big points for that, but bigger ones for the ice cream."

"What's your favorite flavor?"

"Peach."

"Really?" She nodded and he threw his arms in the air and did a lap of the living room, bottle still in hand. This was definitely a happier—and goofier—Nick than she'd seen before.

"Hey, did you guys win today?"

"Oh, we slaughtered them. It was brutal." He took a pull on his beer. "The Red Wheels have been rebuilding for a few years, but we're almost rebuilt. We're mostly putting up shutters at this point."

"Sounds like it's almost time for the decorator," Alyssa said, licking the back of her spoon. Nick had bought the good brand.

"Could be," he said, and something in his voice made her look up and flush. Rip Van Winkle was hot. What if she set off Nick's smoke detector? *I'm sorry, it was just my lonely lady bits responding to your sexy voice and those muscles below your waist that make a "V." Can I touch those things before I see myself out?*

"So you don't mind if I paint the bedroom? I don't want to keep you up." She flushed.

"No, do what you want. If you're having trouble with your boss, I want to help."

So Alyssa went back to the bedroom, and Nick stood in the doorway in his ridiculous orange T-shirt. "Is it okay if I pull the bed away from the wall? But then you'd have to sleep with it that way because you couldn't push it back."

He responded by setting his bottle in the doorway, walking over and grabbing the end of the mattress with a wide grip, and sliding it into the middle of the room. Then he retrieved his beer and sprawled on the bed. He waved the bottle at her. "Carry on."

Was he seriously going to lie on the bed watching while she painted? Because paint fumes were combustible, and she wasn't sure she should be around them right then. What if her lady bits ignited the air and sent a fireball shooting through the building? People would be left homeless.

She cut in around the base of the wall that the bed had been pushed against, trying to angle her backside so it wasn't in his face.

"You want any help?" he said.

"One brush," she said, holding it up, then looked at him from her crouch by the baseboard. "You'd think an artist would have a brush lying around somewhere."

She'd meant it lightheartedly, but he said, "I haven't painted since the crash. I just haven't wanted to."

She winced in sympathy. "Do you have to paint in order to finish your degree? You said you're almost done, right?"

"I think I've actually fulfilled the requirements for the art history major. I suppose I should check on that sometime." He shrugged and rolled his neck. "But I have one more painting for the art degree, and I'm not doing it."

She stood and pulled the ladder over, climbed it, and looked down. "Any reason?"

"I'm a lazy bastard."

"Seems like a lazy guy wouldn't have done the degree in the first place," she said, keeping her eyes on the butter strip she was painting at the ceiling. He didn't respond, and she let it go.

The walls went fast once she had the roller going. He was still lounging on the bed, socks stripped off, wearing his grocery-store-in-October T-shirt. The disco light was rotating in the living room, sending splashes of color through the door and across the far wall. "I guess it's time to talk seriously," he said. She looked over, roller in mid-glide, suddenly alert. "Michelangelo or Leonardo?"

"Leonardo!" She finished the stroke and dipped the roller back in the pan. "You?"

He snorted. "Michelangelo."

She exhaled sharply. "Leonardo was so *smart*—the inventions, the anatomical sketches. His intellect had such range."

"Yeah," Nick said, rolling over to put his empty bottle on the floor. "Leonardo was smart, but at some point you have to admire Michelangelo's physicality. Art is a visual medium—there's a place for the unabashedly physical."

She was done with the room. She set the roller down in the pan and picked a spot of rubbery yellow off her wrist. "I didn't say I don't appreciate . . . physicality." Her voice was breathy.

"Yeah?" He stood up and moved toward her, standing between her and the door. "Do you need help?" He had an erection. He definitely did. The sweatpants were heavy jersey but they weren't hiding that.

"No." Her chest heaved as she sucked in air. The paint fumes had apparently made it hard to breathe. And made her lady parts tingle. They should put a warning on the side of the can. "I just need to clean the equipment. Can I use your bathroom?"

"Or you could just leave it there," he said.

"And let the paint dry on it?" She heard the slight shrill note, but he was talking crazy.

"If you wanted to do something else. Totally your call. You could just leave it."

Was he . . . saying . . . what she *thought* he was saying? "Are you thinking . . . Michelangelo?" She had just coined a euphemism and now she was going to art hell.

"Do you *like* Michelangelo?" He stepped closer to her, and she had to look up because of his height. He rubbed his thumb down the side of her arm, and she whimpered. He grinned, then closed the gap and kissed her. His lips were soft, but his stubble scraped her chin. He pulled back for a moment and looked into her eyes, close enough to make her feel cross-eyed, the warmth and scent of him, the breadth of his chest all she could think about. "Okay?"

She nodded and again pressed her lips against his. He gently caught her upper lip with his teeth, then brushed his fingertips over her cheek as he deepened the kiss. This was nothing like the kiss under the arch that Janet had arranged, or the tentative, gentle kiss a moment ago. It made her warm and achy between her legs.

Alyssa tilted her head sideways to get his neck, play-biting at his Adam's apple and making him groan. He put his hand on the small of her back and pulled her in to him, then held her with a hand on each hip, pressing against her. "I don't think orange is your color," he whispered.

"No. Bad shirt choice," she whispered, and he put his large hands under her T-shirt on either side of her waist, electrifying her skin, then skimmed them up, catching momentarily at the edge of her bra as he lifted the fabric over her head. While her hands were still raised, he stepped into her, his leg behind her, bending her backward and supporting her on one arm. His spread hand covered her back, and his mouth worked down her cleavage, into her bra, and she just had time to be thankful she'd worn the pink lace, before conscious thought cut out altogether. He held her suspended over the bed and pulled back to look at her, tracing his thumb down from her bra line to the top of her pants.

How was he this strong? He was holding her with one arm, and it made his bicep bulgy and oh god, all his bulges were so, so good. He tugged her yoga pants down, and his thumb skimmed over her underwear to just where she needed him. He rubbed a little circle and she moaned and let her head drop back, her hair splaying, and he held her in the air and toyed with her, then gently laid her on the bed.

He pulled his shirt off in a practiced motion and then went for her bra, fumbling for a second when he couldn't find the hook, then realizing it had a front catch. "Tricky," he whispered, unlatching it and letting the lace spread back from her breasts. "Damn," he murmured, his voice husky. He knelt over her, shuddering with need, then pulled her pants the rest of the way down. "Michelangelo?" His voice was husky.

"*Definitely* Michelangelo," she agreed. "Condom?"

His eyes flared wide. "I put them in the fridge!" She put her hand to her forehead and looked up at him, laughing. "Stay right there!" he said, waving a hand vaguely over her and the bed. He ran to the doorway, and then looked back and made an animal growl and flashed his eyes at her. She laughed again. He was back a moment later, still in his sweatpants, ripping the packaging off and lying down on the mattress beside her.

"So this is very cold," he said, setting it aside. "We'll need to find something else to do while it warms up."

"Oh." Her voice was breathless.

He moved over her, holding himself up with one arm while he settled his mouth on her breast, licking her nipple and then sucking it.

The heat and need built between her legs. He skimmed his other hand lightly across her stomach, over her thigh, and then settled it between her legs, rubbing gently while his lips explored her other breast, then climbed up to take her neck in his mouth. His scruff scraped her but his lips were gentle, and his fingers, there . . . She moaned and tilted her hips. He pressed down with his tongue and she spasmed, rocking into him, calling out his name—twice. He continued to lick in gentle circles until the aftershocks subsided. She ran her fingers lightly over his hair, and he looked up at her and smiled.

"Good?" he said.

"Unbelievable." She hadn't been with anyone for two years—not since dating Travis-Whom-She'd-Assumed-Was-Single. She felt a surge of affection for this man and laid her hand over his fingers, splayed across her belly.

He lifted himself higher, and she took advantage of the extra room to roll her legs up and put her feet on his waist, then push down, shoving at his pants. He sprang free, his cock bouncing off her, and then he helped, using one foot to push his sweatpants off a leg. He switched the arm supporting him and slid his free hand under her bottom, lifting her, and tugged her underwear off. His eyes swept over her and she felt shy, but he moaned and pushed his hair back with his free hand. She'd never been with a man who could hold himself up so long, so easily—who could do a one-handed pushup without thinking about it.

Then they were a tangle of legs, wriggling out of the last pieces of clothing till they were both fully nude. She lay beside this man with the body of a god, then lost the shyness, reached down, and gripped him. He shut his eyes and moaned.

"Is it warmed up yet?" she whispered. If it wasn't, she was going to ignite those paint fumes, and her obituary would be scandalous but entertaining.

He grunted an assent before he touched the condom, and when he grabbed it, his eyes flared—not warm. He rubbed it sharply against his hip. Lucky condom, pressing against his warm spicy skin. She took it from him and looked him in the eye as she breathed hot air onto it. Then she pushed it down over the tip of him and unrolled it, feather strokes around his shaft until he was covered.

He positioned himself over her, his expression urgent, then kissed between her breasts, his breathing ragged as he worked up to her neck. She moaned and tilted toward him, and he murmured her name. He needed to hurry or she was going to get there again, without him. He nibbled up to the point of her chin, then settled on her lips, gnawing, and looked in her eyes as he moved his heavy body with authority and shoved into her.

Her eyelids drooped and she dug her fingers into his shoulders. She ran her hands across his back, along his arms, over his neck, keeping her hips moving in rhythm with his. She pulled her fingers through his hair. Oh god. She could fall for this guy. Really, really fall. He cupped her breast and caught her nipple between those strong fingers, pulling slightly. The heat built in her core until she couldn't stand it, could think of nothing but the release coming. She looked down, saw his tight abs arching over her as he thrust, the hardness of his cock sliding into her, and she was there. Her eyes rolled up as she spasmed, grabbing the sheet on both sides. A second later he was there with her, shuddering inside her, their bodies melting into each other's.

When they were coming down from the peak, he rolled his hips, swirling his cock inside her once more—she spasmed again and they both moaned. And then he kissed the side of her neck and rolled off her, panting slightly.

"I'm glad you're okay," he said. "I haven't done that in a while. I meant to suggest you wear a helmet."

She blinked at him and then laughed. "You thought you'd shoot me across the room?"

He grinned sleepily. "It was a concern. You'd have been mad if the paint got messed up, right?"

"Oh, definitely." She paused and then said, "It's been a while for me too."

"Yeah?" He rolled on his side and looked at her, his fist under his chin. "How is that possible?"

"I give off skank vibes?" She cocked an eyebrow at him.

He laughed. "No. You're gorgeous. And creative. And interesting." He reached out to stroke her breast gently. "And these are pretty spectacular."

This guy. How could he be in her life? "The girls are pretty fond of you too," she said, and he laughed. She allowed her eyes one sweep of his body because *wow*. Her compliments to the decorator. She shook her head at the turn this evening had taken. She was having a conversation with Nick Sorensen. In his bedroom. Stark naked.

And then came the part where she had to redress with him watching her, and gather her things. He saw her off at the door, wearing only boxers himself. He put his arm around her lower back, his palm on her hip, pulled her in, and kissed her sweetly. As he pulled away he leaned forward again and kissed the tip of her nose with a little smacking sound. He grinned. "I've been wanting to do that." She laughed. "You want me to walk you to your car?" he asked.

"In boxers?" she said. "You'd scandalize the neighbors."

He grinned. "It would only add to my legend. Okay, there is no legend, but I could start one."

She shook her head, kissed her fingertips, and touched them to his cheek. Then she stepped into the hall, flushed and warm and smelling him on her skin. He watched from his doorway until she reached the stairs, and when she looked back from the street, he was still watching through his living room window. She waved from the car, then sat for a moment as he stepped away from his window, and all that was left to see was his apartment building.

Once he was out of sight, her stomach fell with guilt. She had messed up the contract, and he was going to have his place splashed all over the internet, against his will, and she had known that and slept with him anyway.

She was a horrible person.

CHAPTER NINETEEN

Nick woke up, stretched, and sniffed the air. Paint and sex. His bedroom definitely smelled like paint and sex. And his sheet was wrinkled where Alyssa had grabbed it as she climaxed.

Oh, shit. He'd had sex with the decorator.

The bed still smelled faintly of her, something floral, but not heavy. A June garden when the foliage hadn't yet overgrown its space. She smelled like dappled green light. If he were going to paint her, he'd put her in a long white dress in an early summer garden, stroke in cerulean blue for the shadows in her skirt, maybe some Scheveningen blue. He'd use Old Holland paint or Michael Harding—she was worth it. It would look like something Monet would have painted—except that wasn't his style. What did it mean if you couldn't paint a woman in your own style?

He stood up and padded into his green living room. She'd gotten the shade right. It was light, unobtrusive. It would give the place a natural, outdoorsy feel without calling attention to itself or being too dark. Greens were tricky, and yet she'd made a slap shot from center ice.

But shit. He'd *slept* with her. What was he thinking?

Eric had had an ultrasound picture taped inside his locker.

Tyler, Luka, and Sammy had been happily playing the field.

Dragan had boarded the plane with a ring in his pocket.

And then it all ended.

None of them were slipping the interior designer's panties off. Although Sammy totally would have. Nick smiled faintly. Sammy *definitely* would have approved.

Nick wished he could see Sammy's reaction to Alyssa. Sammy knew a pretty woman when he saw one, and he would have liked her too. Nick was sure of that. He felt like his insides were glowing and Sammy would see that, would give him a warm smile, slap him on the arm, and say, "Don't mess this up."

"I won't," he said out loud. He wasn't sure if he was promising Sammy or Alyssa.

He shook his head sharply. That was wrong, because it's what Sammy would have said when he was alive. But now, moving forward meant leaving his friends behind. Every new thing he did pulled him further away from them. His being traded to Detroit—Sammy never knew about that. Would never know. If Nick married or had children, Sammy wouldn't know that either. And how could that be? Sammy would have given the toast at his wedding, no question. How could he carve a different future, one without these men? They had been great friends. Good men. And he was betraying them, taking his pleasure with Alyssa, watching her paint his walls, the way she brushed the hair out of her face, the way she looked so intent as she worked at the edge of the baseboard. He'd grown hotter and harder as he watched the steadiness of her smooth small hand, and wondered how it would feel if it wasn't wrapped around a roller brush handle. If it was around him.

Going forward was leaving them behind.

He got up, peed, looked at his coffeemaker, and didn't bother. He had to see the therapist again this morning—the team doctor had rescheduled the appointment he'd missed when he was at the museum. Dr. Williams was middle-aged, wore heavy jewelry, and her hair was in short dreads. She was kind, her smile was genuine, and she had a row of framed diplomas on her office wall. Nick would have liked her in any other circumstance—but she wanted to talk about his feelings, and he didn't plan to have any.

Maybe they could talk about Gretzky's records. About how many points you could score for how many seasons and still not be anywhere near his point total. If she wanted to be philosophical, they could discuss why God would have made Gretzky in the first place. Was it a message to hockey players? To fans? And if so, was it a wake-up call? *Look what I can do—I made Wayne Gretzky. Think what I could do if I wanted to lay down an Old Testament smiting.* Then everybody would review the Great One's sixty-one NHL records; mouth, "Oh, fuck" to one another; and shape up.

There was really nothing the therapist could talk about that he couldn't turn into a discussion of Gretzky. But the first appointment had done nothing to make him think she'd be enthused about it. So obviously that was a mark against her.

Nick walked into Sammy's bedroom, shut the door behind him, and stood in the middle of the room. When Nick had moved into the Detroit apartment, he'd taken the larger bedroom. Sammy would've been pissed about that, but if Sammy didn't like it, he could come up behind him and grab him in a headlock and take him down. Or bounce a grape off his eyeball.

"I had sex last night," he said. Sammy didn't say anything. *I'm a guy who talks to an empty room.* "I'm sorry you're not having sex. Although in fairness, I could get busy for a couple of *years* before I'd ever reach Sammy Gonczy levels of doinkitude." He stood silently.

Sammy didn't laugh. "You ever think about how elephants' teeth wear down, and then they starve to death? I think that would have happened to your dick." He stood in Sammy's room for a couple more minutes and then left, closing the door behind him.

In the shower he thought about Alyssa and how he probably had to make things right with her too. He wasn't worried about consent. Alyssa had put the condom on him—thinking about it made him hard again—but she'd been in his place to work, and he'd lain there on the mattress, watching her ass. Which was magnificent. But had that made her uncomfortable? She was having trouble with her boss, and she might not have been able to tell him to go to hell if she hadn't wanted him in there. He was used to being around guys who would tell him to go to hell for anything—if he didn't return the tape roll or he left his skates on the floor. It was amiable and direct, and it made everything so much easier. Not much said, but nothing unsaid.

With Alyssa . . . she'd seemed fine when she'd left his apartment last night. He'd watched from the living room window as she walked to her car. Once she was safely in the driver's seat, he'd turned off the bedroom light and moved to step away from the window, but paused when he realized she wasn't driving off—she just sat there, slumped in the car.

It wasn't the way someone acted after good sex, and it had been very good. He damn well knew she'd enjoyed it—he'd be thinking about her little gasping noises all day. Was she unhappy with him? Did she regret it?

He had been too forward, maybe. She'd been there to work, not be seduced—but he could fix this. On the way to his therapy appointment, he stopped at a flower shop and asked for extravagant pink peonies and white heirloom roses because Alyssa had stopped in front of a painting of a bouquet like that when they'd been in the art museum.

He added a card and gave the florist Alyssa's work address—it was the only one he had.

When he got to Dr. Williams's office, he played on his phone until she let him in, smiling broadly and taking his hand. "I'm so glad to see you, Nick," she said, motioning vaguely toward a collection of furniture. He could sit where he wanted. Sofa, big chair, small chair. She would be secretly evaluating every move. He knew that. It was like being scouted.

"How was your week?" she asked as he sank into the big chair, and she pulled her desk chair around.

"I've been thinking a lot about Wayne Gretzky," he said. *Control the game from the beginning.*

"Who's that?" she asked.

Shit. He was definitely going to have to tell Sammy about this. He'd laugh his ass off.

CHAPTER TWENTY

The sewer department's chairs were arriving that afternoon, but mysteriously, the two little tables were not. Alyssa made phone calls to track them down, then followed up on a table lamp for Nick's living room. It was an antique she was having rewired, and the electrician didn't seem to see the urgency of the project.

She was sitting in her desk chair, looking at a couple of pigeons hanging out by the trash bin outside, when Stacey came to her door. The agency owner held an enormous bouquet of peonies and roses— pink and white and luxuriant and fragrant. For a moment Alyssa thought they were Stacey's way of apologizing for being a jerk for, well, forever. Then she saw the glint in Stacey's eyes as she set the bouquet on the desk and swiveled it so the card in its plastic prong faced Alyssa. The envelope was ripped open and tucked behind the card so Alyssa would know there had been one. Know that Stacey had chosen to open it. The card was plain, pale pink, and in an elegant male script said: *I loved last night, but we shouldn't do that again. I'm sorry if I made you uncomfortable. Nick*

"Did you sleep with a client?" Stacey said as Alyssa was still scanning the card.

No! Of course not! She would never do that.

Nick wasn't just a client, he was . . . different. She flushed, deep and full, and there was no reason to answer. Betrayed by her own circulatory system.

Stacey rocked back and crossed her arms, her lips pinched together. "That is an ethical violation," she said, enunciating very precisely.

This from *Stacey*, who regularly churned through associates, poaching their accounts and stealing pieces they'd found to give to her own clients. Alyssa had lost a Tiffany lamp she'd secured for a client whose grandfather had known Louis Tiffany. It had broken her heart—and she'd already told the client she had something special for her. And Stacey called *her* unethical?

"My personal life is personal," Alyssa said. "You shouldn't have opened the envelope."

Stacey ignored that. "Finish your booty-call apartment." Alyssa's mouth dropped open. "I want my commercial. Oh, and finish the poop project." She walked to the door and stopped with her hand on the frame. "Then you're fired."

Alyssa stared after her as she disappeared down the hall toward her own office. She could not have lost this job. She needed this job. What if the reason for her termination got around? "Ethical violations," people would say, and they'd think embezzlement or painting oak baseboards. There was no way to defend herself if a whisper campaign started. Gossip was the huff and puff that would blow her dream house down. She had worked so hard and dreamed for so long—of owning a home, of having her own agency. And now Stacey was taking it away from her. Punishing her because she'd had sex for the first time in . . . okay, a while.

Good sex, Rip Van Winkle whispered.

Alyssa quickly ransacked her office for personal items, in case Stacey locked her out, then opened the window and lowered the bag out beside the trash bin. She couldn't carry everything, and she wanted those flowers, dammit. They were stunning. When that man sent flowers, he sent *flowers.* Even if the card did say, *"I regret having sex with you and it won't be happening again."*

Was she unethical? Nick couldn't have felt pressured physically, right? He was so much bigger than her, so much stronger, and he had run out for condoms, after all. But then . . . this card. Her eyes pricked with unexpected tears. Things with him had seemed so right—*so* right. The way he had skimmed her belly with his fingers, had cupped her breasts—it was like he was worshiping her. He didn't make love like a man who didn't want to see her again. He just didn't.

She took a deep breath to steady herself, and then carried the bouquet out the front door to her car. She came back in and stopped at Stacey's door.

Stacey was dusting some framed awards, even though they had a cleaning service. She just wanted to bring them to Alyssa's attention. *Bitch.* "Can we talk?" Alyssa said.

"No, honey. You need to finish your work and go away. I can't have you hurting my reputation." Alyssa's cheeks burned and she started to turn, when Stacey said, "I ran a search on you. Your brother is a criminal?"

Alyssa turned back toward her, eyes blazing. "No, he's an educator." That was a lie but her family was none of Stacey's business. "Looks like somebody has trouble with a computer." This was a sore point for Stacey and Alyssa knew it. *Come after my weak point, I'll come after yours.* For a second Stacey seemed uncertain, then she waved her hand. "Inconsequential."

Alyssa took a deep breath to ground herself, then said, "Nick said no to the commercial." She wanted to run home and cry, but she needed to fix this for Nick.

"Did you explain that he signed a contract allowing us to do just that?"

Alyssa flushed.

"Well. Looks like you screwed your client twice." Stacey turned her back on Alyssa and dusted the glass on another award.

Alyssa hesitated for a moment, then grabbed the vase of flowers and a few low-priority items from her office and walked out to the refuse bin to retrieve her bag. Pathetic. But Ryan would have loved her defending him, and the thought made her smile—until she was two blocks away, car motor humming, flowers on the passenger seat, and it occurred to her that she should have acknowledged his past *and* still claimed him. So there was another failure.

If she was going to get fired for sex with a client, though, she was glad it was with Nick. Maybe he didn't want to see her again, and she'd be lying to herself if she said that didn't sting. But god help her, she still liked him. And she could close her eyes and see him whenever she wanted. She could watch his games on TV and imagine him nude, and she knew darned well that when the need was great and she took care of things herself, he was who she would think of.

She was pathetic. Unethical. And fired.

CHAPTER TWENTY-ONE

Gilda set the shakes down at their booth and left. Emma tapped her fingernails on the frosted glass. She had little crystals embedded in the tips of the nails. "What are you going to do?"

"It's obvious what she's going to do," Janet said fiercely. "She's going to come back and work with me."

Alyssa gave her a watery smile. "Thanks." She took a sip of her shake, then said pensively, "I wish I could start my own business. It would be something no one could take away, you know? Nobody could make some stupid decision I don't even know about and then everything disappears."

Emma gave her a sympathetic nod.

"But if I get bad word of mouth, it won't be possible," Alyssa went on. "And I don't think I could swing it financially anyway."

"Start-up is always slow," Emma said, spinning the salt shaker.

"What would it actually take?" Janet said. "Could you work out of your apartment?"

Alyssa drew a finger threw the condensation on her shake glass. "I'd have to have a place to see clients. To show them my proposals, samples—all that. I really need an office space."

"So get one," Janet said. "If you really want to make a go of this."

"I do. It's just . . ." Alyssa was quiet for a moment, worrying a cuticle. Finally she said, "It would take such a big splash to start. An ad campaign so people know I'm there, and getting a work space. It's such a huge gamble." Janet and Emma exchanged a glance. "Stop it, you two," Alyssa said crossly. "This isn't about my father gambling everything away." Janet arched her eyebrows and made fish lips, but she kept her eyes on the tabletop. "I just can't do it right now," Alyssa said.

Janet leaned forward. "I have so many Halloween parties scheduled. I'm actually overbooked—seems the harvest spirit is strong this year." Alyssa gave her a half smile. "Work for me on a week-by-week basis. No benefits, but buckets and buckets of cash."

"When did you get so solvent?" Emma asked.

"It's aspirational. But I definitely can take someone on through spring at least. And there's nobody I want as much as you."

"Aw," Alyssa said. "You're a good friend."

"Yeah, but it's also a smart business decision," Janet said. "You're so good at this stuff, Alyssa. Of *course* I want you."

Gilda brought their plates over and set them down with a clink. The china was white and thick, and the buns glistened with grease.

"Speaking of *good* . . ." Emma said. "You got fired for sleeping with Nick Sorensen?"

"Yep." She dropped her face into her hands dramatically.

"Put *that* on your sign." Emma smirked.

Alyssa lowered her hands and raised an eyebrow. "Designs by Unethical Skank?"

"You are not a skank!" Janet said. "There's nothing wrong with sex. Unless you don't tell your girlfriends every single detail. That would be wrong."

"Very wrong," Emma said. "So what's his best feature? Legs? Chest? Butt?"

Alyssa threw a fry at her. "I actually like him," she said miserably.

Janet and Emma exchanged a glance. "Ohh," Emma said.

"And the card on the flowers told you to kiss off," Janet said, putting the pieces together.

Alyssa nodded miserably. "He said he regretted it."

"Bastard," Emma said. "Let's go . . . do a thing . . . he wouldn't like." She looked at them. "What? I don't know anything about hockey. Maybe we knock his goalpost over?"

"That's the spirit," Alyssa said listlessly.

"Aw, honey," Janet said, sliding a hand across the table to squeeze Alyssa's. "You just have to finish his apartment and that stupid sewer department thing, right?"

"The sewer department's done except for a couple of missing tables. I put everything else in place this afternoon."

"So you finish SexyTime Nick's place and work for me at the same time. There can't be that much more to do on it."

"The design's done," Alyssa acknowledged. "I need to put a second coat on his bedroom."

"Oooh, I'll *bet* you do," Janet said and Emma gave her a high five.

"When he's not around," Alyssa qualified, rolling her eyes. "Then it's just getting everything put in place."

"I have a group of nurses throwing a pirate-themed Halloween party, and I have done nothing for it so far except make sure I have enough plastic cutlasses on hand. And a banker is having a sophisticated autumn-themed dinner at his sprawling estate. There's a caterer, but we're in charge of everything else. I could really, really use you to make the decorations for the front door and the veranda, where people will wander out with drinks. And—"

Alyssa put her hand up. "Sold. I'd love to come back. Thank you."

"Yes!" Janet pumped her arm. "And if you decide you want to be full-time and permanent, you just let me know. I'll figure it out." Alyssa gave her the best smile she could pull off.

Before they were done with dinner Alyssa had backslid to her fifteen-year-old level of professional accomplishment—doing the decorations for other people's parties—and Emma had told Gilda about Nick. Gilda wrapped a cookie for Alyssa to take with her and when Alyssa hugged her in thanks, she inexplicably started to cry.

Alyssa got the second coat on Nick's bedroom when he wasn't home, and checked in by text when she wanted to swap out the bathroom linens because she'd found something better.

Apart from those minimal interactions, the next couple of weeks passed without them speaking at all. As far as she knew, he didn't even know she'd been fired.

She was sitting at the reception desk at the party store, where she took turns with Janet, and Roberta when she showed up. She was eating a tuna sandwich she'd brought from home, and doodling possible signs for her someday-design business when Janet stopped by. "More logos?" Alyssa nodded absently. "That's a lot of logos. You think you'll open the place?"

"I want to," Alyssa admitted. "I guess I could get a smaller apartment if I need to."

"You could room with Mrs. Gilroy."

Alyssa smiled. Mrs. Gilroy was her gerbil. "I don't think she'd share the wheel."

"So," Janet said, back to business, "the nurses' pirate party is tonight."

Alyssa nodded. "I'm prepared! I've got a lot of kitschy decor already in the van. The joke awards are in that box." She pointed by the door. "The hors d'oeuvre trays that look like little ships are still in the back. The caterer will want them immediately, so I thought we'd load them last. Last on, first out." She beamed. The pirate party was going to be fun. She was glad the nurses were going to have a good evening, because she had begun feeling inexplicably lonely for the first time in a very long time. That was the beauty of this job—it brought people joy. Even if she was doing the same thing she'd done in high school and her prospects for a future were sinking and . . .

"You could open a sign-designing factory," Janet said, tapping the desk.

"That would be a graphic design firm."

"Oh yeah."

Alyssa finished the tuna sandwich and went back to work, calculating how many spikes of Styrofoam berries and fabric leaves she'd need for a Thanksgiving party in three weeks. She would also have to text Nick and tell him he wouldn't get his bed for about that long. It was an antique she was having expanded because Nick was a big guy and wanted a king-size bed, but the carpenter had just had a knee replacement and was taking extra recovery time. She really didn't want to discuss his bed with him. It was mortifying—especially since when she'd ordered the bed, he'd suggested she install a goal horn on the headboard that would go off when he scored. She was pretty sure he'd been kidding but kept visualizing another woman's hair splayed across his second pillow.

Figuring out the Thanksgiving decorations gave her a sense of control. She would choose the ribbon when she was actually looking at them—they had tons of ribbons on-site, so that could be a last-minute choice. The party would be fine. She could work for Janet as long as she needed to, and start her business when she could. And soon she'd never have to see Nick Sorensen again. Everything was perfectly fine.

And for the next three and a half hours, at least, it was.

CHAPTER TWENTY-TWO

The Halloween bash was at the home of one of the nurses—a big Arts and Crafts bungalow with pillars in the living room that had narrow glass-fronted bookcases in the bases. "I would kill for those pillars," Alyssa whispered as they walked in with boxes of pirate paraphernalia.

"That would seem more menacing if your cutlass wasn't plastic," Janet said, nodding to the box in Alyssa's arms. Alyssa laughed. The decor was kitschy, lots of orange and black. There were sashes, cutlasses, and cheap felt pirate hats for all the revelers laid out on a table by the front door. It was covered with a black cloth on which Alyssa had sewn a white skull and cross bones. Gluing it would have been faster, but this way she could snip the threads later and reuse the cloth. The appetizers were displayed on trays that looked like little pirate boats and on black glass trays with handles that resembled femurs. They'd made ice cubes shaped like skulls, but they were stashed in the homeowner's freezer to preserve the detail until the guests arrived.

"The drinks island is my favorite part," the homeowner, Melinda Zhang, said.

"Definitely where I'd want to get stranded," Alyssa said, standing back to look with her. They'd put a blue plastic cloth on a card table and piled it with sand to make an island complete with little palms and a wrecked ship that held swizzle sticks. The bottles were behind the island, the glasses to the side. A not-to-scale treasure chest would hold the skull ice cubes and a pair of tongs once the guests started to arrive. The chest was small and would need constant refilling, but it was worth it for the look of the thing. "I'm so glad you decided to have this party," Alyssa said.

"We need to let off some steam," Melinda said. "The hospital has been . . . well."

Alyssa nodded and opened her mouth to say something appreciative of nurses, but never got the chance.

"I need to speak with you," Janet hissed. She gave the homeowner a brittle smile. "Everything's fine!"

The doorbell rang then, and Melinda opened it. Three middle-aged women stood on the porch, beaming. "Happy Halloween!" they sang in unison. Melinda ushered them into her home, and Alyssa ran to the freezer for the ice cubes. Everything else was ready—from the olives to the sugar-cookie skeleton they'd asked the caterer to make as a nod to the guests' profession.

"Did you notice what isn't here?" Janet said.

Alyssa glanced around surreptitiously. "We got it all. I plugged in the purple and orange lights outside. We're good." She dumped some skull cubes in the treasure chest and stowed the rest back in the freezer.

"We are *not*," Janet pronounced. "Where's my sexy pirate?"

"He's coming later," Alyssa said. "After they're drunk, right?"

Janet held up her phone. "Nope. He's at the hospital."

"Well, give him this address. The party's here."

"He's *in* the hospital—with food poisoning."

Alyssa's eyes flew open. "No sexy pirate?"

Janet's expression was determined. "Oh, we promised them a buccaneer. They're getting a buccaneer."

Alyssa waited.

"I need you to call him. Melinda said she wants to do another party at Christmas. These nurses are under a lot of pressure and will need to cut loose on the regular."

Alyssa looked at her, utterly confused.

"Call him," Janet repeated.

"The sick guy? I don't think we want—"

"Nick. Ask him to be our sexy—"

Alyssa inhaled sharply. "Absolutely not! Are you crazy?"

"Yes." Janet nodded. "You already knew that. Now pick up your phone—"

"And ask him to drive to a random house to gyrate for some nurses? Or give lap dances or something?"

"He was just supposed to walk around and be eye candy. Talk like a pirate and have nice abs. Maybe flirt a little."

Alyssa gave her a baleful look. "Nick and I do not have a pirate-based relationship."

"Then call someone else with abs like that. Now."

"There *is* no one else with abs like that."

"Exactly."

They stared at each other over the beverage table while Melinda answered the doorbell and more of her coworkers flowed in, along with the sounds of laughter and chill October air. The guests moved to the hors d'oeuvres table and began munching and telling stories. Melinda made sure they all had their pirate hats.

Alyssa finally thought of the best argument. "There is no way he owns a pirate costume. In fact, I've seen his closet. He has more suits than normal, but he does not own a pair of breeches. Ha!" She folded her arms across her chest and looked at Janet with smug satisfaction.

"The costume's here," Janet said. "And maybe we could get him here too." She gave Alyssa a probing look. "I think you'd like to see him, wouldn't you? You've been mopey," she said gently.

"I'd love to see him," Alyssa acknowledged, and her eyes prickled. "But that's not going to happen."

"Okay," Janet said. "You don't have to text him."

"Thank you," Alyssa said. "We'll just get the nurses good and drunk and tell them he was here."

"That's one plan," Janet said. She walked into the kitchen, leaving Alyssa to wonder what had just happened.

CHAPTER TWENTY-THREE

Nick's phone buzzed twice. He tilted the laundry basket, dumping a tangle of socks and underwear onto his mattress, and walked to the windowsill to retrieve it.

Nick smiled when he saw Alyssa's name pop up. She'd been distant for the past couple weeks. He'd started to text her half a dozen times but stopped when he remembered he wasn't her only client. She was busy. He should respect her schedule. Then he read her texts.

Alyssa: *Hey, so I know this is weird, but I kind of need help.*

Alyssa: *I'm at a party and there's a problem.*

He pitched the laundry basket into the closet and trotted into the kitchen to grab his wallet off the counter, texting as he went.

Nick: *Are you in danger?*

Nick: *What's the address?*

Nick: *Is it a guy?*

Nick: *I'll kill him.*

Alyssa: *No! I'm fine. But we're throwing a party for some really nice nurses. And there was supposed to be a pirate. He got sick and we need a guy to show up.*

Nick stared at his phone.

Nick: *Are you serious?*

Alyssa: *Yeah. LOL. Is there any chance you're interested?*

Nick: *You want me to be a pirate??*

Alyssa: *We sort of need one.*

Nick: *This is so weird.*

Nick: *Address?*

Alyssa: *You're the best!* 😎 *1207 Oak Court. Lots of cars out front.*

Nick: *It'll be a little while.*

Alyssa: *That's okay. They're getting drunk.*

Nick: *If a parrot poops on me, I'm gonna be mad.*

Alyssa: *Ha! See you soon.*

Nick: *Why didn't you ask Ryan?*

Nick: *Seriously. He'd be a great pirate.*

Nick: *You there?*

Forty-five minutes later Nick rang the bungalow's doorbell. He could see—and hear—revelers through the window. A moment later a woman in a cheap pirate hat threw the door wide and said, "Well, ahoy there!" She ushered him into the room, which was festooned with orange and black streamers and filled with women and two men in the same pirate hats.

One of the men lazily waved a plastic cutlass in his direction. "Stay away from my wenches!"

"Aye aye," Nick said, wondering what Alyssa had gotten him into. Janet rushed forward, grabbed his arm, and led him past an inflated mylar palm tree on a desert island and into the kitchen.

"Thank you so much for coming!" she said. Alyssa was sitting behind the kitchen table. She had a little orange paper plate with snacks and was wearing skinny black pants and a white blouse unbuttoned just far enough. Damn but she looked good. He'd missed her. He gave her his most charming smile. It was a little weird that she'd texted him to come cosplay a pirate, but it seemed like a step forward in their relationship—this seemed social, not professional. She dropped her head to stare at him, and it made her hair do that thing, and— Wait, that wasn't a "you look fine tonight, Nick" stare. That was a "what in the actual hell are you doing here?" stare.

He smiled at her. "Um, . . . hi." She had forgotten the cracker that hung suspended halfway to her mouth. "You needed a pirate? *Aargh?*" Her eyes snapped to Janet.

"So," Janet said breezily, "your costume is in the half bath there." She pointed off the kitchen. "You're just local color. You walk around and act sexy and, well, piratical. But you don't have to let anybody grind on you."

"Well, that's good news," Nick said.

Alyssa lowered her cracker. "Janet?" There was more ice in her voice than a Zamboni could smooth in a year.

"My Spidey-sense is tingling," Nick said. Actually, more than that was tingling. Alyssa's blouse was definitely . . . flattering. "I walked into something?"

"Yes," Alyssa said, standing. "Janet's murder. Will you help me hide a body in the woods?"

"Am I supposed to dress like a pirate for that?" Nick said. "I am so confused."

"I may have texted you from Alyssa's phone," Janet said. His eyes flew open. Had he said anything smutty? He hadn't. He was sure. Kind of sure.

Alyssa stood abruptly. "That was *inappropriate.*" Something occurred to her, and she added, "And maybe a felony." Janet squinted sideways at her, and Nick looked confused. "Wrongful use of a telecommunications device. They're regulated, you know!" She turned to Nick and said stiffly, "I apologize for Janet. She—"

"I'm sorry for the misunderstanding," Janet said to Nick. "But we really, really needed a pirate." She turned to Alyssa. "And like you said, there's nobody else with abs like his."

Alyssa gasped and flushed furiously. Nick smirked and stretched his arms overhead, making his shirt ride up. He grinned.

Alyssa stood straighter. "And I'm sorry that my coworker was a phone thief, may she rest in peace."

"I . . ." Nick stood, looking between them. "I'm not sure what to do." Did Alyssa want him to stay? That abs comment had made it sound like it.

"I guess it depends on whether you want to waste your entire trip out here, or dress up like a badass pirate, have some snacks, and party with some really pretty cool nurses—while helping us out." Janet batted her eyelashes.

"I get snacks?" Nick said. Alyssa rolled her eyes. He looked between the women, at Alyssa's purloined phone lying on the table, and at the bathroom door. Sammy would have already had it on and be dancing in the living room with a plastic knife in his teeth. The thought made him smile. He walked into the bathroom and closed the door. The costume was on a hanger on the back of the door. He kicked his shoes off and pulled the pants on—red with thin black stripes that bent around his thighs. These were not pants made for an athlete—they hugged his quads and gluts, and he thought there was a good chance the black sash at his hips would be needed to cover his ass when the seam split. Apparently the average pirate didn't work out.

He shoved his feet into the soft black boots of leather-like vinyl, stuffed the pantlegs in the tops, and gave a trial "Aargh!"

"Sounds good in there!" Janet called.

"The shirt's the wrong size," Nick called. It was white and V-necked with a lace-up neckline, but it was a child's size—seriously, seriously off.

"Nope. It's right," Janet called.

He loosened the laces and tugged it down. It was long enough, it just didn't cover his chest. At all. "Oh," he called. "I get it. I'm a sexy pirate, right?" Janet's earlier mention of not letting people grind on him was starting to make more sense now.

"Burial or cremation?" Alyssa stage-whispered to Janet.

This costume made him look either very hot or extremely stupid. He was going to gauge which by Alyssa's face when he stepped out. If it was the latter, he was staying for ten minutes and calling it a night. But not till he got some of those little sausages in the crockpot he'd passed. Anyway, nobody seemed to have recognized him, which was a relief. He shrugged into the vest, strapped on his cutlass, and shoved the hat on at a jaunty angle. Then he opened the door and stepped out.

"Whoo-ee!" Janet called. Alyssa's eyes danced.

Sexy pirate. Yes.

"Oh my gosh," Alyssa said. "Those pants."

"Yeah, they're a little tight."

"And that shirt isn't really . . . a shirt."

"Guess that's why their timbers shiver." He cocked an eyebrow and smirked when Alyssa sucked in her breath. She was remembering the same things he was.

"Okay," Janet said, grabbing his arm. "Let's get you mingling with the nurses."

"I am so, so sorry," Alyssa said. "But I'm still taking a picture of this." She whipped out her camera and snapped a photo.

Janet pulled him into the living room. "Pirate!" she announced. The nurses erupted into howls and applause. "I fear for my virtue," Nick whispered to Janet.

"Yeah, that's a goner." One of the women turned the volume up on the music, and everyone began to dance. Nick unsheathed his cutlass and gripped it in his teeth. It would keep him from laughing. He danced with a woman in a green sweater for about ten seconds before someone cut in, and then it happened again, and then it devolved into a general melee, everyone dancing together.

A white woman in her sixties danced past him, arms swaying over her head. "Nice intercostals," she said. He'd never thought his rib muscles were his best feature, but if you were drunk enough . . .

Eventually he made his way to the crockpot, found it still had little sausages, and speared some with a plastic cocktail fork shaped like a sword. Then he loaded up the rest of his plate and ate it all. He had damn well earned this. He didn't know what he was doing here, but the food was good. Alyssa leaned against the doorway from the kitchen, her eyebrows raised, her mouth pinched tight but unable to control her smile. He moved past her, baring his teeth and growling "Aargh, matey!" and pitched his empty plate in the kitchen garbage. "Time to go back to my desert island," he said, stifling a yawn.

"I can't believe Janet did this to you. Once again, I am so, so sorry."

"I dunno." He shrugged. "The food was pretty good. I'm willing to gyrate for snacks."

She laughed. "Did you get one of the rum balls?" He shook his head. "The caterers made them because pirates, rum. They're so good." She stuck her head into the living room where the party was breaking up. The first to leave had already retrieved their coats from the bedroom and were saying their goodbyes.

Alyssa snagged a rum ball off a pirate-ship tray and raised it to Nick's mouth. She hesitated at the last second, maybe thinking it was too intimate, but he opened wide and leaned forward so that her fingers were in his mouth. She dropped the cookie on his tongue, and he caught her fingers and sucked them before she extricated them. They held each other's gaze for a long moment, and then she stepped back to an appropriate distance.

Nick chewed the cookie and his eyes rolled back in his head. He moaned. "Well, my hearty, you weren't kidding," he said once he'd swallowed. He had good manners for a pirate.

"They're really clearing out now," Janet said, poking her head in from the living room. "I'm going to start cleaning up. Nick, you were such a good sport. Thank you."

He bowed in swashbuckling fashion, swinging his arm forward and dipping low.

"Just keep the costume," Janet said. "We don't reuse them."

Nick glanced down at his chest. "I doubt I'll need this again, but it'll be fun walking into the building in it." He grabbed his clothes out of the bathroom. When he came out, Janet held out a fifty-dollar bill. "I realize this isn't much, but it's what the other guy was going to get."

"Um, no thanks," he said.

"You more than earned it." He shook his head. "Give it to your abs. They earned at least this much all on their own."

He laughed. "My contract prohibits me from taking outside work except for promotions. I could be in an ad for skates, but I'm pretty sure I'm not allowed to accept your doubloons."

Janet made fish lips and looked at him, then at Alyssa. "Even I feel bad about exploiting him if we can't pay him," she said.

"You could put a couple of those rumballs on a plate for me," he said hopefully.

Alyssa smiled. "Done. And seriously, thank you so much. I'm sorry that Janet has such a black, black heart."

"Yeah, but you're not acting all mopey anymore," Janet said softly, then discreetly left the room. Nick and Alyssa stood in awkward silence.

"Again, the black heart thing," Alyssa finally said.

"Nah, pirates like that sort of thing," Nick said, and then, in case she forgot, "Rum balls?"

Alyssa laughed and piled a plate for him, covered it, and said, "Um, again, thank you very much." He wiggled his fingers, and she pushed the plate at him.

"It was a different night from what I had planned, that's for sure."

"What were you going to do?"

He shrugged. "Pretty much nothing. But in a bigger shirt." She laughed, gave him a warm goodbye smile, and turned to pack up some trays and decorations. He carried the plate out to his car—because . . . priorities. Then he trudged back to the back door, startling Alyssa as she stepped out, almost unable to see over a stack of boxes. He'd had to ignore her all evening because those pirate pants were plenty tight, and he was confident that if he'd gotten an erection, he'd have split them. The party was memorable enough as it was. But now he was going to help.

"I can get those," he said.

"Oh, I'm . . . okay, thanks," Alyssa said, walking ahead of him to pop her trunk. He followed her back in and took the next box, waved to the party's host, and carried it out to Alyssa's car too.

"Could you follow her home?" Janet called. "She has to carry all that, and it's pretty late."

Nick said, "Oh, sure!" at the same time Alyssa hissed, "Janet!"

He turned to her, one eyebrow up. "I don't want to intrude, but maybe I should at least make sure you get in okay?"

Alyssa pulled her jacket tighter around her, arms across her chest. An October breeze made her hair fly, and dry leaves scurried over the yard. "I got your note," she said. "With the flowers."

"Oh." He hadn't expected her to bring that up.

"I get that you don't want to see me again. And that's okay, of course." She hurried on as he started to say something. "But under the circumstances, it was very inappropriate of Janet to text you tonight." She pulled back a strand of hair that floated across her eye.

"I didn't say I didn't want to see you." Had he? That wasn't quite how he'd worded it. It was just that he had been too forward, and she'd sat slumped in her car . . . The flowers had been supposed to fix things. He'd seen her admire a bouquet like that on the wall at the museum. Honestly, it had been damned thoughtful of him to send look-alike flowers.

The wind caught dried leaves and sent them scurrying around their feet, and a few rose up around Alyssa in a small autumnal vortex. He didn't want to go too fast with her. He wanted to grab her and kiss her. He didn't want to explain any of it to Sammy later.

God, he was fucked up.

"I . . . I am fucked up," he said. Clear communication and an honest self-appraisal—Dr. Williams would be proud. Alyssa cocked an eyebrow in a way that suggested otherwise. He sighed. "Um. I didn't mean that note to . . ." He trailed off. How did he explain this? "I didn't mean I didn't enjoy the, uh, evening." Alyssa was watching him intently. This was playoff level pressure, and communication was not his game. "And I didn't mean I wouldn't enjoy that again. I just have a hard time doing enjoyable things. Because of guilt."

"You feel guilty?" she said.

"Basically all the time." He sighed and ran his hand through his hair. "I was really glad Janet texted," he said.

"Yeah?" Alyssa dropped her arms and played with a button on the front of her jacket. *Nervous,* he thought. "Because you assumed it was me and *I* was asking you to play pirate?"

He nodded.

"You didn't think I was weird?"

"No, I thought you were a scurvy bilge rat," he said, and grinned.

She rolled her eyes but smiled. "Well, you certainly took to the role! Maybe they should trade you to Pittsburgh." He stared at her and she faltered. "The Pirates, right? Wait, is that . . .?"

"Baseball?" he said. "Yes." He smiled and shook his head, then pointed toward her car. "I'll follow?"

"Uh, sure. Thank you."

Alyssa pulled out onto a quiet residential street. Nick followed her, his car humming quietly—big engine, small chassis, slick lines. He was thinking about the way her honey hair had blown around her face, how he'd wanted to reach a hand out and pull it away from her eyes. But he'd been too forward the night she was painting his bedroom, and apparently the flowers hadn't fixed it. Tonight, he wouldn't make that same mistake. He'd help her carry the boxes up, get a peek at what her apartment looked like—frankly, he was curious—and then he'd leave. Because he was a gentleman. Even if he was still wearing a hat with a red feather.

CHAPTER TWENTY-FOUR

Alyssa parked outside her building. Was there any way she could run upstairs and straighten the apartment before he got there? Or maybe she could let him walk her to the door and not let him in the building. Yes! That would be the way to treat a guy who'd paraded virtually shirtless all evening because he thought she'd asked him to.

And wow, it had been a better evening than she'd expected. He'd seemed to avoid her while he was in the costume, but maybe he was just . . . dedicated to pirate impersonations?

By the time she got out of the car, he was there beside her, wearing a goofy grin.

"You needed some muscle?" he said. He was standing close and she could smell him, a faint shower odor. That spicy smell was a familiar scent, one that clung to his sheets and to her own skin when she'd gotten home after rolling in his bed, after he'd been on top of her. She'd totally shoved her nose into her arm and inhaled. Was there a nerve running from the nose to the lady parts? She should have asked the nurses.

"Alyssa?"

"Yes!" she said brightly. "You can just dump them in the lobby, and I can grab them from there." He gave her a "yeah, right" look, piled the boxes up, and . . . this was going to be one trip, apparently. She unlocked the lobby door. and he caught it with his foot, holding it for her, balancing on the other foot while holding all those party supplies. Hockey player ankles—handy for late-night apartment entries. She led him into the elevator, pushed the button for the fifth floor, and then smiled at him. "You're an incredibly good sport."

"I have a trophy for that! It was a consolation prize from my Mini Mite days." He beamed at her and she smiled back, then flushed and dropped her eyes. He was exceptionally good-looking. Inappropriately so. His jawline probably violated the municipal code—all sorts of safety risks there. And then the elevator dinged, the smudged silver doors slid open, and they were in the familiar hallway with its coral carpet. Her building was bigger than his, and her apartment was halfway down the hall.

He'd see her place and not be impressed—there was nothing special about it, and she was supposed to be a designer. But how would she explain that she had taste, but no actual money? He had no idea she'd been fired because of what had happened between them. She hesitated outside the door, and he shifted the boxes, waiting, which gave her no choice but to swing the door open and hold it for him.

Nick Sorensen stepped inside her place and said, "Where do you want me to put this?"

Rip Van Winkle raised her hand and said, "I have an idea." *Shut up, lady parts.*

"Um, just on the floor by the wall there would be great." He squatted, which did great things to his thighs.

He set the whole stack down without tipping them, then stood and faced her.

"Oh, crap!" she shouted.

Nick saw her expression and his face fell. "What? Did you forget something? Your phone or . . .?"

She rushed past him into the lavender, white, and silver living room, to where the clear plastic gerbil cage sat against the wall. The lid was knocked to the side, and Mrs. Gilroy was gone.

"Mrs. Gilroy got out of her cage again."

"Who?"

"My gerbil. She's impossible to find. Be careful where you step!" She could hear the panic in her voice.

Nick slipped his shoes off, and there went her chance to get him out of there quickly.

"Gerbil?" he said. She nodded and ran through the apartment: kitchen, bedroom, bath, but no soft brown fur, no shining black eyes looking up at her. "I probably bumped her cage on the way out," she said miserably, sinking onto the sofa. "It's been hours."

"She can't get out of the apartment, can she?"

"I don't think so." Panic swirled in her chest. "Unless she ran out when we opened the door."

"I really don't think she did."

"You can't *know*, though." Her voice was rising.

"I'm very good at noticing small objects flashing past my feet." He lowered his head. "The puck?"

She supposed that was true. She nodded and sniffed.

Nick walked over and sat on the sofa beside her. He put his arm around her and gave her shoulders a squeeze, and it broke the chains she had on Rip Van Winkle, who was now unfettered and cackling wildly. "How do you want to do this?" *Well, I wouldn't mind walking your plank.* "Do you want to go room by room? Or each work from one end and try to flush her out?"

She looked up at him. "I've already taken your whole evening. I don't feel right about making you crawl around to find my gerbil."

"But I have gerbil-finding skills." He flexed the bicep of the arm that wasn't draped over her and gave her a hopeful smile. He was trying to make her feel better.

"You're incredibly sweet. Thank you." She stood and as she did his arm came off her shoulders and brushed down her side, touching her hip for just a moment. She had to remind herself not to jump on him. He had been clear about not wanting a repeat of their night together. And she had betrayed him with that contract—accidentally, sure, but it was negligent. If he knew, he would be angry. Hurt. And he had every right to be. She had to remember that—if he knew what she'd done, he would hate her. It would be wrong to let him touch her again.

Nick dropped to his belly and looked under her sofa. "You vacuum under your sofa. Impressive." He grinned up at her, then belly-crawled behind her side table. How could that be so sexy? Lucky, lucky floor. "You think she ran away because she doesn't like Monet?" He gestured toward the water lilies print over her sofa.

"Of *course* she does," Alyssa said, pretending to be offended. "She has exquisite taste."

"Maybe she's off looking for a different print. A little one in a baroque frame for her cage."

Alyssa snorted. "What do you think she likes?"

Nick rolled on his back and put his arms under his head. "Well, I haven't met Mrs. Gilroy, but Albrecht Dürer's *Young Hare* would seem appropriate."

"Hmm," Alyssa said, laughter in her voice. "You might be on to something." *Me. Make it me.* She crawled into the kitchen, looking for cabinets cracked open. There weren't any—she didn't leave cabinets open. She had left a bunch of craft supplies on the dining room table, though, and she didn't want Nick to see that mess. She was normally very tidy. Had he noticed the mess? She peeked around the end of the cabinets. Was he judging her?

Nick was lying on his belly in the middle of the living room, his eyes sweeping back and forth. He saw her and smiled. "You have to think like a gerbil." He grinned and scooted toward a planter, pushing himself with his toes. "Say, do you tend to leave piles of seeds on the floor anywhere? Because that would simplify the search."

She grimaced. "Is that a crack about my apartment?"

He flicked his eyes at her, then pushed himself up and sat. "What?"

"Do you think it's filthy?"

"Do . . . So, I was clearly talking about catching Mrs. Gilroy." He cocked his head at her, then crawled on his hands and knees to the kitchen cabinet, sat with his back against the living room side, then peered around to look at her. "What's going on?"

"I always feel judged when people see my space. I know that's sort of ridiculous . . ."

"Sort of? Alyssa, you've seen my apartment." He looked around. "Besides, what's wrong with this? I mean, it's sort of girly, but you're . . . sort of a girl." His eyes widened. "You secretly hate the Monet, just like Mrs. Gilroy?

She snorted. "I feel self-conscious about having left a bunch of craft supplies on the table."

"Did you? I didn't notice." She stared at him. "What? How is that a thing I would notice? I mean, if you'd left a ham sitting out, I'd probably notice. Or a bucket of wings." She shook her head in disbelief. "Alyssa, I hang out with a bunch of guys who can barely remember to put their teeth in every morning." She laughed. "No, really. André's left his bridge in the hotel twice this season, and we're like three weeks in."

She laughed again. "I can't believe you thought I felt bad about Monet. They should revoke your diploma, you . . . Kandinsky appreciator, you."

"Eh, Kandinsky's not my favorite." Just then a lock of Alyssa's hair fell out of the messy bun she'd tied it in to look for the gerbil. Nick reached around the cabinet and tucked it behind her ear, then whispered: "I'm more of a Michelangelo guy."

CHAPTER TWENTY-FIVE

Nick looked at her, his eyes steady. She began to breathe faster. Then he leaned forward and kissed her.

She shut her eyes and felt the press of his lips against hers, put her palm on the side of his face, and felt the scratch of his stubble. He deepened the kiss and scooted closer, putting a hand on her back. His strong fingers skimmed up her spine, then played in her hair. She dug her fingers into his shoulders and then brushed feather strokes down his arms. He shuddered and when she opened her eyes, he was looking at her.

"Yo ho ho," he whispered. She smiled. He ran his thumbs across her nipples and then skimmed his palms along the sides of her torso, let one hand cup her bottom and the other rub gently between her legs. She moaned and nipped at his earlobe. She shouldn't do this. She shouldn't. Oh, but she wanted to. "Would you care to show me your desert island?" He glanced toward her bedroom.

"I don't have any condoms in my refrigerator," she whispered.

He hung his head and laughed. "I don't always keep them in the refrigerator," he said. "Just when I'm distracted by the local wench."

"Hmm." She stroked the front of his striped pants and his abs contracted.

He bent forward, forehead on her shoulder. When he spoke, his voice was husky. "I have one in my wallet."

"Mm, pirate treasure." She slipped onto his lap and wrapped her legs behind him, threw her arms around his neck, and kissed him like she'd been stranded on a desert island for years. He kissed her back like he'd missed her like hell. He rolled onto his back and let her ride down to the floor, then reversed the legs so that his were wrapped around her.

"Now you've got me where I want you." He put both hands on her bottom and held her while he rocked up against her.

"Wallet," she whispered. "Now."

He nodded, extricated himself, and grabbed his wallet out of his jacket. He retrieved the condom and waved it in victory. "Pirate booty!"

"I thought this was your pirate booty," she said with a wicked grin and ran her hands over his muscular butt. Then she trailed a hand out to him, intending to lead him into her bedroom, but he threw an arm behind her back and one under her thighs and lifted her. She squealed and scissored her feet as he strode into the bedroom with her, one eyebrow cocked.

He laid her on her blue toile bedspread, then closed the curtains and stood at the foot of the bed, looking at her. "God, you're so beautiful." She felt suddenly shy. He pulled off his pirate vest and the shirt that was mostly ties across his sculpted chest, and there were all those muscles, that hard chest, and the arms that could hold him up while he did things to her. She was already hot and wet and breathing in little shallow gasps as he sat on the bed and pulled her shirt over her head, then traced the lace pattern of her bra with his forefinger. She fumbled at his sash, yanking on it, and saw the touch of a smile on his perfect curving lips. Okay, so he knew she was desperate.

Then his pants ripped, the crotch seam giving way with a creak. He groaned and she ran a finger down the exposed triangle of blue underwear, and he groaned again, deeper. Together they pushed his britches off, and she sat on the edge of the bed, with him standing before her, shaking his ankle free from the soft boot while she shoved his underwear to his knees and then bent to kiss the tip of his penis. He made a soft animal growl, so she did it again, giving it even more attention. His abs contracted and his nipples hardened, and then he pushed her shoulders so she fell back on the bed, and he leaped over her, landing on the far side and gazing at her.

"Fair's fair," he said, and stripped her pants and underpants off together with strong, hard hands. Then he knelt between her knees, shoving them farther apart, and kissed up the inside of her thigh, almost there, and then up the other leg. She moaned and tilted toward him and he licked her there, *there*, and she squeezed her eyes shut. He licked again and again, exploring her with his fingers at the same time.

"Condom," she whispered.

He surfaced and hovered over her. "Yeah?"

She nodded, her chest heaving and glistening with sweat. He lowered his head to kiss her, deeply and fully, dragging himself back and forth across her while his tongue played with hers. *"Now,"* Alyssa said.

Nick grinned, then a look of panic crossed his face. "Where did I . . ." She reached over to the bedside table and waved the package at him. He dropped his head and said, "Whew."

He lay on his back, and she ripped the package off and rolled it onto him. "You're flying the Jolly Roger tonight."

"Yeah, Roger's feeling very jolly." He gave her a wicked look and said, "Prepare to be boarded."

She squealed and he lifted himself over her, shoving her knees apart with his legs, and thrust smoothly into her. They both moaned, and he pulled out, dragged his engorged cock over her on the outside, then thrust back in. She watched his eyes and he watched hers, and she'd never felt such a connection with a man. She kept looking into his eyes as they moved together, rocking, gasping, until she grabbed fistfuls of sheet and spasmed against him, and finally her eyes pulled away from his as they rolled back in ecstasy. A second later he was there, shuddering inside her. They rocked together, her muscles coiling around him, claiming him, and then their breathing slowed, and he gave a final swirl. Wow, did she like that swirl.

And then he pulled out and flopped beside her, an arm behind his head.

He smiled at her and brushed hair away from her face. "I love your hair," he whispered. "I always want to touch it. If you ever want someone to follow you around and push it out of your eyes for you, I want to be the guy." She smiled at him and laid her head in his armpit. "Okay, now you should wash your hair before anybody touches it. My pits aren't really safe territory."

"Well, you are a pirate."

"About that. Did we just name my penis Roger?"

She nodded under his arm and snuggled in closer. "Pretty sure we did."

"See, Roger is not a good name for a dick."

"Did he have a name before?"

"Thor. I called him Thor."

She laughed, rolling on her back. "You did not."

He grinned down at her. "*Of course* I did. Thor is a great dick name."

"Well, my hearty, he's Jolly Roger now."

Nick sighed. "Did you ever name your breasts?"

"Annabelle and Elizabeth," she said without hesitation.

He stared at her.

"What? I thought those names sounded elegant." She laughed. She'd never had this much fun with a man after sex. She was just so comfortable with Nick.

"Which one's which?"

She raised an eyebrow at him. "You'll have to ask them yourself."

He lifted himself and twisted over her, licking her nipples and stroking her breasts. "This one tastes like an Annabelle."

"Works for me." She shifted. "So, Roger's a resilient fellow."

He glanced down. "Um, yeah. Well, hockey players can last for three periods . . ."

"Three!"

"But I only had the one condom," he said, taking it off.

"Mmm. Shame," Alyssa said. "I enjoy having a pirate around."

"I am here for all your pirate needs," Nick said, running his thumb between her breasts to her navel and dipping it in. "Especially burying my treasure." She rolled her eyes, but she was smiling. "Oh! One more thing." He stood, took two strides to the closet and stooped, giving her a great shot of his muscular butt. Then he turned and there was Mrs. Gilroy in his hand, her pointy nose sticking out between his fingers.

"Mrs. Gilroy!"

"She was watching us," he said. "I saw her beady eyes but, you know—priorities." She laughed. He looked seriously down at the gerbil. "Perv."

Alyssa got up, grabbed her satin bathrobe from behind her door, and slipped it on, then led him back into the living room. He lowered the gerbil gently into its cage, and Alyssa set the lid back in place and latched it. "Mission accomplished!" Nick said. He padded naked over to her table. "Is this the stuff that's supposed to be messy?"

"Yep."

He cocked his head. "You're making . . . note cards?"

She twisted her lip sideways. "I was trying different designs for an agency sign. If I open one someday."

His eyes widened. "That's great! You're doing that? Your own shop?"

"Well." She hesitated. "I hope to someday. I'm not in a position to yet." *Also, you're walking around stark naked.* Do that on the ice and I'll bet you could distract the other team.

"It would be nice to get away from that woman, right? The frowny one."

She hesitated. She didn't want to explain that she'd gotten fired—and definitely not that it was over him. "We'll see." She shrugged.

"You would be great! You're a terrific designer, and you're good with clients. You seem organized. Are you organized?" He sounded excited.

She laughed. "I am organized."

He threw his hands up. "What's stopping you? Go for it!"

"Nick, it's not that easy. A million things could go wrong."

"A million things could go right!"

"It's dangerous. Things can fall apart just like that!" She tried to snap her fingers. He tilted his head and looked at her, clearly unimpressed with the attempt. "One minute everything's fine, and the next you're knee-deep in debt and have a lease for some commercial space that you can't use because . . . the end tables didn't come in, say, and you can't finish a project."

He lowered his head and gave her a look that was clearly meant to be serious, but a smile kept breaking through. "Are end tables a known hazard in your profession?"

"Yes! Many things can go wrong with end tables."

He gave her squint eyes. "You might have warned me before you put some in my place."

She waved a hand dismissively. "Throw them overboard if they get rowdy." She flipped the logo designs face down. "But seriously, it's dangerous to start a business, and I'm not in a place to do it right now."

"Huh." He opened his mouth, shut in, and then took a breath. "This is about your dad, right? And what happened afterward?" He flipped the designs back over, squinted, and stepped back.

"*No*, it's about . . . well, maybe."

He nodded, apparently satisfied with the admission. "Things can get better, you know. People heal." He hesitated, then plowed on. "I was perfectly content living with one chair and a mattress on the floor. I didn't want my place turned into a home."

"And now?" She sounded breathless.

"You're making a home for me, and I like it." He flushed and looked back at the sketches scattered over the table.

There was something in his voice when he said that she was making a home for him—she wasn't sure he meant just the apartment. His apparent embarrassment added to the impression. While he looked at the sketches, she eyed his torso—wide shoulders, narrow waist, muscular butt. He looked like he should have been carved from marble and propped in front of the Parthenon.

"I like the one with the extra scroll on your name, but it's not clean enough. It would be hard to pick out at a distance."

"That's what I thought," she said.

He left them face up on the table, tapped them with a knuckle, and gave her a significant look. "Tell me something. Why do you like designing people's houses?"

"Because it makes it a home." She struggled to find more words, then just said, "It feels important to me." He nodded and opened his mouth, but then she said, "It's like being the groundskeeper. You guys couldn't play the game without the groundskeeper, right? They make the place work for you."

"For us that would be the Zamboni driver." He cocked his head at her. "Didn't take you for a Zamboni driver, Compton."

She responded with a vaguely automotive sound, and he laughed. Then he collected the pirate costume, wishing he'd thought to bring his own clothes up. He tied the black sash low to cover the ripped seam. "Pirate walk of shame," he said, and Alyssa laughed.

"Do you want to borrow a sweater?"

He looked at her quizzically. "Do you have something big enough?"

She looked at his shoulders and winced. "No."

He gathered his keys and wallet and hesitated at the door. He leaned close to her, smelling of skin and sex, and whispered, "If Mrs. Gilroy posts photos on the internet, I'm suing." She was laughing when his lips brushed her cheek with a quick kiss, and then he hustled down the hallway in his red striped pirate pants, ripped in the front where she couldn't see. But the view from the back was amazing.

CHAPTER TWENTY-SIX

After practice that night, Nick rapped lightly on the door to Sammy's room, then walked in, closed the door, and leaned awkwardly against the wall. "Hey," he said. He walked to the windows and looked out. His room was bigger, but Sammy got better light.

Well, no he didn't.

"I had sex with the decorator again. The one who's doing our living room." He turned and looked at the empty room and tried to imagine Sammy's bedroom furniture in it. It shimmered like a mirage and disappeared. Just an empty room. "In my defense, I was wearing a pirate costume." He gave Sammy a moment to absorb that. "I thought you wouldn't mind. How many chances does a guy get to have sex as a pirate?" He ran a thumb over the window ledge. "I just thought I should tell you."

He left the room and went to the kitchen, surveyed the stacked glass containers of chopped fruits and vegetables, and settled for carrying six containers, a fork, and a glass of water to the living room. The furniture had already been delivered, and Alyssa had carted away his

188

old chair. It was going to a homeless shelter, apparently—not the one Vanessa worked with. He set the glass containers down with a clink. He couldn't imagine Alyssa homeless—and trapped in a car with Ryan. How had that even worked? How had they done homework?

He'd felt homeless when he left the hospital, but he'd had enough money to live indoors. He was emotionally homeless, maybe, but Alyssa had been the real thing. He flopped down on the new sofa and imagined her as a kid, long-limbed and a little scrawny, maybe in a unicorn stage. Had she been the right age for that? He flipped the TV on and popped the lid off the broccoli container. No point trying to cook any of it. A hot meal would be nice, but he ran through smoke detector batteries pretty fast.

He found a documentary on George O'Keeffe and a Colorado game and flipped back and forth between them. He was fine. He had baby carrots. He had a bookshelf with books on the floor in front of it because the little knickknack crap Alyssa was going to put on it wasn't there yet, and she didn't want him arranging it himself. As if it mattered where a fake avocado went. Or maybe a fake duck. Would she do that to him? Anyway, he was fine.

O'Keeffe died at the end of the documentary, and Colorado won their game. Neither ending pleased him, but neither was a surprise either. He looked at his phone: 12:11 AM. Which was 6:11 AM Zagreb time. He scrolled through his contacts, felt an old wound ooze as he saw the names: Sammy, Tyler, Eric, Luka, Dragan. He found Dragan's girlfriend's number and called. It rang six times, then he heard the familiar voice.

"'Allo?"

"Hey, Mia. It's Nick Sorensen. Is this too early?"

"No. Is not bad time. How are you, Nick?" Her accent was thick.

"I'm good. Fine. How are you?"

"I'm fine. We're lying, yes?"

"I guess so." He was quiet for a moment. "Can I ask you a question? It's personal."

"Personal?"

Her English had never been as good as Dragan's. "It's a question I shouldn't ask, but I want to."

"Like what is my real hair color?"

He laughed. "Like that."

"Sure. You ask."

"Do you think you'll ever get married?" Silence stretched forty-five hundred miles and then back. "I'm sorry if . . ."

"Yes. I will get married." She paused, then went on. "I will always love Dragan. I will love him most. But in a few years I will find some good man and make life with him. Now I have question for you."

"Okay."

"Why you ask this?"

He rubbed his fingers over his mouth. "I may be having trouble moving on. I thought if you were, it would shame me into it."

"Moving on? Like you have new roommate? Or best friend?"

"I don't have either one. But I recently got a second chair."

"Oh, Nick. You be better. Dragan would not want this."

"Yeah." He stacked the empty food containers. "I miss him."

"Of course." And then she was crying.

"Jesus, Mia, I'm sorry."

"I miss little scar on his left shoulder," she said, sniffling. "Do you remember?"

Nick spun the remote control on his coffee table. "He said he got it from a fishhook."

"Yes. We made joke about me, I forget how you say, but I fished him."

"I remember that scar." But he'd forgotten it. Hadn't thought about it since the plane went down. "Do you remember his singing?"

She laughed. "O moj Bože, at least I don't have to hear that again." They were silent. "I would give my own life to hear again."

"Yeah." They both sniffed. "It really was bad, though."

She laughed. "You make me laugh and cry. Thank you. But I get ready for work now."

"Do you need anything? You have enough money?"

"I have job. But thank you for question. All your questions. I like to think of Dragan. It makes my makeup bad, but I like to remember."

"Yeah," he said. "Okay. Thanks for taking the time." They said goodbye and he carried the food containers to his sink, dumped them in, and decided to wash them in the morning. He wouldn't have if Sammy were there. Sammy would have sprayed him with the kitchen sink hose if he'd left dishes around. But Sammy wasn't there.

The next morning he met his counselor again. He'd given up on trying to discuss hockey. She wanted to talk about his feelings, and he had things he could tell her about. Progress. She would be happy, and he could get out of there. Maybe if she gave the coach a positive report, he'd let Nick stop going. And that really would be best for everybody.

At ten o'clock Dr. Williams motioned him in. Nick sat in the big chair again. He figured it looked defensive, but he was a big guy. Let her write down whatever she wanted—he was going to be comfortable.

"How have you been?" she said warmly.

"Great!" he said. She raised an eyebrow. *Overselling it, Nick.* "I made progress on multiple fronts."

She sat back and folded her hands at the wrists. "That's wonderful! Tell me."

"Well, I scored a hat trick in the game against Toronto . . ." The wrinkle over her nose creased slightly. That wasn't the thing to lead with, apparently. "I went to a party, and I talked to an old friend. Oh, and all the furniture's been delivered, so my living space is almost normal."

She gave him a slow clap. "That's all fantastic! What did you enjoy the most?"

He tried to suppress the smirk working at the corner of his mouth. It was definitely burying his treasure with Alyssa. Although that hat trick was a pretty close second. "Um, not sure I can prioritize."

"Sure," she said. "Who was the old friend?"

"Um, Dragan Novak's girlfriend. He was on his way to propose to her when the plane went down."

"She wasn't on the plane, right?"

"No. He sent a limo for her. It dropped her off at the designated spot, but he never showed up. So she knew. I think about that sometimes—her standing there by all these white flowers and lights reflecting in the water and knowing something happened."

Dr. Williams let him squirm for a minute. "How is she doing?"

"She sounded pretty good, really. I made her cry."

"Did you cry?"

He tapped his fingernails hard into the arm of the chair. He didn't want to talk about this. "Did I tell you last time that Gretzky scored ninety-two goals in an eighty-game season?"

"Okay," she said. "Let me ask you this—do you still think you should have died?"

He sucked in a breath. She wasn't afraid to ask straight questions. "Yeah. I guess I do."

"Did you ever think that maybe you're not the one whose path went wrong? That maybe the other guys should have lived?"

He blinked a couple of times and looked out the window. Finally he said, "Oh, and one of the guys from the team invited me to Thanksgiving. I'm not going to go, but it was nice of him."

She twisted her lips, making sure he knew she'd caught the change of subject. "Why aren't you going?"

He shrugged. "It's a pity invite I think. Thanksgiving is family time."

"Maybe he thinks of you as family."

Nick snorted.

"Did you think of Sammy as family?" Dr. Williams asked.

He paused. "Well, yeah. But that's different."

"So you can love, but not be loved?"

He gave her a sour look.

"What are you going to bring to the dinner?" she pressed.

"I really don't plan to go."

"But it's a feast. It's meant to be shared."

He brightened. "That's a good point. I do enjoy food."

By the end of the session Dr. Williams had persuaded him to start keeping a journal, and he'd told her about Sergei Fedorov's five-goal game. She'd smiled and said, "Maybe you should tell that to the journal."

"The journal already knows," Nick said, grabbing his jacket. "It's a pretty well-known game."

She laughed and said, "See you next week. I want you to tell me what you're going to bring to that Thanksgiving dinner."

As he left her office, Nick thought about that. He still wasn't sure he was going to accept Devin's offer, but if he did, he should take beer and meat. You could never have too much beer and meat.

CHAPTER TWENTY-SEVEN

Alyssa stroked mascara onto her lashes with a straight wand. If you were using a curved wand, what even was the point? It was like using bumpers while bowling. Go big or go home.

She'd put enough mascara on that she could probably catch a bird with her lashes. At some point she needed to stop. She sighed and capped the tube and stared at herself in the mirror. Her eye makeup looked different, but not too strange. She'd just applied it with a heavier hand than usual. A guilty hand, connected to her guilty, guilty heart.

"I am a bad person," she told the mirror. It mouthed it back at her. She glanced at her watch. She was putting the final touches on Nick's apartment, and then he was going to meet her there for a walk-through when he was done lifting weights. Which meant that he would be even more muscley, and that didn't seem fair. She had taken some chances with his apartment, and not counting getting the right shade of green for the living room, the risks were all in the accessories, which could go horribly, horribly wrong. He'd been living with most of the furniture for a couple of weeks now and seemed happy enough. But she had a few surprises in store and was regretting it.

And then she had to tell him about the commercial and how her mistake with the contract had made it possible.

Alyssa cleaned out the rest of her office at the agency that morning, gave stiff hugs to a couple of other designers who were in, and left her key on the front desk. She remembered after she was in her car that her polka-dot umbrella was behind the door, but she didn't go back for it. She drove to Nick's apartment building, a route that was familiar by now. She parked and carried a box up, terrified that she would trip and break all the contents. She rapped lightly on the door, just in case, and scraped the key he'd given her in the lock. And then she walked into his apartment and took a deep breath. It smelled like man. She put the box on his antique French country dining table and ran a finger over the gorgeous patina. If she could be reincarnated as furniture, she was pretty sure she wanted to be that table.

Alyssa made four more trips to her car, then unboxed everything. She spread an autumnal runner down the length of his table and set it for two, thought it looked lonely and added two more plates, then decided that pressured him to have more people over, and he clearly was not a guy who entertained. She put the two extra place settings away. The centerpiece was a small yellow mum in a green plastic pot that she'd wrapped with burlap shot through with gold and amber metallic threads and tied with raffia. It would last longer than a floral arrangement.

She installed the lamp she'd been waiting on and pulled the first framed print out of the stack. They'd talked about it—she wasn't comfortable choosing paintings for a guy with an art history degree, so he'd chosen the art himself. He had educated taste, and where she might choose a Paul Klee print for him, he might have preferred . . .

Michelangelo.

Oh gosh. She could never again look at the Sistine Chapel ceiling without having impure thoughts. She pulled out her steel measuring tape and found the center of his bedroom wall and hung a pastoral landscape at the foot of his bed. It showed a farmer with a worn face heading home with a herd of sheep on a hill. The style was modern and masculine, but the effect was comforting. Nick could literally count sheep if he wanted.

Alyssa added a couple of throw pillows to his bed, even though she was pretty sure they'd wind up in the closet, and angled a chunky knit afghan over the back of a chair. She nailed up pictures, a mix of abstract and nineteenth-century European reproductions, in the bathroom and kitchen, and propped one up on the front of the living-room bookcase. The main wall space in the living room had a bold modern painting that Nick had purchased at a gallery a couple of weeks ago. He'd texted to tell her it worked with the wall color. Based on his description she had been sure it wouldn't, but when she got there and found it leaning against the wall, four feet by four feet, she had to admit that he was right. It added some masculine energy to the space.

She had sculptural reproductions too, mostly Greek and a small Nike of Samothrace with her wings spread for his kitchen counter. The goddess of victory could watch over his cooking efforts.

Alyssa got all the art up—and it was a lot—including photos of his parents in his bedroom, and a photo of him and a cousin laughing, a candid he'd shown her when she demanded to see family photos. She'd blown it up and positioned it so he'd see it when he walked in. He had a family that loved him. He hadn't lost everything, and he had more left than some people ever had to begin with.

Then she went back to the car, retrieved a bottle of wine with a bow and put it on the counter, and installed the plants—in the kitchen, living room, dining room, and bedroom. He'd said he would kill houseplants, but she was going to make him prove it. He had been so drawn to landscapes at the museum. Besides, taking care of something was important, even if the something was a sago palm in the corner—it was a step back toward living. And the foliage added to the calm, country feel of the place.

The bathroom didn't have a window or much counter space, so she left it alone, and he'd told her not to go in the spare bedroom, which was such a waste. She would have liked to have made it a studio or put a whole garden for him there—the light was good enough. She could have installed a water feature, maybe on the wall. It would have been a beautiful space to meditate. But for some reason Nick insisted that it stay empty.

Why pay for a two-bedroom apartment and only use one bedroom?

The last touches were things she'd pulled from storage: a Greek bust she'd seen in the article about Nick and Sammy that he'd shown her on his laptop, and three large shells with twinkle lights inside that made them glow softly. She arranged them on top of the bookcase, the way they'd been in his Boston apartment.

He would recognize them. They'd be easy enough to put back in storage, but if it angered him it would be hard to justify. *I thought you needed a baby step like this. A small link to your past.*

She had the whole place looking beautiful. She smoothed the wrinkles out of a rug in the entryway and took photos of her work. She wouldn't use them for advertising, but she did like to keep track of her designs.

She had stacked the boxes by the door, to carry back down to her car, and was standing in his bedroom, checking things one last time, when he pushed the apartment door open. Startled, she rushed out of his bedroom, as though she'd been doing something wrong. Which she wasn't. It was normal to inhale deeply. Oxygenation was important.

"Hey!" he said. He sounded happy to see her. She blushed and tried not to think about pirate pants. "How's Mrs. Gilroy?" Her blush deepened.

"Oh, she's seen things."

He laughed and looked around the room. "This looks fantastic. Seriously, Alyssa. When the coach made me do this, I was pretty pissed, but he was right. It feels different in here." She beamed. "I'm gonna make the plants sign a legal waiver, though." He grinned at her, and the world's supply of handsome went way up.

"Oh, I got you something!" He walked to his refrigerator and pulled a mug out from behind a glass container of chopped broccoli. "This was the only place I was sure you wouldn't look." She laughed and he handed the mug over. It said "Zamboni Driver" above a picture of a Zamboni. "It's for your fancy coffee in your own agency. To remind you that you're good at this, and you should be in the driver's seat."

"Ah," she said, tucking the mug into her bag. "Thank you." Her eyes misted. "That was actually incredibly sweet."

"Right?" She laughed. He tilted his head and looked at her appraisingly. "Your problem is you've never read your own scouting report." She cocked an eyebrow and gave him squint eye. "No, seriously. A scout would say you have good design IQ, move very well, and are solid in your own zone."

"I am?" She felt slightly breathless.

"Yeah. You have the potential to play upward of twenty minutes every night at an extraordinary level." She flushed. Why was this sexy?

Nick went on. "Alyssa Compton plays well on the periphery but will also go straight to the net and get her nose dirty."

"I will not!" Alyssa said, then added, "Although I don't actually know what that means."

He waggled an eyebrow at her. "Compton changes gears effortlessly and works equally well on the forehand and backhand. She's able to keep playing hard on a long shift." Her face and neck felt hot, and she wondered if she had invented a new shade of red. "Imaginative offensive player with an arsenal of moves and superior balance . . ." He stopped and his mouth pulled sideways. "I may have strayed from your professional abilities."

"I kind of had that impression," Alyssa said.

Nick rubbed his cheek ruefully, and his stubble rasped. "But seriously, it can help to see your strengths written down. You're good at this, Alyssa. The only criticism a scout would make is that you need more confidence."

"Hmm." She absently touched the outline of the cup in her bag and thought about that, then looked around the room. It *was* good. He was right—she was solid in her zone.

He glanced around the room too, then his eyes flickered and locked on the top of the bookcase. The shells. He gave her a sober look, then walked across the living room and looked at them, his back to her. She couldn't see his expression, but his body was absolutely still. She had made a horrible, horrible mistake.

He reached a hand up, tentative, and touched a shell as though to see if it were real, had substance—that it wasn't a ghost. Then he lifted it down and cradled it in both hands. He said nothing. Alyssa stopped herself from speaking four times before he turned to her.

"Tyler's dad has a fishing boat, and he grew up by the ocean. He was weirdly interested in it. Whales, fish, seaweed, coral reefs—any of that. He spent most of a plane ride once expounding on the different types of sand—and we were flying to San Jose, so it took hours. We almost threw him out over Colorado." He smiled at the memory.

"After Sammy and I got our new apartment—the last one we had—Tyler showed up with this big box. He put it on the table and said it was a housewarming gift, and beamed at us. So Sammy and I looked at each other, right? And Sammy opened the box, and there were three big shells in it. And he said, 'Wow, this is amazing!' And Tyler was so pleased with himself. He picked them off the shore himself and told us all about them. These, as it turns out, are queen conch shells, which are made of calcium carbonate and occasionally have pearls. Non-nacreous pearls."

"Very impressive," Alyssa said softly. Nick's eyes hadn't moved from the shell in his hand. He was seeing the memory, and she didn't want to jar him away from it.

"Oh, indeed. So Tyler finally left, and Sammy said, 'What the fuck are we supposed to do with these?' And we about fell over laughing. It seemed like such a random gift." His eyes were wet. "Tyler was giving us the ocean, which he loved more than anything. He was sharing his passion. I wish we'd been nicer about it."

"You didn't say anything mean, though."

"No, but we laughed our asses off after he left. I walked over to the bookcase and put them on top just to get them out of the way, and said, 'There.' Then we just shook our heads."

"Who put the lights in?" Alyssa asked.

Nick finally looked up at her. "I did. About three days later I thought about it, ran past the hardware store, and got some tiny lights and rigged them up. I'd turn them on in the evening, and they gave the most beautiful soft glow—like if you could see butter."

"You can see butter," Alyssa said, and instantly regretted it.

He gave her a wan smile. "I mean if the taste were a form of light—the softness and smoothness."

"Creamy light," Alyssa said, and he brightened.

"Yes, that's it. They gave creamy light, and the shells became one of our favorite things in that apartment." He turned the conch over in his hand. "And we never told him. I never one fucking time told him how much we enjoyed them."

He walked back to the bookcase, looked intently at the shell on the right, then moved it to the empty center spot and replaced it with the shell in his hand.

"You can tell which is which?" Alyssa asked.

He nodded, then took a deep breath, shoved his hands in his pockets, and glanced over at the large bust she'd paired with a Boston fern in the corner. "You know I'm gonna flip those fronds over his head so he has green hair."

"Poor old Greek dude. First the Persians invaded, and now this."

Nick gave her a smile. "Somebody took Western Civ."

She polished her fingernails on her blouse and gave him a smug look.

Nick stepped toward her and said, "Seriously, this is really amazing. It looks like a home." He nodded to himself, then stepped into the bathroom and bedroom to look around. "The living room has more modern accessories with traditional furniture, and the bedroom's straight . . ." He looked for the word.

"It's European country. Casual, but refined. An undertone of elegance."

"Totally what I was going to say," he said with a wink. "Seriously, though, it feels more restful in the bedroom. Less energy in the accessories."

"I wanted to play it safe in the bedroom," she said, then blushed furiously, thinking of the pirate shirt he had hanging in the closet.

He saw the flush and smirked. "I owe you a final installment." She named the figure and pulled out her card reader, and he handed her his credit card. Once she'd processed the transaction and had shoved the reader back in her bag, he said, "So that concludes our business relationship, right?"

She nodded. It was a strange way to put it. "I've enjoyed doing your apartment so much, Nick." *Also doing you.* "Thanks for the opportunity." She gave him a warm smile, but her stomach clenched.

"There's something I . . ." They said at the same time and stopped.

"You first," she said. When he heard what she had to say, he wouldn't want to speak to her again.

He ran his hand through his hair and left his elbow pointing up. "I wondered if I could take you to dinner sometime."

Her heart exploded in valentines and violin solos. She could see them dancing on a veranda under the stars, her in a red dress cut to here, and him in a black tux. Or sitting beside each other on his sofa, reading, with their stocking feet propped on the coffee table. And every once in a while, he would tap her foot with his just because he was glad she was there. And she would tap his foot back. She could be happy with this man.

And then she crashed back to reality. If she'd ever had a chance with this guy, Stacey had blown it for her.

"I can't. I'm sorry. It's . . ." He looked surprised. Clearly he'd thought he had this in the bag—just because he was funny and gorgeous and smart and, well, she'd already slept with him twice. "Nick, I made a terrible mistake at the very beginning of us working together."

"I'm sorry you feel that way," he said, and she paused, confused.

"Oh! I don't mean . . . That wasn't . . ." She took a breath and plunged ahead. "The agency—Stacey—uses one contract, and I typically use another. One that I feel is a bit more fair to the client. And when you dropped by that day and I chased you to your car, she handed me a contract. And it was hers."

"So she gets credit for your work or something?" He looked confused.

"No, it's worse than that." She squeezed her eyes shut for a moment. "Her contract says the work can be used in advertising." She waited for him to catch on, but he just stood there. At least he'd taken his hand off his head. "She wants to do a commercial showing your apartment."

He screwed his mouth sideways. "She hasn't even seen my apartment." Then his eyes opened wide. "Wait. Has she been here?"

"No! No. But . . . she will be."

"I'm not doing that. My home is"—he hesitated—"a retreat. I have a pretty high profile in Detroit. I get recognized buying laxatives, you know? I don't want the world seeing my conch shells. It's a personal space." He paused again. "What I have left of Sammy is here." She waited for him to explain what that meant, but he opened his mouth, shut it, and then just said, "I don't want strangers in my space, even digitally."

"I know," she said miserably. "But the contract says she can."

He shrugged and his shirt hugged his shoulders and skimmed his stomach, and her eyes pricked. She wasn't just losing a chance at happiness with this man—she had hurt him. He'd opened up to her, and she'd exposed him to this violation of his privacy, and now he was going to hate her.

"I'm going to hire a lawyer," he said. "I'll sue if I need to."

Oh god. This was a nightmare. "I understand," she said. "I'm so sorry. And I'm sorry I handed you the wrong contract. But you know, you could have *read* it." He looked surprised. "Did you read your contract with the Red Wheels before you signed it?"

"Not really," he said. "My agent checked it out. He said it had everything we wanted and I was clear to sign. So I did."

She shook her head. This was not entirely her fault—Stacey had set her up, and Nick hadn't done his due diligence. But she was the one who'd gotten fired. So she turned and fled, leaving the boxes for him to throw away because the tears were starting, and she needed to get out of there.

CHAPTER TWENTY-EIGHT

Devin and Vanessa's Thanksgiving dinner was set to be served at one PM. At twelve thirty Nick loaded his car and drove carefully over. It got him there ten minutes early—long enough to greet everyone, not long enough to get caught in a conversation. They'd sit down, he'd stuff his face, and then he'd leave. He would see people, but not really interact—it would make him and his therapist both happy. He pulled up in front of the house—the driveway was roomy but it was parked up. He was a one-trip guy, so he loaded up and strode to the front door. When he came here to lose money at poker, he came in through the garage, but that didn't seem right for today. He would make a respectable appearance—Devin had told him that Vanessa's parents would be there.

He didn't have a finger free to ring the bell, so he kicked gently at the door. So much for respectability. Vanessa shouted, "Come in!" at the same time that a man in his early sixties swung the door wide.

"Let me help you with that," he said, standing back and trying to figure out what he could take without making Nick drop something else.

"I got it," Nick said. "If you could just clear a path for me." The man swept ahead of him, scooping up two preschoolers and shouting, "Food-laden stranger coming through!"

"That's Nick," Devin called. "Nick, this is my father-in-law, Mike Cowling."

Nick grunted a hello and set a short, wide vase of mums, cream roses, and cattails on the counter, then let a pumpkin pie and a pecan pie slide down his arm.

"This guy's got skills," Mike said.

"You should see him on the ice," Devin said.

Nick fished a bottle of wine from under his arm and then smacked a lump wrapped in thick deli foil onto the counter. Devin gave it a poke. "What's this?"

"Ham. In case you'd been counting on having leftovers for supper."

Devin laughed. "You're eating the whole turkey, eh?" He took Nick around, introducing him to Vanessa's mother, Vickie, her sisters, brothers-in-law, and their kids.

Vanessa waved from the kitchen. She was flushed and several strands had come loose from her messy bun. She looked cheerful and stressed and like she meant business. Nick felt a stab of envy. Devin got this every day—someone making his place a home, filling the space with smells of meat and rolls and gently bossing everyone as the table got set and the glasses filled. It was what Dragan and Mia had wanted to make together—a home. A family.

"Nick, you afraid to sit next to a five-year-old?" Devin called.

"I fear no mortal," Nick said.

"Bad call," Vanessa's sister said cheerfully, scooping up a squirming boy with a cowlick and a red stain down his shirt. It was a Red Wheels jersey—he was wearing his Uncle Devin's number.

"I'm a superhero," the kid said as his mother lowered him onto a chair at the big dining table, where Devin had added several leaves.

"What's your superpower?" Nick asked. The kid frowned in concentration. "Burping?" Nick suggested.

The kid brightened. "Yes!"

Vanessa's mother leveled a finger at him. "You're a bad influence," she said.

"Vickie's a kindergarten teacher," Devin said, pushing past the last stragglers at the table. "Don't mess with her."

"That's right!" Vickie said, beaming.

"She's threatening to put Rolf Bjornson in timeout," Devin said.

"For the hit he laid on you in Vancouver?"

Devin nodded, then shouted over the hubbub, "I'm saying grace now. Listen or go to hell."

"Wow," one of Vanessa's sisters said.

Nick lowered himself into the seat beside the superhero, thankful he didn't still need the cane with this many people and chair legs around. Devin said the blessing and then carried a turkey on a platter to the table while Vanessa's parents broke into song. "Here's the taters! Here's the meat! Thanks to God now eat eat eat!" They high-fived each other across the table and Vickie Cowling giggled.

"They have a song about turkey?" Nick stage-whispered to Vanessa's older sister, seated across from him.

She rolled her eyes. "They have a great marriage. It's a lot for the rest of us to handle."

Mike, Vanessa's father, took over the carving while everyone else passed heaping bowls of sweet potatoes with mini marshmallows and brown sugar, green beans with onions and bacon, a bowl of mashed potatoes for each end of the massive table, cranberry relish and cranberry salad, beets with pineapple, homemade yeast rolls with parmesan crumbles on top, and stuffing with and without giblets, which Vanessa's sister referred to as "boy stuffing" and "man stuffing." When she asked which he'd like, Nick hesitated, then said, "Boy stuffing." This raucous crowd didn't seem judgy, and he'd be damned if he was eating giblets if he could get out of it. She handed him the bowl over the head of her little girl, seated next to her. Or somebody's little girl. Nick had kept the couples straight but had gotten confused when it came to the kids.

They all tucked into the food with determination, and the conversation died off. Nick managed to fork in some of everything except the giblet-laced stuffing. "This is wonderful," he said several times, and Vanessa beamed. When the little superhero was done with his food, he ran his finger around in the leftover gravy. His mother opened her mouth, but Nick leaned over and said, "Hard to keep a grip on your stick if you have gravy on your fingers."

The little boy processed that, then nodded soberly. "Thanks for the tip."

"You bet," Nick said, unable to suppress a smile. This clattering, laughing, butter-passing crowd all crammed around one giant table was exactly what he wanted life to be. What it should be but wasn't really. This was the facade that covered a world where planes slammed out of the sky, and tables had an empty chair.

He didn't realize his face had gone sober until Vickie Cowling said gently, "I'm glad you could join us today, Nick. I'm sorry your parents missed out on seeing you, though."

"My mom's sisters are coming over, and my dad's brother will be there. I didn't want to travel."

"Well, it's our gain," she said warmly. "Refill his wineglass," she ordered vaguely, and one of Vanessa's sisters obeyed.

"Thought travel would tire you out too much?" Devin said. Nick nodded. Devin was great—terrific player, nice guy—but he kept an eye on things. Filing information away. Nick didn't need him knowing how often he sat in his chair and stared out the balcony window until it was time to do the next hockey thing—practice or lift weights. How hours could go by. How hard it was just to get up and move.

It was getting easier. Alyssa had gotten rid of that chair, for one thing, and the new ones faced the sofa.

"A B C," the little superhero burped.

"Greyson!" three people said at the same time.

"I don't remember the rest of the alphabet."

"Try to burp the NHL teams," Nick helpfully suggested, sipping the wine Vickie Cowling had ordered up.

"There are more teams than letters," Greyson's father said, as if Nick's idea was not, in fact, helpful.

Greyson belched out a couple of team names, and Vanessa shot Nick a dirty look that she couldn't quite pull off because she was also laughing.

"Did Alyssa get your job done?" Vanessa said as people began to filter into the living room and the family room off the kitchen.

"Yeah. Looks real good."

"I'm glad. I was afraid somebody else might have to finish it."

"How come?" Nick said.

"Well, because she got fired." She sounded surprised that he didn't already know.

He stared at her.

"It was a few weeks ago," she explained. "She called me because the agency owner accused her of unethical behavior, and she was afraid I'd hear about it through the grapevine. She wanted me to know it wasn't some financial impropriety or something. She was really embarrassed."

"She got *fired*?" His mind raced. Was that why she'd been stand-offish at the end of the walk-through? Had she been afraid she was going to get fired? "Wait. It didn't have anything to do with a commercial, did it?" What if she'd told Stacey he'd refused, that he said he was getting an attorney. Surely Stacey wouldn't have been mad enough about that to fire her. It wasn't Alyssa's fault he didn't want his place on TV.

"No, a client sent flowers with something inappropriate in the card. Stacey opened it."

A chill settled over Nick. "When was this?"

"She called me around Halloween. I think she'd been seeing the client, and Stacey didn't like it, which is ridiculous. I don't see anything wrong with that."

"She finished my apartment after that," he mumbled, thinking through the timeline, wondering if anyone else could possibly have sent flowers to her office. No, it had to have been his flowers that caused the problem.

Vanessa put a pile of silverware in the sink. "It's a shame. She really wanted to be a decorator—and she was good at it."

Nick thought about the pile of papers and sketchbooks on Alyssa's table when he'd gone over after the nurses' Halloween party. She'd been designing a sign for her own agency, but when he'd asked, she'd said she wasn't opening a shop right then. More thinking about it for the future. What had the card with his flowers said? *Thanks for last night, but we shouldn't do this again.* Something like that.

The reason they shouldn't have done it again was because of his own guilt about living—but he hadn't said that. Anyone who would have read the card would have assumed he'd meant "We need to keep things professional."

As if she'd done something wrong.

He'd gotten her fired.

But after that, she still finished his apartment. She still slept with him a second time. And she'd said nothing about being out of a job.

He reached back for his wineglass on the table and emptied it. "Did she say anything about what she's going to do?"

Vanessa shrugged. "She's back to party planning now. It's what she used to do. Opening her own agency would be hard. Not enough people know her."

"Huh." He thought about the designs scattered on the table at her apartment—signs for an agency of her own. One that no one could take away from her.

"Nick!" one of Vanessa's sisters called. "You're needed at the air hockey table."

"I should be going," Nick said. "I've imposed on family time enough as it is."

Someone clucked in the other room. Nick sighed, lowered his head, and strode toward the family room. He was not putting up with clucking. Five games and nine pony rides later, he went to the bathroom, and on the way back was waylaid by a preschooler with a trembling lip. "I can't find You Nork," she whispered.

"Is that a problem?" he asked. She nodded soberly, eyes brimming with tears. "Okay," he said. "Let's see what we've got." And that's how he came to crawl around on the floor of a guest bedroom, looking for a puzzle piece, and then he had to reposition Kentucky from its temporary spot on the West Coast. Once he'd reestablished the traditional state boundaries, he grabbed his jacket and made for the door.

Vickie Cowling called from the nook off the kitchen. "Come sit with me. I want to talk to you for a minute."

"I really should go," Nick said.

"That's a bunch of hooey." Vickie walked to the kitchen island, grabbed his arm, and shoved him gently toward the seating area. "You save our spots. I'll just be a minute. Say, what do you drink?"

"The bitter tears of goalies."

Devin snorted.

"I think you drank too much to drive yourself," Vickie said. Nick opened his mouth and then shut it. Had he? "Just go sit on the sofa.

Devin can drive you home in a few minutes." In the kitchen Devin shrugged at him, so Nick went and sat on the sofa, unsure what else to do.

A moment later Vickie walked into the family room, holding a bottle of vodka and two shot glasses, and shooed everyone else to the front of the house.

"Join me?" she asked, setting the bottle down with a clunk.

"Um, sure," Nick said. "I really didn't drink too much."

"I know it, sweetie." They drank and Vickie poured them both a second shot. Nick raised an eyebrow but tossed the second drink back. Vickie coughed, her eyes streaming, and Nick jumped up and ran to the kitchen for a towel and a glass of water. Vickie wiped her mouth, then dabbed her eyes, and finally in a hoarse voice said, "Thank you."

"You using your sexy voice on me?" Nick said. "I don't want to get in trouble with your husband." That made her laugh and she coughed again.

"It just went down the wrong way," she said. "Let's try again." Nick was sitting beside her now, and she poured him a third shot and gave herself water.

"I don't drink very much," he said, and tossed it back. The burn was warm and good. "A guy who's lost as much as I have should be careful."

"That's good advice," Vickie said. "What have you lost?"

"My best friends. Five of them. They died in a plane crash last year."

She nodded. Clearly she already knew. He'd gotten good at telling when someone didn't know, but he seldom ran into anyone who didn't. "You doing okay?" she asked.

He gave a small snort. "No. I am *really* messed up."

She sat back in her seat. "Tell me about it."

He shrugged. "Everything I do is something they don't get to. But also, I have no choice but to eat and pee and score goals. So what am I supposed to do?" Vickie nodded sympathetically. "I mean, I had pirate sex with my decorator while the gerbil watched, and that seems like crossing a line." He was vaguely aware that the vodka seemed to be talking on its own.

"I see." Vickie refilled her shot glass with vodka this time.

"I did everything the other guys did—know we were going to die, fall out of the sky, crash, get hurt. I went through every damn thing they did except just for the heart stopping part. And I did rehab and they didn't have to. And now I'm pretty sure I'm going to feel crushingly guilty every time I have swashbuckling sex. Or, you know, regular sex."

Vickie tossed back her drink and coughed. "I hope you don't," she said, patting his leg.

"Actions have consequences, and you don't know what they'll be. You don't get to choose. I changed into a blue shirt—Sammy died. I slept with a woman I really like, someone I feel like myself with, and I got her *fired*. And I didn't even know it! I feel like a giant fucking bull in a tiny fucking china shop. I destroy something every time I move." Through the vodka haze he was aware that that was a lot of swearing. "What do you do again?" he said thickly. "For a living?"

"I'm a kindergarten teacher," Vickie said.

"Oh, fuck, I'm sorry about the swearing."

"That's okay, honey." She patted his knee reassuringly.

"What am I supposed to do?" he said miserably.

"What would *they* do? If they'd been the ones to survive?"

"Eh." He gestured dismissively. "Any one of them would have been better at this than me."

"At surviving?"

"Yeah." He stuck his glass out and Vickie poured. Nick knocked it back. How many was this? "I am really bad at this surviving business. Like fifth line bad."

She patted his hand. "Seems to me you're doing okay at it."

"I have big seashells," he said. Vickie tilted her head in confusion, and he realized vaguely that could sound dirty. He clarified, "I have shells on my bookcase again." He wiped his nose on his knuckle and made a strangled choking sound. "I really, really miss Sammy."

"There we go," Vickie said softly.

CHAPTER TWENTY-NINE

Thanksgiving morning, Alyssa had the car loaded early. Two stiff shallow boxes she'd saved all year because they fit a pie perfectly were nestled in the back seat footwells. One was a pumpkin pie with leaves, made from the extra dough, that she'd scored to make veins. She'd had to do an image search for a maple leaf to make sure she got the veining right. Her mother would notice. The other pie was banana cream. It wasn't Thanksgivingy, but it was Ryan's favorite, and if she didn't make it, they wouldn't have one. And she had a slow cooker of sweet potatoes that she'd need to plug back in when she got to her mom and stepdad's, but as long as no one lifted the lid, they should be ready in plenty of time.

Alyssa also had a box of three different designs of Thanksgiving napkins, shiny turkey confetti, appetizer picks shaped like maple leaves, and a roll of French-wire ribbon in an autumn plaid. And Emma had sent a bouquet of orange lilies, peach roses, and burgundy mums for her mom. She drove slowly, careful not to upset anything, and pulled into the driveway of her parents' two-story brick home with the understated pillars by the stoop. Her mother had autumn topiaries flanking the front door, and her stepfather had mowed the lawn. It was a very presentable house.

Her stepfather, Bill, opened the door for her and kissed her on the cheek as she went past with the pies. He was a tall man with steel-gray hair, wearing a zip cardigan over a dress shirt. Ryan was sprawled in front of the television, watching football. He lifted a lazy hand in greeting and shouted, "Throw it! Throw it! Throw it! No!"

"Apparently something happened in the game," Alyssa's mother said from the kitchen. "Hi, sweetie." Alyssa gave her mom a quick hug, and as they pulled away, her mother brushed her blouse to smooth any wrinkles or brush off any crumbs of failure Alyssa might have left on her. Okay, she'd never actually said that. Alyssa's mom was fifty—a circumstance she'd considered a catastrophe and met with a quiet face-lift and a shopping trip to Chicago.

Alyssa's stepfather sat on the sofa beside Ryan, watching the game, and Alyssa and her mother worked smoothly in the kitchen. "Gravy!" her mother said brightly at one point, and Alyssa laughed. "Not much of a segue there, Mom."

"Gravy needs no segue." Her mother pulled her whisk out. "It needs a lot of pepper, though." She stuck her hand out, and Alyssa handed over the pepper tin. "So, you're sticking with party planning for now?" Her mother's eyes didn't come off the pan or the whisk.

Alyssa had told her mom that she was leaving Stacey's Interiors over the phone the previous week, with the vain hope that they wouldn't discuss it on Thanksgiving. "Yes, I think so," Alyssa said, and walked to the hutch to get the plates with turkeys. They were fine china and used exactly once a year. Her mother also had a set of plates for Christmas; one for Easter, with eggs around the rim of the dinner plates and a bunny on the dessert plates; and a set of regular fine china for non-seasonal celebrations: birthdays, anniversaries, and the like. The Easter set was the cutest, but the Thanksgiving dishes had a grim autumnal quality—an awareness of the coming winter. Not so much a celebration of the harvest as an announcement that all things are ended by the scythe.

"You going to put those on the table or just stand and look at them?" her mom said.

Alyssa set the table, ending with using the ice tongs to put the correct number of cubes in each glass.

"Did you give Bill four cubes? He's only taking four now."

Alyssa removed one of the ice cubes from his glass and dropped it in the sink.

When they gathered at the table, Bill said grace and they spread the napkins in their laps, then passed the dishes counterclockwise, as God intended.

"Bill," Alyssa said as they ate, "you know how they used to bake potatoes before hockey games? And they used the foil from them to keep their hands warm?"

"Yes?" her stepfather said, his eyes twinkling.

"Wait, what?" Ryan said.

"Well, I was at Devin Nillson's house and mentioned that, and . . ."

"You didn't," Bill said, laying down his napkin.

"There were a bunch of players there," Alyssa continued, "and none of them knew about the potatoes. Do they just drink Gatorade for energy now?"

Her stepfather and Ryan exchanged a glance. "You told her that?" Ryan said.

"I . . ." He shrugged. "It seemed harmless. I was trying to bond."

"What?" Alyssa said. Then she narrowed her eyes at him. "Wait— it's true, isn't it? The potatoes?"

"Um, no," her stepfather said.

Her mouth dropped open, and she remembered Nick dissolving in laughter. "Does that mean there was no chicken either?"

Her stepfather shot a guilty look sideways at Ryan, who howled.

"That's too loud for the table," their mother said. "Manners."

"You are unbelievable," Alyssa said, blushing bright pink. "Now a whole hockey team thinks I don't know anything about their sport."

"Yeah, they were gonna figure that out anyway," Ryan said, then to their mother, "My compliments to the turkey. This is great."

"Thank you," she replied. "How are things at the school, Ryan?"

"Fine," he said, reaching for the sweet potatoes.

"Are you applying anywhere?" she asked, ripping off a piece of her roll and buttering it without looking at her son.

"Why would I apply someplace else? I have a job."

"Well, you won't be staying there longer than necessary. I thought you might be testing the water."

"What do you think I could get?"

"I don't know. But surely you don't plan to stay there long term."

"I'm a janitor, Mom."

"Well, yes, but you could at least phrase it differently," she said brightly. "You could say you're a sanitation technology specialist. Something like that."

Alyssa gave a quiet snort and snuck a peek at Ryan.

"I'm a janitor. There's no need to call it something stupid—that just makes it sound like it's not good enough for you. And since it's what I do, you're making it clear that I'm not good enough for you."

"My God, Ryan, the drama," their mother said, rolling her eyes. "Always the drama with you." They ate silently for a few minutes.

"I helped create a mural on the cafeteria wall—a big tiger. They liked it." He raised his eyes to meet Alyssa's—a fleeting look begging her not to turn him in. "And the art teacher and I are becoming friends. Her kids painted it in."

"Oh. So you didn't paint it yourself?" their mother said. Ryan was visibly shrinking.

"That's great, Ryan!" Alyssa said. "I'll bet the kids love it."

"Yeah," he said. He shoved a roll in his mouth and chewed mechanically.

Their mom turned to Alyssa. "How's it going working with Janet? I just don't understand why you gave up a prestigious job working for one of the best respected designers in the area to go back to what you did in high school." She clinked her fingernails on the foot of her glass. "I don't understand it."

You would if you'd seen Nick Sorensen's butt, Mom.

"I hope to open my own interior design shop someday, but I'm not quite ready," Alyssa said.

Her mother threw her hands up. "Then stay with the good job until you are! Honestly, Bill, it's like the children want to be as unimpressive as possible."

"If you need some start-up money, I could front you something," her stepdad said, ignoring his wife. "I can always pull a few more teeth."

"Thanks," she said, "but I want to do it myself. I don't want to borrow money."

"Everybody borrows money, kiddo. If they didn't, nobody would buy a house till they were sixty."

She shrugged. This wasn't buying a house—it was starting a business. Her business. And if she took money from her parents, she'd have to take advice from them too. They'd try to make decisions for her. There would be quiet judgments. It would be . . . unpleasant. But in a tasteful sort of way.

"Pie time!" she said brightly. She stood and smoothly lifted the plates. "Just sit there, Mom," she said, but of course her mother didn't. They worked quickly clearing the table, then her mom brought out the pumpkin pie and ran the mixer for whipped cream, and Alyssa put the banana cream pie in front of Ryan.

"That's not an appropriate Thanksgiving pie," her mother said, her upper lip gathering.

"It's appropriate in my stomach," Ryan said. He cut a giant wedge and slid it on his plate. "Thanks, Lyss." She smiled. It was good to see him happy. "Hey, did you tell Bill about doing Nick Sorensen's apartment?"

"I did! He helped me choose a picture." She didn't add that Nick had vetoed the whole first design.

"See?" her mother said forcefully, laying her fork on her dessert plate with a clang. "That is the kind of opportunity that you won't get working at a *party store*."

"Do you even know who he is?" Alyssa was genuinely curious.

"Well, no, but he's obviously important."

Her stepdad laughed. "He's a hockey star. A fast forward with a complete game, great puck control, really terrific ice sense, and—"

Her mother threw her hands up. "I'm sorry I said anything."

Her stepdad grinned. "So you've gotten to know him, huh?" *Oh, Bill, I seduced him in a Mellow Yellow bedroom.* "What's he like?"

All she could think about was that yellow bedroom, and she needed to say something that was not about that. "He has a double degree in art and art history. Almost." Her mother raised her eyebrows. "He had to finish a project he never got around to."

"It would be hard with his schedule," her stepdad said.

"Yeah."

"Alyssa?" her mom said. She looked up. "Will you help with the dishes?"

Ryan lifted another piece of banana cream pie onto his plate and took it out onto the veranda, letting the cold air in briefly before the door slid shut behind him.

"No," Alyssa said. Her mother looked shocked. "I'm going to have more pie with Ryan. And later we can all wash the dishes together." She thought of Nick's statement that sometimes you had to crush someone on the boards to get a little respect. It made her smile. She wondered what he was doing today.

"So you're leaving it all for me," her mother said.

"No. I'm saying I want to talk to my brother, and then the guys should help too."

"No can do," her stepdad called cheerfully. "I have football-watching responsibilities."

Alyssa cut a thin wedge of pumpkin pie, slipped into her jacket, and followed Ryan onto the veranda. "Hey."

He looked over, surprised. He was standing at the edge, looking over the back yard. "What are you doing out here? This is *my* getaway spot. You usually go to your bedroom."

She smiled ruefully. "I wanted to talk to you." There was a look of alarm in his eyes. "You look scared."

"This can't be good."

"See, that breaks my heart. Siblings should be able to talk without scaring each other."

"No, I mean just that you want to. It's got to be something serious. So out with it."

"It doesn't have to be something serious, but that's my point." She took a bite and collected herself. "I just want to say that I'm sorry. When you were having trouble, and . . . I wasn't very supportive."

He shrugged. "I embarrassed everybody."

"You're a good guy, Ryan. I mean, you need to work on punctuality. And you should help with the dishes. But I'm sorry I wasn't there for you." She shoved a crumb of pie crust across her plate with a tine. "It's easy to have things go bad. We both know that. And it scared me. Putting distance between us felt like it shielded me from having more things go bad for me." Ryan looked at her quizzically. "That's so stupid when I say it out loud." She sighed. "I . . . should have reached out more. I'm sorry."

He stared at her. "You're serious."

"Oh my god, were we so bad that you can't even believe I'm sorry?"

"No," he said. "No." And he wrapped an arm awkwardly around her and gave her a quick squeeze. "Um, thanks for bringing banana cream. Even though it's not *'appropriate.'*" He smirked.

"Maybe being appropriate isn't the most important thing. Maybe you should eat the pie you like."

"I will get you to the doctor right away." He grinned at her, swallowed the last bite, and then licked his plate.

"Ew. My newfound tolerance has limits."

"Of course it does, Lyss. Of course it does."

Alyssa stuck her tongue out at him. She set her plate down on the railing and pulled her jacket tighter as a November breeze lifted her hair. "Can we talk about when we lived in the car?"

He gaped at her and his head snapped toward the house, checking to see where their mom was—Alyssa would have done the same thing. He finally nodded, but the look he gave her was deeply suspicious.

"I'm not sure how to say this." She took a breath and looked at him. "I know you got in trouble sometimes . . ." He snorted. "But it seems like you made it through okay." He just stared at her. "I mean, a friend has recently helped me realize that I have some issues related to that time. I have the impression you don't. I hope that's true."

Ryan tilted his head and opened his mouth, then shut it and shook his head in apparent disbelief. Finally he said, "You try to be perfect and never admit anything's wrong because Mom imprinted her bullshit on you."

"That obvious?" Alyssa said ruefully. "But you seem . . . not to be trying to be perfect." She'd tried to phrase it carefully but winced internally at how that sounded: *You're a happy fuck-up!* "I mean," she said hurriedly, "I think you were young enough not to have . . ." *Noticed? Been imprinted with Mom's bullshit?* "Been affected so much."

Ryan let out a little sigh. "Toward the end of the time we can't talk about," he said flatly, "I started to go through puberty. Like the beginnings. Kids called me Rank Ryan and Compost Compton."

Alyssa stared at him, horrified. "Ryan. I'm so sorry. I didn't know."

He shrugged. "One time the gym teacher called me 'Compost.' He'd obviously heard it, and instead of telling the other kids to shut up, or, you know, getting us help, he just used it too. Everybody laughed."

"My god. Ryan." Her eyes filled and she began to sniffle.

"I never tried to be perfect because I knew I couldn't keep up. I'm the one who had to pee during Mom's date. I was the one who messed *everything* up."

"You were younger!" Alyssa said. "You had a smaller bladder."

He shrugged. "You know how I got into drugs?"

Alyssa shifted uncomfortably. His drug use—and his dealing—was the other thing they didn't talk about. But maybe it was time the silence ended. "You fell in with those guys," Alyssa said softly. "Jerome and his crew."

"Yeah. And you know how I met them?"

She shook her head. She'd assumed it was something sordid.

"I had detention with Marco B.'s little brother, Caspar. I ran into him a few years later when he was with Jerome. I started hanging out with them."

"Okay." She didn't like hearing about this, but she'd brought it up. Ryan had gotten detention for a month for breaking into the nurse's office to steal drugs. And the nurse didn't even have much in there—just Tylenol and something for menstrual cramps.

Ryan looked at her like he knew what she was thinking. "I walked into the nurse's office, and Mr. Thompson walked past like six seconds later, and then I was in so much shit. The nurse said I'd 'broken in' because she was supposed to be there to guard the room, and she wasn't." Hurt splashed across his face. "And nobody believed me. Not Mom. Not you."

"Ryan." Alyssa started to cry softly. "I'm so sorry."

"You know why I walked in? I wanted a deodorant. Some group had donated supplies and they were for us—the kids—and I thought it was okay just to take one." He looked at Alyssa, his expression flat now. "Once the nurse said I'd broken in, they assumed it was for drugs. I mean, what else? That's how I wound up spending two hours after school every day for a month with those guys. I wanted a deodorant."

Alyssa sat heavily on the deck, her knees pulled up, rested her face against her knees, and cried. She finally choked out, "Why didn't you just ask the nurse for one?"

He shrugged. "I walked by, and the room was open and nobody was there. I could get a deodorant without explaining to an adult? You weren't the only one who was embarrassed, Lyss." She nodded and pushed herself up and stepped across the deck to hug him. He held her tight. She thought about Nick's take, that the things Ryan had gotten in trouble for didn't seem that bad.

Finally Alyssa wiped her face and took a deep breath. "Let's go do the dishes with Mom."

Ryan stared at her. "Are you kidding me? Haven't we suffered enough?"

She gave a small sniffly laugh. "I want to ask her something, and you should be there."

"Oh god," Ryan moaned, but he followed her inside and remembered to bring his plate.

In the kitchen, Alyssa picked up the dish towel and smiled tentatively at her mother. Ryan stood awkwardly, near her shoulder. "Well," Linda said. "You decided not to leave all the work for me after all?"

Alyssa poured a last drip of water out of the gravy boat before drying it and handing it to Ryan to put away. "Mom, when we were living in the car . . ." Her mother looked absolutely shocked. She glanced sideways toward her husband watching football in the living room. "He knows, Mom," Alyssa said dryly.

"It's Thanksgiving," their mother hissed. "This conversation is inappropriate. Let's all enjoy ourselves, shall we?"

"Why was it so important that no one know?" Alyssa asked.

Her mother blinked and tightened her mouth. Her whole body seemed to clamp down—her face, her shoulders. She dropped the dishcloth in the water and crossed her arms. "I don't see any point in revisiting—" she began.

"But why was it?" Alyssa persisted.

"Because people take advantage of you," her mother said. "You need to look like you're doing okay. Fake it till you make it." She turned back to the sink. "I can finish this myself—you two are too busy traipsing down Memory Lane."

"Madame didn't take advantage of us," Alyssa said. "She helped."

"She risked everything!" Linda snapped. "Don't you understand? I was so afraid I'd lose you." She looked back and forth between her children and whispered again, "I was so afraid they'd take you away."

This time Ryan started to cry, and Alyssa pulled them both into an embrace. Her mother resisted for a moment, then wrapped her arms around them. Nick wasn't the only one who had work to do, Alyssa thought ruefully. Maybe she wasn't runner-up for being messed up, after all. She might have nudged him out of first place.

CHAPTER THIRTY

The Red Wheels had one road game, wedged in before a long home stretch after Thanksgiving. It was a quick jaunt to Quebec, where they lost in overtime on a stupid bounce, but ugly goals still counted. They flew back that night.

Nick was nestled into his seat, earbuds in, too jacked up from the OT loss to fall asleep. They all were. His mellow evening playlist had ended, and he'd been listening to progressively weirder songs for the better part of an hour when the backup goalie shouted, "Oh, Jesus! Oh, Jesus!" in a full panic. Nick pulled the earbuds out and turned around, and his breath caught. The guy was pushed back against his seat, elbows out, staring out a right-side window. "Oh, Jesus!"

"It's . . . on fire," Devin said dumbly, in shock.

Then the flames flared, and the inside of the cabin reflected orange.

And Nick was falling inside again. How could there be so much empty space within yourself?

The guys erupted, jumping out of their seats and rushing to the right side, hunched over, staring at the engine trailing fire through the night sky.

The pilot crackled on the speaker. "Yeah, we're experiencing a starboard engine failure. Please remain calm and fasten your seat belts."

The guys ran for their seats, buckled up, and turned to Nick. Everybody on the damn plane—like he'd carried this to them. Like he was the Typhoid Mary of aviation disasters. He stared blankly back at them. Then they fumbled for their phones. A big-deal sports reporter, traveling with them to cover their GM's rebuild strategy, sat in the back. Bad luck for him, riding with the team this flight. But Nick was oddly calm—maybe the fire was good luck for him. Because he hadn't wanted to survive without his friends—and now maybe he didn't have to. He could unbuckle.

Guys were making quiet phone calls and texting, thumbs flying over the keyboards. It had been like this the last time—the panic, the shock. They'd texted then too. And then Sammy, Tyler, Luka, Eric, Dragan, and he had reached across the aisle and over seat backs to hold hands. Dragan had apologized, over and over, saying it was his fault they were on the plane. He finally stopped when Nick had said, "It's a privilege to die with you guys," and the others had nodded. As they entered the final tailspin, they'd just looked at one another. They were past talking. Their eyes said everything.

Nick blinked and was back here, seeing the Czech rookie hunched over, his face in his hands. There was one gift he could give these guys that no one else could—one final gift, maybe. He could talk about the thing he never talked about. He took a deep breath, unbuckled, and stood.

"Take your seat!" the coach barked.

"Maybe later," Nick said. He looked out at his teammates. They stared at him, faces drawn, hoping he held some secret to survival.

"You know I have some experience with this, right?" His voice was casual. The guys shifted. "This isn't a crash." He pointed out the window. "That's an engine fire. There's a big difference, okay? I'm not shitting you. This isn't a crash." He was totally shitting them. It wasn't a crash yet, but he had no idea what was going to happen.

"That's not a little fire," André called.

"Nope," Nick said. "It's a pretty good fire. But it's not a crash. Just a story to tell your wives and girlfriends when you get home. Think what great sex that's gonna turn into." A couple of the guys smiled.

"You need to sit down," the coach hissed.

"Eh." He stretched and yawned, deliberately casual, and looked at these men. He felt a flood of affection for them. God, they were terrified.

"We're going to try to land in London," the pilot's voice crackled. "Ground made the decision. We'll just get her down, then work on getting you guys back home."

The team rumbled in approval. London was a few miles across the Canadian/U.S. border from Detroit. And a safe landing—anywhere—was good. They were fighting off the panic, although the right sides of their faces glowed orange with reflection from the engine that still burned.

"Sit down, you idiot!" the GM called. Nick sat, found the ends of his seat belt and held them, one in each hand.

"Those lights you're seeing are London," the pilot said. "We're going to set this firebird down and then go get very drunk." The guys laughed a little. The plane straightened and wobbled, and then shook.

What if it crashed and he died this time? My god, his parents—after all they'd been through. He'd heard his mother tell friends about getting the phone call—they said they'd taken him to the hospital, and when she'd asked if he was alive, they'd said he was in surgery and there was no update. She never made it through the story without crying, and his father always had to finish it. They lived in fucking Minnesota, in the Arrowhead. His dad had loaded the car wordlessly and driven them to the Duluth airport. The trip took three hours because it was dark, and it was January, and it was fucking Minnesota. And then they sat in the airport until a flight left at one PM. What if their phone rang in the night a second time?

The plane rocked. "Sammy," Nick whispered. "The fuck, man?" He remembered the first time he saw Sammy, in the orange juice line at hockey camp. They were friends by the time they set their trays down.

One wing tilted up and then the plane straightened. "Oh god," Leif moaned. They flew another ten seconds, fifteen, and the lights of the city were behind them.

The pilot's voice came back. "I wasn't able to line up for the final descent, so we're just going on to Detroit. We have decreased maneuverability, and I don't want to try to circle back around."

The plane rocked again, hard, and Nick said, "We're doing okay, boys. Put your shoes on and make sure they're tied." He thought about Alyssa. About the way she trailed her fingers over a table. The way she kneaded them into his shoulders. How determined she was to make him help choose the paint color for his living room; how she'd talked him into having some plants. She was life—she was the future. And he had a choice.

He shoved the ends of the buckle together. He wanted to live. Fuck him, after all his moaning, he wanted to survive.

As they began their descent, Nick called back to the reporter, "What day's your story coming out?"

"Um," the guy said. "Um." Sorting it in his mind. "Sunday."

"When you write about the Red Wheels, make sure you tell people that we're brave and handsome. I'm not sure they'll be able to tell from the photo."

The reporter exhaled softly, as close to a laugh as he could get. He clearly understood what Nick was doing—extending the future past the next two minutes. Ahead were the lights of the terminal. Even from this distance they could see people standing inside, hands pressed against the glass. Two lines of rescue vehicles, flashers already on, stood ready to rip toward them.

And then the plane descended sharply—it was going down, one way or the other. It bounced on the runway, landed again, fishtailed, and swung off the runway into the grass. A good landing, really.

"Emergency exit on the left side," the pilot said, all business, but André already had it open. The big inflatable slide billowed out, and André launched himself down it, popping up at the end. They filed out efficiently, following him down the slide. Nick touched two fingers to his forehead as he passed the pilot, then jumped out into the night, the cold air bracing on his face.

In the terminal, Nick checked in with each guy, making sure he had someone to be with that night. Checked with the pilot too. It was like he was the host of the emergency landing. Everybody had a place to go but the reporter who was doing a story on them. "I booked a hotel room," the guy said. He was a fifty-something white guy, thin strands of hair hovering over his head so you could see his scalp underneath. It was like an old-guy halo and Nick felt a surge of tenderness for him. For all of vulnerable, fucked-up humanity.

"You think you'll be okay alone?"

"Yeah. I'm going to call my wife. What about you, Nick? You okay?"

"Yeah, I'm good. And I've got somebody to talk to." He chucked the guy in the shoulder, lifted an arm to his teammates, a couple of whom already had wives running at them. He pulled out his phone and opened his thread with Alyssa. How should he phrase this? *Almost died, but didn't. Just FYI.* And then a thumb's-up emoji? It would be better to call. Delivering a bad diagnosis or breaking up required a phone call, not a text. Probably an aviation near-miss was in the same category. His thumb hovered over the phone icon by her name.

But she'd said no when he'd asked her out. Who could blame her? He'd gotten her fired. And with her background, the struggles she'd had? Of course she was angry with him. He pocketed the phone.

And then he went home. He picked up a bottle of whiskey on the way. He carried it and two glasses into Sammy's room and sat on the floor. "I've got something to tell you," he said, pouring for them both. "You aren't going to believe it."

CHAPTER THIRTY-ONE

The next Monday Nick parked by his apartment building and threaded his grocery bags down his arms. What was the point of having biceps if you weren't going to use them? He was on the second stair when he realized someone was standing outside his door, and he was on the third stair when he placed her. That gruesome woman Alyssa worked for. Had worked for. She looked like she'd stepped out of a Hieronymus Bosch painting. There was a cameraman behind her.

"Can I help you?" he said, going up the stairs and sticking his key in the lock, but not opening the door.

"I'm Stacey Treblor. I own Stacey's Interiors," she said. "I never got an answer to my calls or texts, so I just popped by to take a look at the place. I'm sure Alyssa told you we're featuring it in our next marketing campaign—congratulations!"

"Yeah, no."

She went on as if he hadn't spoken. "I'll just see what we're working with now if it isn't tidy, but if the place is in good shape, we can go ahead and get some basic footage. I'll want to bring in some flowers later and maybe some food to stage it."

"Not interested." Nick nodded to the cameraman and turned the key but didn't open the door.

"The thing is, Mr. Sorensen," Stacey said, her voice chilled, "you signed a contract that gives us the right to do this."

He sighed and turned to her, the bags draped down his arms. "Will the ad generate enough revenue to overcome the cost of litigation?" He was betting he had deeper pockets, but he wasn't sure. He probably made more a year, but she'd been around a lot longer.

She cocked her head. "You'll lose. A contract is a contract. And if you sue us, it will bring even more publicity to my business." She smiled.

Well, shit. That was probably true.

"How are you going to get in, since I'm never going to let you?"

"I'll sue *your* ass off," she said. "And then I'm going to make a series of ads of your place. The harder you make it to get in, the more ads I'm going to run." She tapped a navy-blue fake fingernail on his chest and turned to go.

"Game on," he called, then pushed the door open and dropped the bags. He hadn't planned to hold them quite that long. He locked the door, then stepped to the window to watch her go. She looked up as she pulled away and gave him a wave that didn't engage her wrist. An old girlfriend had shown him that move once and explained it was how the queen waved so she wouldn't tire her wrist out greeting peasants. He'd thought the queen should get her ass to the gym more often. That was just embarrassing.

Nick thought about things while he put the cold food away. The freezer still had the remains of the ice cream he'd bought when Alyssa had been over, painting. They'd had such a good time that night. And again at her place. This woman was funny and smart and knew things about art. This was a woman he could talk to. And then he'd asked her out, and she'd turned him down.

She'd also left him with ice cream in his freezer, which was a temptation he didn't need. He wasn't a guy who drowned his sorrows with sweets. But he could chop the hell out of some carrots. He got a cutting board out and slam-sliced until he figured the downstairs neighbors were calling the police.

When he had his refrigerator containers refilled with ready-to-eat vegetables, he drove to his therapist's office. Dr. Williams was waiting for him and ushered him right in, laying a hand on his forearm.

"Nick. I read about the engine fire. How are you?" She looked at him closely.

He shrugged. "I'm okay." She tapped her fingers together in an "I don't believe you" gesture. "You know what I was thinking when we were going down? This time, I mean?"

"No," she said softly.

"I thought about my parents and how much this would suck for them—if I died after all that effort to patch me back together. But then I thought about Sammy." He hesitated. "He was my best friend for years. We knew each other from hockey camp even before we were in the AHL."

"He's the one you avoid talking about," she said. "You change the subject whenever he comes up."

"Um. Yeah. So anyway, I was thinking maybe I was about to see Sammy. And at the last minute, I buckled my seat belt anyway."

Dr. Williams clasped her hands and pressed them against her mouth. Her eyes were wet. "That's progress, Nick." She reached behind her, to her desk, and picked up a piece of paper. "I read the article about it. The reporter talked about what happened on the plane, how you calmed everyone. How you calmed him." She picked up a pair of reading glasses. "This ending! His final paragraph is a single line: *'One more thing: the Detroit Red Wheels are brave and handsome.'*"

Nick smiled. "Yeah, he did a good job." He tapped his fingers on the armrest of the chair.

"I want to hear more about Sammy," she said.

"I want to tell you about the Richard Riot."

She sighed.

"No, this is gonna be good," he said, leaning forward. "Oh, and I was thinking next week we should meet at the public rink. You need to learn to skate."

Her eyebrows shot up again. "Would you be comfortable talking about your life at a public rink?"

He hesitated. "Well, no. So it would be good for that reason too."

She rolled her eyes. "I'm not going to learn to skate."

He sighed loudly. "You need to take some chances. Try new things." No reason he couldn't parrot that shit back.

She cleared her throat and redirected the conversation. "What do you have coming up?"

"Los Angeles comes in on Tuesday, then St. Louis . . ." He caught her expression. "You mean me personally?" She nodded and her dreads rocked. "Um." Crap. What *was* going on? He needed something that sounded emotionally healthy. "Hey, I'm going to a party! Devin's hosting the team and a few random friends."

"Sounds like a big gathering."

He shrugged. "Probably not everybody will go. It may not be as big as the Richard Riot." There. He was back on track.

Three hours later he had retained an attorney—Dr. Williams's brother-in-law, who came highly recommended; scanned the design agency's contract and emailed it to the attorney's office; and gone in to the rink to take some laps in a pair of skates he was breaking in. His thoughts went around with his feet: Alyssa had dug her fingers into his shoulders. Alyssa had licked the outside of his ear. Alyssa had refused to go out with him.

The situation was confusing and irritating, but at least his apartment was finished, and he wouldn't have to see her again.

CHAPTER THIRTY-TWO

Alyssa slit open the cardboard box, careful not to let the blade cut deep. The box was filled with paper napkins, and she could ruin the whole top layer if she were careless. It was an appealing thought, really—she felt like stabbing something. Napkins weren't her first choice, but hey, life was tough. She laid the box cutter aside and flipped the flaps up. Valentine napkins—all pink and lavender, the visual equivalent of granulated sugar. She flipped through—one stack had tiny hearts with sayings: "I Do," "Yes," "Love You, Baby," "Hot Stuff." One design was scrolly interconnected hearts, and a third had a fat Cupid raising his bow, his forward thigh obscuring his boy bits. How could a baby that age have the dexterity to nock an arrow? Seemed unrealistic.

All the Christmas items were already on the shelves. The Valentine's Day items would go out the day after Christmas, coexisting with New Years' stuff for a week. Some people would pick up Valentine things when they came in for New Year's party supplies, but wouldn't bother just for Valentine's Day itself. January could be a slow month in party planning.

The door chimed and Alyssa looked up, pushing a strand of hair back from her eyes. It was a customer with a sleek black bob and . . . holy cats, it was Krystelle Rohrbach, looking exactly like she had in high school except for the tailored powder-blue suit. In high school she'd worn designer jeans and expensive sneakers.

"Alyssa?" Krystelle said, popping her eyes and pushing her head forward like a turtle. But turtles don't generally throw your pencil pouch down the stairwell. Or invite you to run for lunch with their crew and then leave you stranded at McDonald's, so you have to walk back to school, and your heel bleeds from the blister you wind up with, and you get detention for missing fifth period and . . . "Oh my god! It's you. You're still working here?" She looked around, eyes wide, like a journalist investigating a prison camp.

"Hi, Krystelle," Alyssa said. "How can I help you?"

"Wow, this place hasn't changed. I used to buy glow lights here for my lake parties. You remember those."

Of course she did. She'd heard all about them. She'd just never been invited.

"Are you looking for anything specific?" *A sense of decency maybe? We have those next to the curly ribbon.*

"So probably you're up to date on me. I married Trace Arnold and his medical practice is just thriving."

"Trace Arnold?"

"He was a senior when we were sophomores. You remember Trace! Everyone was in love with him."

"Oh," Alyssa said vaguely. She did not remember him, but she did want to sell Krystelle whatever she was here to buy.

"Anyway, I'm planning a Valentine's dinner for the other doctors in his practice. Not on Valentine's Day itself, of course—we'll be sprinting off to Cancun." She gave a radiant smile.

"What date are you looking at?" Alyssa said, leading her to a consultation corner. It was a couple of folding chairs with a chipped Formica table between them—a hundred steps below the consultation rooms at Stacey's Interiors. Alyssa had never been so aware of the store's shabbiness. The floor was concrete, the shelves powder-sprayed cream and riddled with little holes, as though Party Barn was too cheap to pay for a whole shelf. The overhead lights were suspended metal hoods with exposed fluorescent bulbs. There was no attempt to make it . . . presentable. It was the kind of place you went to buy red drink cups for your high school kegger when your parents were out of town. Janet had worked hard and given it a reputation for party planning and staffing, but she wasn't one to think about the appearance of the store itself. Alyssa should have done something about that. Immediately when she began working there. Before Krystelle Rohrbach Arnold walked in.

"I'll need it catered, of course," Krystelle said. "You can arrange that. And I'll need you to set everything up—decorate the place and be there to serve and troubleshoot, and then clean up after us."

"Well, the caterer would do any serving," Alyssa said.

Krystelle waved a hand. "Arrange it however. But if you're in charge of the party, I expect you to be there to make sure everything runs smoothly."

"Sure," Alyssa said. "Is this at your house?"

"Yes. We have plenty of space." Krystelle went on to detail her house, which rooms would work for serving, for mingling, where the help could refill glasses.

The help.

This wasn't why she'd gone to college or stayed up late learning about the stain absorption of different woods or . . . Krystelle was still talking. When it finally ended, Alyssa smiled brightly, showed her out, and shoved the paperwork into a folder with a savagery she normally reserved for expired coupons.

"Easy, cowboy," Janet said from the back. "Everything okay?"

"No. That was the girl from high school who thought she was better than everybody else, even though she wasn't nice or talented or smart."

"And now we get to take her money?"

"And now I'm her 'help.'"

"Aw, screw her. What's her theme?"

"Valentine's! So I can sprinkle Cupid confetti on her stupid table while my own heart remains unclaimed."

"That's a straight-up lie."

"We're out of confetti?"

Janet looked at her. "Lying liar from Lyingtown."

Alyssa stuck her tongue out and went back to unpacking boxes. She was almost done when her phone rang. She glanced at the screen—Vanessa.

"I'm having a party tomorrow, and you should come." No hard feelings about the homeless shelter job, then.

It took Alyssa a moment to respond. "I should? I mean, thank you. I think I can . . ."

"Oh," Vanessa said. "I should tell you that Nick's okay. He seems really good, actually. I thought you'd want to know."

"That's great," Alyssa said. She had no idea what Vanessa was talking about. "Is there some reason he wouldn't be?"

There was a beat of silence at the other end of the phone. "Well, because of the crash. I'd have thought this would be hard for him— being in another plane that almost went down." The world stopped for one beat, two, and then Alyssa realized that the beating was her own heart. "Alyssa?"

"Their plane almost went down?" She felt like her throat was lined with sandpaper.

"Oh no—you didn't hear? It was on the front page of the newspaper and, well, everywhere." Alyssa had been heading for the sink in the tiny staff lounge, to get a glass of water, but now she detoured to the computer. She nudged Janet sideways with her hip and ignored her stare. She had a tab open and typed "Red Wheels AND airplane" in the search bar before Vanessa spoke again. "Nick always asks if you've been over . . ."

"He does?"

"Yeah, and I had the impression you were getting close. I mean, it's obvious he likes you," Vanessa said. "I thought you'd want to know. Because no matter how cool he acts, that had to have been traumatic, right? Devin says he calmed everyone down, though."

"Oh my god," Alyssa said as photos came up of the team's plane approaching the airport at an angle, one engine engulfed in flame. What must Nick have been thinking? She should call him. Immediately. She needed to get off the phone, but Vanessa was talking again.

"I'm sorry I told you so abruptly. Because there is a little something there, right?"

"I don't . . ." Alyssa said. "I mean, I've enjoyed his decorating project. It's always rewarding to, um . . ." Why couldn't she just admit she liked him? That he had helped her understand she had unfinished business in her family? And that she lusted after him most of the day?

Vanessa laughed and saved her from flailing on. "So, about the party. A bunch of friends are going to be here. Commissions, Alyssa! They'll see our house, they'll love our house—because of course they will. They'll say, 'Who did that gorgeous thing with the topiaries in the entryway?' and I'll say, 'She's right here! Hire her.' And you get rich and famous. And also have a good time."

Alyssa laughed. "You're wonderful, but you don't have to do that."

"I want you there anyway. As a friend. It's on a Tuesday night because of Devin's stupid schedule, but you're less likely to have a conflict, right?"

Alyssa smiled. "What should I bring?"

"Nothing! You don't have to plan this party or design the kitchen or anything! Well, you already did the kitchen. Be here at seven!"

Vanessa said goodbye and they hung up, and Alyssa was grateful that she hadn't said a thing about her dodging the homeless shelter job. She started to call Nick six times but talked herself out of it each time. Would he want to talk about being on a second plane with an engine fire? What if he were in the middle of something that he had to concentrate on, and she made him think about it again? She settled for reading every article she could find about it and watching the clip of the plane landing eleven times.

Finally Janet said, "You planning to do any work this afternoon?" Alyssa nodded absently and watched the clip eight more times. Finally, she stowed her phone on a shelf and unpacked Valentine's Day supplies, from the kitschy to the lush, until closing time. No one else came in for party planning, but she sold two bunches of Mylar balloons and persuaded a man to go with a pretty floral motif instead of buying paper plates that read "Over the hill" for his wife's birthday. One small step for humankind.

She worked most of the weekend, but she doodled a little with the design for the sign for her someday-agency and texted Ryan to see how he was doing. He responded entirely in emojis, but at least she'd reached out.

When Tuesday arrived, she flipped the "Closed" sign exactly at six and scurried home to shower. It was going to be great to have something to do. She'd already met a couple of Vanessa's friends, but a whole houseful of women would be fun. It had been a while since she'd had time for a girls' night. She added a shimmer shadow along her brow bone and felt a stab of guilt. Janet and Emma would hang out with her if she ever made the time. They needed to do more than lunch at Gilda's.

She always put effort into her makeup, but she was putting on her A face for tonight. She chose a cute outfit she'd found at a discount outlet the last time she'd made time to shop with Emma. It looked good with a complicated wedge that was too much for most occasions but would be perfect for tonight. Then she decided the wedges were fussy, and she was not fussy—she was sleek and sophisticated. So she slipped on a soft black sweater that showed off a phenomenal necklace she'd bought herself as a graduation present, and switched to shiny black flats. She was having a good hair day, and it survived the sweater change.

Alyssa knew the route to Vanessa's house by heart. She enjoyed the drive now, and when she pulled up to the French-style mansion, there were already a dozen luxury cars parked in the driveway. It wasn't going to be hard to find her vehicle when she left, she thought ruefully. She knocked on the front door and it opened instantly—and there was Devin, Vanessa's hunky husband and the captain of the Red Wheels.

"Hey, Alyssa," he said, pulling the door wide for her to come in. "Don't cost me any money."

She smiled. "No new throw pillows?"

"I would definitely throw them," he said, laughing. "Let me take your coat."

She shrugged out of her jacket and handed it over, then made her way into the home. Its rooms were so familiar—she had their dimensions memorized. She was distracted looking at the furnishings she'd selected, the art and plants and a table that had gotten pushed out to make more legroom, when she realized that the room wasn't filled with women. It was couples and a few single men. She scanned the room quickly—every guy there could choke a gorilla with his thighs. It was a team party—that's why Vanessa had said it was planned around Devin's schedule. Of course.

It would be rude to leave immediately, but she couldn't possibly stay if Nick was there. She was pretty sure he wasn't—she didn't see him. And then a deep, familiar voice behind her said, "Well. Look who's here."

CHAPTER THIRTY-THREE

Alyssa turned. Nick was standing there wearing a red shirt. He'd clearly bathed in handsome before driving over. "Alyssa."

"Hey," she said softly. "Are you okay? From the other day?"

"Sure," he said. Then he turned to speak with a gorgeous brunette squeezing past him. Somebody's wife, but she caught the snub.

"Well," Alyssa said breezily to Filip, standing nearby, "where are the drinks?" He pointed, and she went to get a glass of white wine.

She found Vanessa and asked if she needed help with anything.

"I need you to sit down and enjoy your drink," Vanessa said.

So Alyssa did. She found a spot in the family room, off the kitchen, where a couple of other women were sitting. She'd just settled in and introduced herself when their husbands showed up, one of them deep in a conversation with Nick. He sat down on the sofa opposite her, still talking to the guy. When he saw her, his gorgeous eyes pinched a little.

The guy's wife said, "Nick, do you know Vanessa's friend, Alyssa?"

Alyssa gave him a tiny smile. "Uh, yeah."

He gave her a small jerk of his head. "I don't think they hold up as well," he said to the guy he'd walked over with. "And you have to sharpen them more often." They kept talking about some brand of skates the other guy was endorsing. She didn't expect him to nibble along her collarbone here in public—although she'd have let him if he'd tried—but he was being standoffish—rude even. And she hadn't done anything to deserve this. Well, except give him the wrong contract.

Alyssa fell into conversation with the woman next to her—was it worth planting ornamental cabbage as late as it was already? Do you really need to put celery and carrots in when making chicken stock? How often do other people vacuum their sofas? Not often, right?

And then Nick's friend wandered off in search of snacks, and the woman Alyssa was talking to excused herself to find the bathroom. Nick turned and looked at her with obvious reluctance, like a detective at a crime scene lifting a tarp. "So," he said. "How have you been?"

She shrugged. "Fine. You?"

"Fine." They were silent. Nick sipped his beer. Alyssa played with her bracelet. "I wish you'd said yes when I asked you out," he finally said.

She stared at him, stunned. He couldn't want to see her socially now. Could he? He was pissed about the ad, and they hadn't spoken in weeks. He hadn't looked very excited running into her here either.

"It didn't seem like a good idea. Because of the situation with the agency." *Your contract. I used the wrong contract.*

"Oh." He tapped his fingers on his glass, and there was another long silence. "I thought you might call. After the emergency landing the other day."

Ah. He had wanted her to check in. That explained part of his pissiness. "I didn't even know about it," she said. "Alyssa told me when she called about tonight."

A look of hurt splashed across his face, and it occurred to her that he might have thought she followed the team more closely than she did. Maybe he hoped she wanted to, because of him. "I often see Red Wheels news," she amended. "I've just been so busy."

He gave her a small nod. Then, out of nowhere, he said, "Did I tell you that I saw Monet's *Rouen Cathedral* exhibited once?"

"No." She sat forward. This was interesting.

"It's tight in on the building, right? So it should be all hard lines and sharp angles, but it's not. It looks like a bar of soap that got left in the bath water." He looked pleased with himself.

"It does not!"

"It *does*. It lacks definition."

"I cannot believe you said that!"

"Van Gogh was by far the better Impressionist."

"You take that back!" People were beginning to look at them, but she was not going to let that go.

He leaned forward. "Van Gogh has an energy. A sense of movement. Have you ever really looked at his clouds?"

"They're too strong! They look like you've worked so hard your whole life, and then those stupid clouds come in and blow everything away. I mean, *Wheat Field With Cypresses* looks like the backdrop of *The Wizard of Oz*." His jaw dropped, but she didn't care. She felt mean—just as mean as he was being, going after Monet. "Like the set for a *high school* production of *The Wizard of Oz*."

"Oh, that's bullshit!" Nick said. André turned to Devin, who'd wandered over and stood behind him. "My parents fought a lot," he whispered, "but even they never went after *Wheat Field With Cypresses*." Devin cracked up. Alyssa shot them a look over her shoulder.

"I don't like Monet. Nick said. "I've never liked Monet." He leaned forward, his face hard and angry, biting his next words. "He doesn't draw well."

Alyssa knew she was shaking. She set her glass down because she didn't need wine on her charcoal pants. "You like Kazimir Malevich's *Woodcutter*, right?" She clearly remembered him talking about it, but she wanted to get him on the record. A crowd had gathered, and there were going to be plenty of witnesses to everything he'd said about Monet.

He nodded.

"It's all line and no charm." She shook her head. "It looks like Malevich made it for geometry class."

"It's a masterpiece!"

"It's some guy cutting wood! He looks like the Tin Man," she said, suddenly realizing it was kind of true. "You only like art that relates to *The Wizard of Oz*." She laughed harshly.

His face darkened. "Monet painted water lilies during World War I. Talk about not reading the moment! All that misery going on—millions of soldiers dying, all the empty chairs at people's tables—and he paints a bunch of fuzzy flowers."

"He was trying to bring beauty to a hurting world!"

"He didn't care how much the world hurt. And he was a liar too." He jabbed a finger at her. "You can't trust Monet."

She drew her breath in. This was directed at her, not a dead French artist. Even angry she understood that.

"He's trying to make it look like he's painting something in the moment, right? Like this is how the river looks this *one* instant."

"Yes, and it's beautiful!" she said.

"But he didn't paint all of it wet. Some of those quick impressions were actually done over a week. He let the paint dry between sessions." She opened her mouth, but he held his hand up. "They've proved it with the brush strokes—whether the paint bled or not. They know if he was painting wet on wet and *he wasn't always*." He sat back in triumph.

"He can paint any way he wants," she said, offended.

He sipped his beer. "You can't trust Monet."

"I don't think they're fighting about art," Devin whispered. André nodded. Alyssa shot them another look and they clamped their mouths shut.

She stood, her mouth tight, and smoothed her black sweater. She was so glad she wasn't wearing complicated wedges right then. "You have a poker tell. When you have a crappy hand you take a drink." A half dozen guys groaned. This revelation was going to cost them some money on poker night. "You sip when you want to stall or you have nothing. You're a *sipper*." She leaned forward. "You were drinking just now because you know that's all bullshit. Monet painted beautiful things, and there's a place in the world for beauty. So you can take World War I and cram it up your butt." She spun on her heel, blurry eyes turning the whole party of staring people into a watercolor.

Nick stood too. "Oh yeah? Well, I really liked Michelangelo, but some people only *pretended* to. People should be clear on their feelings about Michelangelo."

She whirled on him. "I *loved* Michelangelo, but you clearly don't trust . . . Monet. So what am I supposed to do?"

"This is why I don't go to museums," André said.

"Yeah, I'm not following this," Devin whispered back, "but they both turned bright red. Did Michelangelo paint a lot of smut?" Alyssa wheeled on them. She'd had enough of their little asides. Maybe they thought this was funny, but she didn't. Then she realized she was in Devin's house and thought better of ripping into him.

She went to retrieve her jacket instead, but Vanessa met her with it, threw it over her shoulders, and then wrapped an arm around her as Alyssa walked toward the door. Everyone gave way as they pushed through. Behind them Leif said, "We get to talk about World War I and his butt, right? I mean, we're not letting that go?"

"I don't normally kinkshame," André said, "but that's excessive even by my standards."

"They're sleeping together, right?" the Czech forward, Jakub, said. "Nobody is this stupid with someone they're not sleeping with."

Vanessa squeezed Alyssa tighter, and they stepped out.

"I am so sorry," Alyssa said. "I didn't mean to make a scene." She never wanted to make a scene. That was low class and embarrassing. Not something a woman in a tasteful pearl necklace would do.

"Alyssa . . ." Vanessa started, then trailed off. She squeezed her friend's upper arm and just said, "I'm sorry about whatever happened back there. I'll tell Devin to make Nick apologize." She smiled.

Alyssa squeezed her eyes shut. "It's complicated. But I am so, so sorry I ruined your party."

Vanessa laughed. "This doesn't even register. Do you have any idea the kinds of things these guys will do? I'll tell you sometime about Rolf Ingersoll wedging a jet ski in a tree." She shook her head. "Insulting Van Gogh doesn't begin to compete."

Alyssa gave a little laugh that was half sniff. "Yeah, but the other guys know how he feels about Monet now. They'll probably trash-talk him a lot."

Vanessa gave her shoulder a little rub. "I think you misunderstand team dynamics." She smiled warmly, and Alyssa got in her car and pulled carefully out.

CHAPTER THIRTY-FOUR

The following day, Nick clicked the edge of the chair in the lawyer's office with the tips of his fingernails. He kept them short, and so he had to get the angle just right in order to get the click. It took a little bit of concentration. Finally Dante Freeman looked up from the desk and laid a hand across the contract as though keeping it from blowing away. He had a chunky ring on one finger that would have weighed down a whole book.

"Yeah, there's nothing you can do about this."

Nick grimaced and twisted his head to the side in disgust. "Seriously?"

Dante nodded. "The contract is clear. The agency has the right to use images of the finished work in promotional materials of all kinds. That includes print, online, and TV ads. He looked up at Nick. "You really want to block it?"

"Absolutely."

Dante rolled his thumb along the backside of his ring and looked at the contract Nick had signed, the one Stacey had tricked Alyssa into giving him. "You could try paying her off."

Nick pulled his head back. "What?"

"Just offer her cash to rip up the contract. If you do that, let me draw something up for you that terminates the relationship."

"So you're suggesting . . . I bribe her?"

"No, it's business," Dante said matter-of-factly. "Happens all the time. She gets money and you get privacy."

"Doesn't that mean she wins?"

"Is it actually a competition?" the lawyer asked.

Nick thought for a moment about Stacey's smirk when she stood outside his door with a cameraman. "Might be," he said. "I'm not sure."

"Well, you'd better decide. Because you're going to have to deal with this woman one way or another."

As he took the stairs down to his car, Nick thought about what the lawyer had said. Was it that bad if his apartment was all over the internet? What was the worst thing that could happen if people in Detroit saw the soft green walls Alyssa had painted for him, or the luminous yellow in his bedroom? It's not like they'd know what happened during the painting. His place looked great, and he hadn't cared what anyone thought even when it didn't. He reached his car, swung in, and gripped the wheel, looking straight ahead. Why did this bother him so much? He admitted the answer to himself: it damn well *was* a competition. And Nick hadn't gotten into the NHL by not caring if he lost.

Stacey texted him twice while they were in Buffalo having their asses handed to them by a worse team. He ignored the first text because he wanted to, and the second because the coach was reading them the riot act.

Friday morning, his lawyer called. "Stacey Treblor called me. She says you've been ignoring her texts."

"Yeah. I also told her to bother you instead of me, and she kept texting anyway. Is there a harassment suit in that?"

"No." Nick made a guttural noise and filled a glass with water. "She's coming over at two PM today with a cameraman. If the time doesn't work, you can set another one, but you have to set something up today, or she's ready to file a breach of contract suit."

"She might get some bad publicity from that," Nick said, pouring the water into a ceramic pot holding some plant that had defied the odds and was still alive.

"She'd get publicity. Then people would know the ads are coming, and they'd get more traction."

"So what do I do?"

"You let her in today at two, or you arrange another time. She has a legal right to enter when you're present and to take photographs or film the place. She can't touch anything without your permission, but she'd only want to bring in flowers or something like that anyway."

Nick thought about that for a minute. "She can't touch my stuff?"

"No. Does that help?"

"Yeah. It does—thanks." Nick signed off. He moved the shells into Sammy's closet. They were personal. Then he finished watering the plants, got the apartment ready for Stacey, and played a game on his laptop until two o'clock. When his doorbell chimed, he buzzed her up, standing outside the door while she and a cameraman climbed the steps. "Hi," he said. "What time would you like to come through?"

That made her pause awkwardly on the step.

"The lawyer said you wanted to come through today or set a time," Nick said.

She looked up at him. "We're here now. You knew we were coming now."

"Right," Nick said. "So let's set a time. How about Monday afternoon?"

Stacey stomped up the stairs. She had to switch to the left side of the staircase because of the way he was standing. He knew how to take up space and how to make the opponent take a longer route to get where they were going.

"I intend to come through now," Stacey hissed. The cameraman looked deeply uncomfortable.

"Huh. The lawyer said we could make an appointment for a later—"

"But if you let me come all the way out here . . ." She glared at him. He didn't flinch. He'd been stared down by NHL defensemen. "You're just trying to make this as difficult as possible."

"Yep," Nick said. He was kind of enjoying this. He was absolutely going to drag it out and make this as hard for her as possible. It served her right, and not just because she was strong-arming him. She'd also fired Alyssa—and humiliated her in the process. If he could make Stacey walk the long way up a staircase or have to return another day, he was damn well going to do it.

"If you don't let me in, I'm suing for breach of contract."

He shrugged. "Then you can walk through, but the cameraman can't come in today." He turned to the man. "Monday afternoon. Say, one o'clock?"

"Works for me," the guy said. He looked relieved not to go in. Nick guessed he hadn't known much about the situation—that Nick was unwilling to have his apartment featured in this ad.

Stacey's nostrils flared. "Alright, Mr. Sorensen. I'll do a walk-through now so I know what I'm dealing with. Then we'll come back to film on Monday at one."

Nick hesitated at the door. Maybe what he'd done was stupid. Okay, it was definitely stupid. "Did you fire Alyssa because of me?"

Stacey gave him a smile as warm as a Zamboni towel. "Yes."

Nick waited for some explanation, some excuse, but she just stood there, looking smug. He swung the door wide open.

He'd pulled his living room chairs over to the entry and laid them on their sides. There was a three-foot triangle inside the door. To get beyond, you had to climb over furniture. "Remember, you're not legally allowed to touch anything," Nick said, squatting and leaping over a chair cleanly, landing lightly on the other side. He stood back to give her room. Stacey stood in the triangle, fuming at him, then took her shoes off and climbed over his chair, stepping on the side of the arm. He pulled his phone out and snapped a picture, and the cameraman quietly raised the camera and filmed a few seconds, lowering it quickly when Stacey turned around. Nick gave him an appreciative grin. Probably nothing could be done about her touching his stuff, but it was worth documenting.

Stacey strode around the place, opening his kitchen cupboards—which seemed entirely unnecessary and designed to maximize the intrusion. She walked into his bedroom and looked around, then adjusted the angle of the quilt folded at the end of his bed.

"You're not allowed to touch things."

"Get over it." His eyes flew wide at that. Her acrylic nails tapped his bedside lamp, turning the nightlight feature on and off. "Not the lamp I would have chosen," she said.

He thought about that. Alyssa had never said anything about that lamp, just showed him how it worked. She could have easily said, "Flip the top switch for reading, touch the base for middle-of-the-night-panics." But she hadn't. She'd left him a little dignity—and he'd insulted her stupid pond flowers. He'd been hurt when she rejected him, and he'd been petty.

"We'll be back on Monday at one o'clock," Stacey said. "Have your furniture upright. I'll be bringing flowers for the table." She turned back to look at him. "I won't put any incriminating cards in them."

"I'll try to hose the place down. I'm hosting an orgy tomorrow so it'll be iffy." The cameraman laughed. Stacey walked over his chair again and climbed over. She was pretty limber for her age, he'd give her that. "Hey," he said to the cameraman as she left, "can I talk to you for a second?"

"Yeah," the man said. "I'm sorry about this. I didn't realize it was a problem."

"Can I hire you to make an ad for me?" Nick said. "I'll pay you twice—"

"Don't care," the guy said. "Nick Sorensen? I'm in."

Nick mass-texted his teammates. He was going to need help to pull this off. Because what did he know about marketing?

Nick: *Party at my place right now. Urgent. Pick up food and drinks, please. Bring women.*

Nick: *This is not a drill.*

Nick: *Wear pants. You're going to be on camera.*

Then he sat at his computer, opened a design program, and sketched out the sign he'd seen in Alyssa's apartment, the one for the business she hoped to open. He wasn't sure he had it exactly right, but it was close. He had an eye for that kind of thing. He hit "Print" and handed the paper to the cameraman. "Can you do the whole thing? The editing and, I guess, producing?"

"Sure," the guy said. "My years of film school will finally pay off." Nick shook his hand.

His teammates arrived half an hour later—eleven guys, six with their wives or girlfriends. A few other guys had texted that they were intrigued but out on a lake or otherwise occupied, and a few guys hadn't seen the text yet. Eleven Red Wheels were more than enough. Nick threw his door open and let them stream in. "Get everything," he said to the cameraman, and the man nodded, filming silently from the corner.

Devin walked in with a bottle of wine and a tray of cookies. He stared at the apartment. "Alyssa is amazing," he said. "This place sure looks better than the last time I saw it." Nick beamed and glanced over to make sure the cameraman caught that.

He was about to shut the door when Jakub, the Czech left wing, walked in wearing a purple suit. He had this week's girlfriend, a leggy blond in a low-cut dress, on his arm. He clunked two bottles of vodka on the counter. "Emergency party!" he shouted. "I am here for you, Nikolai!" He patted Nick's cheek.

Pretty soon the disco light he'd bought when Alyssa was painting was rotating with a soft grind, and they danced. Then one of the guys turned the TV to a game, and they tumbled into his living room to watch. They snacked, told jokes, poked fun at one another, and laughed. Even Nick forgot the camera was there, and once he'd explained his plan, the other guys had ignored it too. Considering it was a party for show, they had a lot of fun. When it was over, they collected the leftovers and wandered out, complimenting his place and thanking the cameraman, who beamed and asked for autographs.

"You can get it done?" Nick asked him.

"It'll be tight, but yeah. I texted the station while I was filming, and you're good for tomorrow."

"Seriously?"

"Yep. I explained and they rearranged some things. Basically, once people knew it was for you, they made it work."

Nick tightened his mouth. It was the crash. Dead friends got you favors, but also that's why you needed them. "Thanks so much. I can't tell you how much I appreciate this." He shook the man's hand.

"I'd have done it just to see Jakub Cermak sing 'I'm a Slave 4 U.' That was . . . something."

Nick laughed. "Yeah, I was afraid he was going to strip a little too far."

"Let's shoot the intro, and then I can get to work," the man said. "There's a lot to edit."

"Basically anything with Jakub . . ."

". . . needs to be cut," they said together, then laughed.

Nick stood in his living room, ever so slightly drunk, loose from hanging with his friends. Turned out he had friends who would answer the emergency beacon of a cheap drugstore disco light and show up in the middle of the afternoon, no questions asked. God, this was a good life. It was. He should be more grateful.

"Hi, I'm Nick Sorensen," he said. "And this is my apartment. Alyssa Compton decorated it for me, and she did a great job."

CHAPTER THIRTY-FIVE

Alyssa pushed through the Party Barn's door on Sunday morning, registering the chime. It was the same one that had dinged when she was in high school, but the sound made her happy. It sounded cheerful and optimistic. *Ding! Here comes fun.*

The day went downhill from there.

"So Roberta's sick again," Janet said.

"She called in at least? So that's . . . good?"

Janet shook her head. "She's actually sick. But it gives us a problem because tonight is Krystelle Rohrbach's Christmas party." She batted her eyelashes.

"That's a Valentine's Day party."

"No, she called *yesterday* and wanted to add an event in December—because, of course, it's not a busy month for us. And she wanted it for this weekend. It's a party for kids from her school."

"That's a little tight," Alyssa said, frowning.

"Yeah, but she threatened to cancel her other party if we weren't 'professional enough' to pull this off. So I said yes. Possibly without getting the details first."

"Janet."

"Anyhoo," Janet said breezily, "with Roberta out of the picture, you'll need to staff it tonight."

Alyssa sighed. "Sadly, I can do that."

"A caterer's taking care of the food and drink. We just do table service and decor."

"Christmas themed?"

"Yes." Janet moved off toward the storeroom, then paused at the door. "Oh, one more thing: you have to dress like an elf." She swung the door shut fast behind her.

Alyssa stood in the store, staring after her, then shouted, "You can kiss my tinsel-draped butt!"

Someone cleared their throat, and she turned to find an elderly man in an overcoat. "Hanukkah napkins?" he said.

She squeezed her eyes shut.

For the rest of the day, she sold glittery green tree-shaped confetti and napkins with poinsettias and spools of plaid ribbon as the pine-scented jar candle at the checkout filled the room with cloying cheer. When the sun was low enough to glare off the cars in the parking lot so it blinded you if you stood by the cash register, Alyssa snuffed the candle out. Janet sat cross-legged on the floor, shoving inflatable Rudolphs on a shelf. She looked over at Alyssa, one eyebrow raised.

"I have Christmas in my lungs," Alyssa said. She made a fake hack.

"Your lungs are atheists?"

"Apparently. I feel like I can't breathe."

"And you blame the candle?" Janet said.

"Yes." She drummed her fingers on the counter. "My mother sent seven texts today."

"Were they supportive reminders of how much you are loved?"

"They were not. They did question whether my education was worth the expense considering where I now work."

"We should do something socially inappropriate to get her back."

"I could wear white pants." She jutted a finger at Janet. "Not winter-white wool. I'm talking straight-up white linen."

"You brute." Janet pushed the last Rudolph onto the shelf and stood, rolling her neck. "Have you checked the elf costume?"

"I wore it last week at the Children's Hospital, and it didn't need cleaning. I'm good to go. But *you* wedged this party into our December schedule. I think you should distribute elvish cheer tonight."

"The Rohrbach woman specifically asked for you. Said you'd want to see the kids or something."

Alyssa gave a soft snort. She liked kids, but she'd rather be home with a magazine or a book. Or she could watch TV, but not a hockey game, because she didn't think about hockey or players or jawlines or where a vein wrapped around his left wrist and snaked over his hand. There were a lot of things she'd like to stay home and not think about.

But money was good, so while Janet stayed to close the shop—they were open until eight o'clock through New Year's—Alyssa went home with the elf costume on a hanger in a bag, heated leftovers, and then shoved her legs into red and white horizontally striped tights. The costume came with green shorts and a green vest over a white blouse, and a red hat with a large jingle bell that she put on at home so she could bobby pin it in place at the right angle. The curly-toed shoes rode in a box of decorations she was taking to Krystelle's.

Alyssa let the GPS get her there and was glad to have it. Krystelle's house was in a subdivision full of doctors and other random monied people. The streets twisted past Greek Revival and Georgian homes, and one pillared monstrosity that seemed like a set rejected from *Gone With the Wind* when the director decided not to be that pretentious.

Alyssa parked around by the triple garage and carried two boxes of party supplies up to the side door. She had to knock with her knee. Krystelle answered in a green blouse and black velvet skirt, swinging the door wide. "Come in! You can set your things down on the counter."

The interior of Krystelle's house was more tasteful than the exterior. She'd had someone do it, but it was still a little too much—more mirrored surfaces and gold faucets than Alyssa thought were strictly necessary. Not her house; not her business. She put the boxes down where Krystelle pointed and slipped on her elf shoes with their curved, jingly toes, then went off to consult with the caterer. Party Barn was supplying the plates, and she stacked them beside a serving dish that smelled divine.

"Little sausages?" she asked the caterer.

He shook his head. "Portabellas stuffed with maple-glazed sausage."

"Pretty fancy for a kids' party," she said, stringing a garland of Santa faces along the front of the table.

The caterer poured ice into a wine bucket, then stabbed two bottles of rosé into it and topped off the ice. "This isn't a kids' party," he said, giving her a curious look.

Alyssa looked at the beverage table. There were three more wine buckets. This was not a kids' party. Alyssa did an emergency mental run over the decorations. They were heavy on traditional Santa and elf themes, and all in red and green, but people often liked that at Christmas. Some people were disappointed by a burgundy, gold, and ivory scheme. The caterer was looking at her. "Krystelle said it was for her kids' classmates? She spoke to my colleague," Alyssa added. *Not my fault.*

The caterer shrugged. "We were told food and beverages for sixty adults."

Alyssa ran into the kitchen, her toes jingling. "Krystelle?" The host was in a powder room off the kitchen, door open, freshening her lipstick. "I think there may be a misunderstanding with the party," Alyssa said, smiling thinly. She did not want to look incompetent in front of Krystelle "better than you" Rohrbach. If she had the same job she'd had back in high school, at least she could do it well. "We thought this was a kids' party, but the caterer's putting out wine."

"No, it's for adults," Krystelle said. She pulled out a compact and patted her forehead.

"You wanted me in an elf costume, though?"

Krystelle turned. "Oh, it's adorable! Everyone's going to love it."

"Your kids' classmates?"

"No, *my* classmates. Well, ours, I guess. It's just a little impromptu reunion of our graduating class. When you're not working, feel free to mingle and catch up. Everyone will love to hear what you're doing these days." Krystelle smiled brightly. "Just because you're the help doesn't mean you can't have fun." Alyssa was still processing that her high school class was about to see her in red and white striped tights and shoes with tips that curled. She wasn't ready to add "the help" to that. Krystelle looked out the window, and Alyssa followed her gaze and caught headlights up the street. "Guests!" Krystelle said, clapping her hands. She smoothed her dark green silk blouse. Alyssa was wearing green too, but the effect was very different.

Alyssa ran into the front rooms and strung up a garland of stockings and some twinkle lights by the time the doorbell rang. Krystelle's husband, Trace, answered it. He was wearing dress pants and a white shirt with a candy-striped tie. "Come in!" he boomed. It was Jake Turner, who had been quarterback of the football team and captain of Quiz Bowl and was not, it turned out, any less dreamy than he had been in high school. A willowy redhead with porcelain skin and huge eyes was on his arm. She wore a deep emerald sheath dress and black heels, and looked amazing. Alyssa glanced back at the Santa garland she'd strung on the front of the food table. Turning made the bell on her hat jingle.

"Alyssa?" Jake said. "Hey, how are you?" His handsome brow furrowed. "Is this a costume party?"

"No," Alyssa said brightly. She was going to stab Krystelle with a candy cane and stuff her body up the chimney so Santa could find her rotted corpse. As the party wore on, Krystelle got in more little digs, and Alyssa thought of more Christmas-themed murder methods. Trampled by reindeer? Strangled with curly ribbon? Poked a thousand times with the business end of an ornament hook? Krystelle could meet a deadly but festive end.

That wasn't how the evening turned out, however. There wasn't much for her to do after the initial setup, which she accomplished before the guests arrived, so she spent as much time as possible hiding in the kitchen. Krystelle regularly herded her into the living room or asked her to check on the napkin supply, forcing her out among the guests. She got roped into conversations about the art teacher who'd been arrested on drug charges the year after they graduated, and the secretary who decided at age fifty to get in shape, and then swam the English Channel at age sixty-two.

Just a couple years ago, Alyssa had attended the five-year reunion in a blush-pink linen outfit with wedges that worked perfectly with her purse. She had been an associate at Stacey's Interiors, one of the top interior design firms in Detroit. Now, Krystelle held Alyssa's upper arms from behind while she explained to everyone that Alyssa was back at her high school job! The Party Barn! And it would be great if people hired her because it looked like she really needed the work. Then Krystelle gave her a little shake and Alyssa's hat jingled.

Alyssa avoided her former classmates by hiding in the kitchen. What would Nick do in this situation? He sure wouldn't be standing pressed against the counter on the far side of the refrigerator, to avoid detection. For one thing, even a big stainless steel model like this one would do nothing to hide his bulk. Also, she'd seen him take on Stacey. Krystelle was nothing compared to the agency owner. Krystelle was mean, but she wasn't as smart as Stacey. Or as talented. Alyssa thought about that for a moment. What exactly did Krystelle have going for her? Money. And . . . absolutely nothing else. She was still the same selfish, unpleasant person she'd been in high school.

Alyssa might not be working her dream job now, but she had trained for it and could do it again someday. And right now she was working with a dear friend, doing things she genuinely enjoyed. Was she challenged? No. But she still found joy in her work. Good grief, she was a grown woman who got to play with balloons and plan parties all day. And there was a man in her life who was artistic and thoughtful and kind. He'd remembered how she liked her coffee. He'd sent flowers like those he'd seen her admire in a painting. And he'd been brusque at Vanessa's party because he'd been hurt that she hadn't checked in after the plane's engine fire. That meant he cared. You couldn't get upset with someone you didn't care about.

She was not upset with Krystelle, she decided in that moment. She wasn't worth it. Alyssa went to where she'd stashed her bag and pulled her phone out. She texted Vanessa.

Alyssa: *If you still need someone for those rooms at your church, I'd be happy to help.*

There. She was done hiding from her past.

Krystelle's husband poked his head in just then. "Need you out front for a minute," he said. Alyssa nodded and dropped the phone back in her bag. She straightened her felt vest and strode into the living room. Her old classmates—the ones who would attend a party hosted by the Rohrbach-Arnolds—were starting to line up in front of the fireplace.

"Alyssa! Get in here!" Krystelle called. Alyssa moved over to the group and saw the photographer when she was past the eight-foot tree. He motioned her in, and she stood in the back row, hiding behind Elizabeth Frantini.

"What's this about?" Alyssa whispered, leaning down over Elizabeth.

"Krystelle gets all her parties in the gossip column of the newspaper," Elizabeth said. "She's so well connected, and the society reporter just loves her."

"The *newspaper*?" Alyssa said in horror, right as the photographer snapped the photo.

"Well, it'll be on the website too," Elizabeth said.

CHAPTER THIRTY-SIX

Alyssa checked on Mrs. Gilroy when she got home, took a shower, wrapped herself in a fluffy bathrobe, and sank onto her sofa under the Monet *Water Lilies*. She opened her laptop and logged on to a TV app. There was a baking show, but she'd missed a couple of episodes and wanted to catch up before watching the contestants make European landmarks in gingerbread. She watched a couple of minutes of a wedding show, but the bride wasn't a raging narcissist, and the groom seemed thoughtful. Where was the drama in that? Ah . . . it was an outdoor wedding, and they didn't have an indoor backup. She knew where this was going, and as a party planner, it knotted her stomach. Hard pass. She began to scroll through her social media sites.

She'd pulled the afghan over her shoulder and shoved harder into a throw pillow when a sponsored ad came on, and Nick Sorensen's big stupid face was on the monitor—and he was standing in his apartment. She sat bolt upright, fatigue forgotten. So Stacey had made her commercial. But how had she gotten him to be *in* it?

"This is my apartment," Nick said. "Alyssa Compton decorated it for me, and she did a great job." Her mouth fell open. The camera panned the living room, dining room, and kitchen—the elegant furniture, the art, the sculpture on his kitchen counter, the plants—still alive. He had teammates over, guys she recognized, and they were laughing, dancing with their wives, throwing popcorn into one another's mouths. Just quick glimpses of strong young men at ease together, and then there was the rotating disco ball that splashed colored light. When the commercial ended, there was her logo for the business she intended to start but hadn't yet. The business whose launch party she had mentally planned down to the champagne glasses.

How dare he? The business was *hers*, or would be when she was able to open it. *She* would choose how to advertise, and it wouldn't be an online *commercial*. Okay, she'd never be able to afford a commercial, but that wasn't the point. How dare he? She picked up her phone and stabbed it. A minute later he answered.

"Hey, Alyssa?"

"Do you want to explain the ad I just saw online?"

He hesitated a second, picking up on her tone. "I got a lawyer to see if I could stop her from getting in my space." Alyssa squeezed her eyes shut. "He said no. So I beat her to the punch. If I have to let everybody in Detroit in my living room, *you* get the benefit from it—not her." He sounded extremely pleased with himself.

"Did it occur to you to call me before you did that? To *ask*?"

He hesitated again. "No?" She exhaled sharply into the phone. "But it's a good ad, right? And it gets you off to a good start with your new business."

"I wasn't ready!"

"The game comes at you fast," Nick said.

"This is not a game," Alyssa said, fighting tears.

"This was *nice* of me." His tone was defensive.

It *was* nice of him. She hadn't wanted him to do it, and he should have asked. But he was definitely trying to help. Even in her anger she understood that.

"All you have to do is sit back and answer the phone," Nick said.

"Oh my god. You put my phone number on it?" She'd seen it but hadn't processed what it meant.

"Well, yeah. You don't have a website yet, so how else will they get a hold of you?"

"I was going to get a second number! When I got around to doing this, which isn't right now."

"You could still get a second number. You could make the new one your home number if you want. I don't see what the problem is."

"The problem is," Alyssa said, biting her words, "that you took a decision that was mine and did what you wanted, and I don't think it was even to help me. I think you were trying to outmaneuver Stacey."

There was silence at the other end of the phone. That had hit home. "You know what?" Nick said. "None of this would have happened if you hadn't given me the wrong contract." He scored a direct hit. "I paid for the ad to run for four days. I won't renew it. You can decide whether to take the opportunity or sulk."

"That's unfair!" she said.

"We all have to get out of our comfort zones sometimes, Alyssa." His words were heavy with more meaning than she could even begin to understand right now.

She started to answer, but he hung up on her. She stared at her phone. "I was going to have a launch party," she whispered. "There would be pink cookies." She set her phone down and wiped her eyes.

Then she saw that while they'd been talking, she'd missed three calls.

CHAPTER THIRTY-SEVEN

Nick scored a Gordie Howe hat trick in the game against Philadelphia—a goal, an assist, and a fight. Dave Taylor cross-checked Jakub Cermak in the neck, and as soon as Taylor was far enough from Jakub's prone body, Nick took a swing at him. In a second it was a full scrum, one big fight and little side fights. Their goalie came out and stuck his giant mitt over the face of one of the Philly players, effectively taking him out of the melee. It was a good technique. Nick wasn't the best fighter in the league, and he wasn't even close, but if you smacked your stick over his teammates' vertebrae, he was coming for you.

He got in his second fight of the night when Alyssa called while he was on the bus on the way to the airport. She was pissed about the ad, and he'd had to take the call in front of his teammates—who had dropped everything to come help him get the ad shot. It was embarrassing.

The next day he had a purple abrasion on his cheekbone from the fight with Taylor. Too bad he didn't have a therapy appointment. Dr. Williams would ask about it, and it would get them talking about hockey, which was the right thing to talk about. He didn't want to talk about the argument with Alyssa.

He ordered flowers for his Grandma Sorensen's birthday and considered returning his overdue library book, but he didn't feel like it, and the fine would help support the library. He was a bad boy and a virtuous citizen all in one. He yawned, stretched his arms overhead, and flopped onto a sunny spot on the floor. Cats knew what they were doing. He'd already lifted weights that morning, and now he just felt lazy. No need to do anything until practice except avoid vengeful librarians.

He rolled his head and looked at his naked Christmas tree. His parents had always made putting the tree up a big deal. He suspected it was because he was an only child and they'd never wanted him to feel like he was missing out on big family moments. Nick hadn't made a big deal of it since he'd been on his own, but he and Sammy had always put a tree up. They'd skipped the wassail and carol singing that Nick's parents thought were an integral part of bringing a fir inside. Although he and Sammy almost didn't get a tree one year when they couldn't find one without any low branches. Sammy had wanted to be able to have sex under it—he thought that would lend some seasonal gaiety to his carnal activities. They finally found a tree that Sammy thought would do—but he was wrong, because he and a blond barista had brought it down.

Nick hadn't planned to put a tree up this year, but then the apartment was so fucking depressing without one that he caved. He knew he'd miss it if he didn't. Dr. Williams had been delighted, and it was almost worth the trouble just to see her look so happy about it. He'd come to really like her. Still, Nick wasn't sure he wanted to decorate it. Alyssa would probably have great ideas for what to do with it. She'd have coordinating decorations and a color scheme or something. What he had was a shoebox of ornaments from home, mostly penguins in

Santa hats from his childhood penguin phase. Alyssa would find his ornaments deficient.

Nick sighed, rose effortlessly from his cat sprawl, and retrieved a string of lights from the coffee table, unspooling it as he walked around the tree. Then he opened his box of ornaments and pulled a penguin in a sleigh out of the tissue paper. Last year he and Sammy had decorated their tree together. Sammy also had a cardboard box that his mom had sent his first year away from home. Neither one of them had bothered to pick up anything more. Had his mom hung those ornaments on her tree this year, or was the box in a spidery corner of their basement?

His phone rang and he answered it with the sleigh dangling from its hook on his finger. The caller ID said "Stacey's Interiors." He was looking forward to this conversation.

"Sorensen." That usually threw people off. It was a good way to answer the phone when it wasn't going to be a friendly call.

"Hi, Nick. I saw your ad." Stacey didn't sound as upset as he would have liked, but she'd probably gotten herself together before making the call.

"What did you think?"

"Looks like you throw boring parties," she said. He raised his eyebrows and lifted the ornament off his finger. Stacey had come out swinging.

"We cut the footage of Jakub Cermak," he said. "He violates FCC standards."

"I don't know who he is, and I don't care," Stacey said. "But I'm bringing a cameraman out this afternoon to get my commercial, as planned."

He pulled his head back and stared at his phone for a moment before returning it to his ear. Was she stupid? "I already made a commercial. I beat you."

"You developed an interest in your apartment, sugar. Now I get to film a better version and make it clear that the work was performed by Stacey's Interiors. And since Alyssa Compton no longer works here, you'll be getting a cease-and-desist letter on airing your ad."

Had she actually called him "sugar"? He wanted to say "You can't be serious," but she clearly was. He yawned into the phone. "Today's not good."

"Be there or I'll have the landlord let me in. I have a letter from an attorney to wave in front of his face."

Nick thought for a moment. You scored by sheer speed or by faking out the goalie. Sometimes you needed to do both. "Four o'clock?"

"One," Stacey said. "On the effing dot. Per our agreement."

Nick laid his phone down and thought for a moment. Then he retrieved the shells from the top of the living room bookcase and carried them back to the safety of the closet in Sammy's bedroom. "Hey, buddy. I gotta do a thing. I can't let this woman beat me. You would understand." He looked around the empty room, gave the doorjamb a single pound, and walked out.

Nick pulled everything out of his kitchen cupboards while he called his landlord. "Javier? Nick Sorensen. You got any open apartments?"

Forty-five minutes later his first teammate showed up, answering his second emergency text in a week. It was Leif. "You're a spontaneous guy, Nick." He clapped Nick on the shoulder. "You decided to move? Before practice?"

"Yeah." Nick raked his hand through his hair. "That building two blocks north? My new apartment's in it. I haven't actually seen it yet."

"You . . ." Leif shook his head. "I saw movies, ja, in Sweden? But they didn't prepare me for Americans."

Nick grinned. "The landlord's waiting over there with the keys. How 'bout we take something big on the first trip so we clear some space?"

Leif blew air out. "How 'bout we leave the big things for the defensemen? You have boxes yet?"

"No, Devin is going to pick some up. Shit, I didn't ask him to get tape. You think he'll think of it?"

Leif shrugged. "He's captain for a reason."

"Because he thinks of tape?"

"We'll find out." The goalie swept Nick's toaster and fancy ass coffeemaker off his counter and headed out the door. Nick threaded a couple of dining room chairs over each arm and followed him, pulling the apartment door shut with his foot as he left. By the time he'd met with the landlord; signed the lease without reading it because he trusted the guy, who rented to several Red Wheels—and because Nick obviously had not learned a thing; dumped the chairs; and walked back to his apartment, four other guys were there.

Leif explained the situation. "Nick is having an American moment. He is moving to a new apartment because the frontier is closed, and he has a restless spirit."

"Yippee-ki-yi-yay," Nick said.

"You're moving on an emergency basis because the frontier is closed?" André said.

Nick shot Leif a look. He'd have to insult herring later to even the score. "You want to grab one end of that sofa?" he said.

"Yeah, okay," André said.

By noon everybody who could come was there—ten guys, an assistant coach, and the locker room manager. They'd moved the living and dining room furniture and decided that the most efficient way to move small things—dishes and books—was in boxes that they passed from one guy to the next. They weren't close enough together to just hand them over, but it was easy to walk a box a few yards to the next guy and get back in place before another box got to you. When they passed the Christmas tree from hand to hand, the guys sang "O Little Town of Bethlehem."

In Nick's old apartment, Devin looked up from where he was taping the bottom of the last box he'd brought. "Should I run out for more? I forgot how much more stuff you have now."

That was Alyssa's fault. "Yeah, there's still a bunch of books."

The assistant coach walked in, waving two empty boxes in front of him. "The boys in the new apartment are unpacking. They said you can rearrange later if you want, but for now you've got fresh boxes."

"Well, that solves that," Devin said. "Perfect timing."

Nick took the boxes and dropped them on the kitchen floor. "You guys are all right."

"We're actually pretty amazing," Devin said.

"And gooood-looking!" André called.

The apartment emptied quickly. His teammates could do to a closet what they did to a buffet. When their Czech rookie walked out with a floor lamp gripped in his fist, the place was empty. Nick turned slowly. Was there anything lonelier? At the same time he could see the desolate white hole it had been before Alyssa, as well as the elegant space she'd created for him. He stepped into his bedroom and ran a thumb down the soft butter wall. He wasn't ever going to forget her painting this room. That was a good night. He walked back out, checked the balcony lock, and thought of Alyssa trapped out on that balcony when he'd gotten home from a road trip. He wouldn't mind stepping out of the shower again and finding her trapped out there, rapping lightly on the glass. But that wasn't going to happen.

He walked into Sammy's room, crossed to the window, and rested his hand on the sill. He addressed the middle of the room. "I'm moving, Sammy. It's a two-bedroom, but I need to tell you I'm going to use the spare bedroom as a studio. You can hang out there if you want." He fell quiet for a moment. "I hope you'll come with me, but I got to be honest. I didn't feel you over there. In the new place. Maybe 'cause there were guys there you didn't know." He took a couple of breaths. "Anyway, if this is goodbye . . ." He blinked and hit the windowsill with his knuckles, trying to hurt them so he wouldn't feel. "If this is goodbye, I love you, man."

He walked to the closet shelf and took down the shells. He had large hands and could handle three shells. Besides, he needed to get over to the new place to thank the guys. He stepped into his empty living room with its soft moss walls. Shit, he really didn't want to leave this place.

Devin popped his head around the corner. "Hey, we're having a team meeting at four thirty." He picked up on Nick's mood, and his head disappeared, the sound of his footsteps trotting down the steps hollow, as though the whole building were empty. Nick just needed to thank the guys and hand his landlord the old key, and then he could find out what this meeting was about. Probably their penalty killing. That had been weak.

Nick grabbed all three shells and stepped into the hall, pulling the door shut with his foot. He was halfway down the steps when he caught sight of the landlord at the bottom, letting Stacey in the door to the lobby. The same cameraman trailed her and shot Nick an apologetic look. Nick trotted down the rest of the stairs, cradling the shells tight to his chest.

"I'm here to film my commercial," Stacey said triumphantly. Her upper lip, puckered with wrinkles that channeled her lipstick, pulled up in a sneer.

274

"Have fun," Nick said. "Also, screw you."

Stacey clucked her tongue against her front teeth. "Such a mouth on this one. But your apartment is going to make me money."

"Ooh," Nick said, feigning confusion. "You're in the wrong spot if you want to get into my place. I don't live here." He cocked his head. "Of course, you don't have any right to enter my new place because nobody from your firm decorated it."

Stacey gave him a hard stare and then stalked upstairs and pushed open the door to his old apartment. She stared into the empty space and then wheeled. "You're willing to *move* to avoid a tasteful commercial that features your living space?"

"I'm willing to do about anything to win."

She stared at him, her jaw tight. "Does he still have a lease for this space?" she asked the landlord.

"He does not," Javier said cheerfully. "And I can't tell you where he lives now. Tenant confidentiality." He smiled broadly.

Stacey hissed and began to descend the staircase, trailing one finger on the railing. When she spoke, it was to Nick. "You are a deeply disturbed man."

"You have no idea," he said. He nodded at the door, and Javier opened it for him. Nick strode off, cradling the shells. Stacey had fired Alyssa and cost him a chance with her.

Without all this Stacey crap, he *knew* he would have had a chance. They were good together, and not just in bed. Alyssa wasn't only gorgeous, she was fun, and she'd cared enough to confront him about his coffeemaker. She'd tried to pull him into a better place—had literally given him a better place to be. But she'd been clear at Devin and Vanessa's party—she wouldn't go out with him because of what had happened with the design firm. He'd gotten her fired.

He turned at the small fountain with a bench, behind his new apartment. It was the kind of landscaping no one would ever use, but it made the space more attractive. Maybe he should try painting it sometime. He wasn't very good with water. Monet had him there, although he'd never admit that to Alyssa.

And then he looked up, and there she was.

CHAPTER THIRTY-EIGHT

Alyssa watched Nick walk down the sidewalk. He was cradling the shells Tyler had given to him and Sammy, but he had a curiously triumphant look on his face. She had come here to explain herself and, she hoped, to make amends, but his expression was infuriating. He looked . . . smug.

"Oh, hi," he said, as though he hadn't seen her coming, and set his jawline to "extra full of himself."

"Hi," she said. "Taking your shells for a walk?" He flushed. But he stopped and looked at her, and now she had to say something. She gripped the folder she'd brought with both hands and realized that she probably looked like a chipmunk. "I wasn't sure I was clear when we talked on the phone."

He started walking again, and she fell into step. "You were pretty clear."

She inhaled sharply. He wasn't going to make this easy. "I thought maybe I sounded ungrateful. It's that I've wanted my own agency for forever. I used to draw floor plans for my doll house and rearrange the

277

furniture. When I was little—before Dad gambled and lost everything."

"You played with the furniture instead of the dolls?" That made him smile.

She laughed. "Well, yes. And I painted throw rugs and little pictures for the walls. I was definitely more into the decor."

"Hey, would you carry one of these shells?" he asked. "I don't want to drop them."

"Oh." She stuck the folder under her arm and took the top shell, aware of what it meant to him and that he was trusting her with something important. "Um, why are you carrying them around the block?"

He grinned. "I moved. Today." She stared at him. "Stacey still wanted to film at my place. I thought beating her to it would keep her from making her own commercial, but she doesn't give up." He glanced at her ruefully. "Usually I like that in a person." Alyssa laughed. "So I called the guys and moved this afternoon."

"For real? You just . . .?"

"The contract says she can film in a space you designed and I live in. But I don't live there. So I win."

She let that sink in. "You would do basically anything to win."

"Yep."

They'd reached his new apartment building. The layout was different from the place she'd been in. It had stairs on the outside and was five stories tall. "My apartment's on the top floor," he said. "Do you mind carrying that up?"

"No, that's fine." She hadn't said what she'd come to say, but now there were the stairs and hockey players milling around, and she was throwing elbows out to protect that shell, and when they got to the top floor with its dark blue carpet and white walls, there were even more players.

"Home sweet home!" Devin called cheerfully, and opened the door for them.

Nick walked in first and looked around. "You guys did good. Looks nice."

Like heck it did. The dining table cut off the natural traffic flow; the coffee table was too close to the sofa; and the floor lamp was turned so the task light would illuminate a spot on the floor, not his book if he sat on the sofa. The coffeemaker was as far from the sink as possible and . . . maybe not even by an outlet? The walls were white, the—

"Alyssa?" She blinked up at Nick. "Can I have the shell?" His hand was out, and she realized he'd already put the other two on top of the bookcase. Which was four inches off center. What was *wrong* with these guys? She handed him the shell and watched his butt as he walked to the bookcase, and his shoulders as he stretched up to put the final shell in place. He turned back to her, and she was aware of the other guys milling around, so she said, "Nice view," and Jakub, the Czech in the loud shirt, laughed out loud. She flushed and waved toward the large windows that overlooked the building across the street. That wasn't where she'd been looking, and Jakub had obviously noticed.

"What's in the folder?" Nick asked.

Her face grew hotter. Circulation was really a stupid idea. "I thought if I showed you . . ." And that was dumb too. He wouldn't care about pink cookies or champagne flutes. She blinked and held the folder across her chest.

Nick turned to his teammates. "Hey, I owe you guys big time."

There was a rowdy chorus of agreement. "You can thank us with beer!" someone shouted.

"I'll do that. Now head out and let me talk to Alyssa for a minute, okay?"

The guys moved off cheerfully, slapping one another on the back and coming up with slogans for a Red Wheels Same-Day Moving Service, several of which were obscene.

"You want to sit down?" Nick asked, waving toward the seating area. "I have a really nice sofa."

"You do," she said, and walked over and sat on its edge, slanting her legs princess-style.

"I'll probably need to have it painted," he said. "The room. Not the sofa." This was as close to him being a chatterbox as she'd ever seen. Was he . . . nervous?

"I felt like I wasn't clear on the phone, and I just wanted to explain."

He nodded. He was listening. Was there an actual chance to fix this?

"I've wanted to have my own agency ever since I was a little girl. I also wanted to own a magical pony farm, of course."

"Naturally." He smiled and it warmed his eyes. He sat beside her, turned toward her, his shoulders bulky and his pants straining over his thighs. His hands rested on his knees, and she tried not to stare at them, but they were good hands—strong fingers, gentle when they stroked down her abdomen.

She cleared her throat and hastily flipped the folder open, fanning it so he had some idea just how much it contained. "These are my launch party ideas. I had plans for invitations and decorations and . . ." She hesitated, then decided to tell the truth. "I've probably spent a dozen hours choosing which font to use."

He smiled again. "Which one did you choose?"

She threw a hand up. "I haven't decided yet! I don't have the party all planned yet. I'm not ready."

He nodded slowly. "You didn't really want to start a business. You just wanted to have a party."

That made her bristle. "No," she said deliberately. "I wanted to start a business, but I wanted to do it right. *Appropriately.* And I wanted to do it my way, when I was ready."

He studied her. "How would you know when you're ready?"

That made her stop. "I'd know. And I wanted to do it by myself."

"You'd do it *all* yourself?"

"*Yes.*"

"No help from anybody? Nobody giving you a little boost?"

"No. I'm capable of doing it myself."

"I don't think you are." She stared at him. His voice softened. "Alyssa, nobody can go it alone. You know what would happen to us if we took the ice without Leif?"

"He's the goalkeeper, right?"

Nick sighed. "Yes."

"Probably the other team would score a lot. Although maybe it wouldn't matter because apparently your defense is really bad anyway."

He raised an eyebrow at that.

"My stepdad has opinions on defense."

"Coach says pretty much the same thing." He sighed and raked a hand through his hair, and that was just an unfair distraction. "Everybody needs a team, Alyssa. You'd have an easier time in life if you understood more about hockey."

"I'd be better off if I took swings at smelly toothless dudes?" She flushed. That might have been a little unfair, but Nick grinned.

"That's not the whole game," he said. "It's not all that fun." He pondered that for a moment. "Okay, yes, it is." He grinned at her again, and she had an urgent desire to find a block of cheddar and grind it on his face. She was pretty sure his jaw really would slice it cleanly. "Can I ask you something?"

She nodded and he turned serious. "Why can't you have a launch party now?" She blinked and looked down at her folder, which she held in a death grip. "Lemme see," he said gently, and when she didn't move, he pried her fingers up, one by one, a smile playing at the curve of his mouth where the softness of his lips gave way to rugged stubble. He slid the folder out, raised his eyebrows for permission, and when she still didn't say anything, he flipped it open.

"So you've got a lot of stuff in here," he said. He lifted three stapled pages with possible icing recipes for the writing on the cookies. "Some women don't put this much thought into their weddings."

"Oh yes, they do," she whispered. He grinned at her and looked through the folder with attention. It made her feel naked. Not the fun kind.

"You have seriously planned the kickoff," he said. "I will grant you that. But Alyssa, why not open your agency? Since you clearly want to? Have the party, make the"—he turned a paper upside down and then back again—"whatever this is. There are links to rental places—tents, chairs. Tulle by the yard?"

"It was just a thought," she said. "I don't think I'd use any tulle, though."

"Huh. Well, it's important to know your stance on tulle. We always make sure we have that straight before we hit the ice."

She rolled her eyes. "You're making fun of me."

"No! I'm . . ." He ran his eyes comically back and forth, looking for a way out. "I'm making fun of tulle." He smiled, pleased with himself.

She bumped his shoulder, an easy, intimate gesture that she immediately regretted. "I'm sorry my competitive streak ruined your party plans," he said, waving the folder and then handing it back to her. "And I'm glad you explained. In my defense, I didn't know you had your entire life planned out in detail. I genuinely thought I was doing something nice for you."

"You were," she mumbled. "But it felt like you were taking over." He nodded and they sat silently for a moment. "It's such a gamble—starting a business. So many of them fail. Long shots don't pay off."

"You're talking to a guy who fell fifteen thousand feet in a tooth-paste tube. I'm a living long shot."

"But that would never happen again."

"I sure as fuck hope not," he said. "This is about your dad, right?" She didn't say anything. "He gambled on things he couldn't control. A throw of the dice, right? Or the turn of a card? You're not gambling on chance: you're betting on yourself."

They sat silently for a moment. She'd never thought of it that way before. Then he stroked the back of her hand with his thumb, just once, but she felt it everywhere. "I wish you'd gone out with me." He looked back and forth between her eyes. "I know I should have apologized for getting you fired. I mean, I didn't *know* you'd gotten fired because you didn't tell me, but once I heard about it, I should have reached out. The commercial wasn't just to beat Stacey. It was also the apology." He smiled ruefully. "A little late and inarticulate, maybe."

"It's not your fault she fired me."

"It is, though. It was because of the flowers, right?"

"Yeah. Well, a lot of things, really. But you can't be blamed for sending flowers!"

"You were mad about it, though." He shifted. "You said so at Devin's. I thought we . . . hit it off." She flushed. "You were willing to have sex with me, but not let me take you out to dinner." His tone was faintly accusatory, but he looked hurt, and his stubbly chin was so close that it took a moment to process what he'd said.

Then she was outraged. "That's *not* fair."

"I mean, if you only like me in a pirate costume, I could buy another one." He waggled an eyebrow at her.

She gritted her teeth. She didn't need to visualize the way those striped pants had curved over his thighs, over his bulge. "Are you kidding me? How could you have asked me out? And then blame me for saying no? Of *course* I said no!"

Anger flashed in his eyes. "So you blame me for getting you fired, you refuse an apology, and you blame me for making an ad for you to try to help you. Which, by the way, was a pain in the ass for all the guys. I made them show up to help me twice this week, with no notice."

"I don't see how you—"

"You slept with me twice. You let me play with your breasts and lick your clitoris—"

"Oh god," Alyssa murmured.

"But you're horrified at the idea of being seen in public with me?"

She stared at him. He opened his mouth, but she stood so she could tower over him. She realized too late that this move put Rip Van Winkle right by his mouth, and the things he'd just said had definitely gotten her attention. Rip Van Winkle was wide awake and looking for trouble.

"You were mad at me for giving you the wrong contract, which, might I remind you, *you* never bothered to read." She stuck a finger in his face. "Don't say anything—it's true. And okay, I screwed up, but it was sort of understandable, and you could have been nicer." Her eyes flashed hot with tears, and she flushed with humiliation. She would not cry in front of him.

"Alyssa," Nick said, and she looked away, a traitor tear spilling down her cheek. She wiped it angrily. "Did you think—"

"Oh, hell." He threw his arms around her and pulled her into his chest, which was warm and smelled so familiar. His sweater was soft, probably cashmere, and was going to have mascara all over it. She pulled her head a little lower so her eye was lined up with a black stripe across his pecs. That would minimize the damage to his woolens. She sniffed and he tightened his grip on her and leaned in by her ear so his breath tickled and sent shivers racing down her spine.

"I wasn't mad about the contract, Alyssa." He said her name almost as a reproach. "How could you think that? That I'd be so distracted by your ass in my bedroom that I'd stick a pack of condoms in the fridge, but I'd turn around and refuse to see you because of an honest mistake? Without even talking about it?" She sniffed and tried to raise her head, but his arms held her tight. "How could I ever be angry with you?"

She talked into his hard chest. "You need to let go of me, or I'll be using your sweater as a tissue."

He dropped one arm but kept the other draped around her. "That's not as big a threat as you think it is." He smiled. Then he angled his head. "You've been angry with me for getting you fired, though." He held his hand up. "I get it. The card I wrote to go with the flowers was stupid. We had mind-exploding sex . . ." She smirked. He gave her a look but went on. "But then you looked so unhappy afterward."

She was confused. "I was definitely not unhappy. I mean, I may not have been able to form a coherent sentence afterward, but . . ."

He laughed softly and waggled an eyebrow at her, but then he said, "In the car. You just sat there."

She looked up at him, searching his face. "You saw that?" He nodded. "I was looking at your apartment building and thinking about what I'd done to you."

A look of understanding crossed his face, and he squeezed his eyes shut for a moment. "It's why I sent the flowers. Why I got you fired."

She ducked her head and fished in her purse for a pack of tissues, then tried to wipe her nose discreetly.

"Can I ask something else?" he said. She nodded hesitantly. "After the engine fire—I thought you might call. Or at least text."

Her mouth twisted to the side. "I really didn't know until several days later. I kind of feel like we can blame that one on my stepdad." He nodded agreeably. "When I did find out, I was afraid I might . . . reopen a wound."

"Like I wouldn't know about it if you didn't mention it?"

"Well, it sounds silly when you put it that way."

"I guess I just wanted you to care," he said. He flushed. "I have a home because of you. And I don't just mean the apartment." He struggled to find the words. "I'm glad I'm alive. I'm glad I'm with you." He leaned forward and kissed her neck, his stubble brushing her skin. She shivered involuntarily and glanced sideways in time to see his smile. He moved his lips around to the front of her throat, then nibbled down and over to her collarbone. He placed his large hands on her waist and pulled her against him, then pushed under her blouse and skimmed her abdomen lightly, raising goose bumps.

CHAPTER THIRTY-NINE

Nick put one finger on the front of her bra, deftly released the clasp, and cupped her breasts as her bra slid back. He caught her nipples between his fingers and gently pulled, rising slightly to trap her mouth under his own and ride her down to the sofa. And he was on her, the bulk of him, heavy and hard, and his erection already throbbing against her leg.

She wrapped her legs around him and ran her fingers lightly over his back, skimming over the skin where it dipped between muscles. He groaned. She bit gently at his earlobe, and his breathing became raspy. "Time for a fridge run," she whispered, and he looked at her. "That's where you keep your condoms, right?"

He laughed, a deep-throated, masculine laugh that made his belly move, and since it was on top of her, she felt as well as heard it. "No, I just needed to stash them fast that night. I didn't want you to think— you know."

"That the decorator wanted to talk about Michelangelo?"

"Yeah," he said, nibbling along her collarbone. "That."

"Oh. Oh. Get a condom. *Now*."

He grinned at her and stood, then stared out at his new apartment, arranged by his teammates. "I don't know where I keep them."

"Wallet?" she said.

"I never replaced that one." He exhaled in frustration, then looked down at her and ran a finger along her lips. "I'll be right back." He ran into the bedroom, and she heard drawers opening and slamming shut.

He ran back out, doing a comic-style run with exaggerated arm movements. "Bedroom cleared!" He dashed into the bathroom, and hard objects rattled and more drawers slammed shut. "Bathroom cleared!"

"Where were they?" Alyssa said. "Before?"

"In the bedside table. And a drawer in the bathroom."

"And they're not now?" He shook his head, standing in the living room, a look of wild desperation on his face. She stood and grasped his shoulder firmly. "Remember, you're the guy who found Mrs. Gilroy. You can do this!"

"I want to do that," he said, waggling an eyebrow at her. "That's why I need the condom." She flushed but put her hand out flat. It took him a second to understand, and then he laid his hand on it and shouted, "Go, team!"

"Yeah, that!" she said, a moment too late.

He laughed and turned in a circle, then launched himself at his bookshelf, feeling around behind the books. "So that makes no sense," Alyssa said. She walked into his new bedroom. The walls were white, but the windows were great, and the trim was better in this apartment—a little more graceful and Old World, and more in keeping with his furnishings.

"I hear no sounds of ransacking!" Nick called desperately. "Do you think we could just use a sock?"

"No, we can't use a sock!"

"I have some big ones. Like a boot sock."

She cracked up and rummaged through his drawers, peeked under the bed and on the closet shelf, then moved into the bathroom. He'd trashed it. He'd dumped his things into the bathtub—razor, toothpaste, comb, steri-strips to hold the edges of cuts together. But definitely no condoms. It suddenly occurred to her that maybe he was out. She didn't want to think about the implications of that.

"Alyssa. Come here." His voice was strained.

She popped out of the bathroom and found him in the kitchen, standing beside an open cupboard door. He tipped his head toward it and she shot him a curious look, walked in, and tilted her head. She didn't see anything but some plates one of his teammates must have unloaded for him. He put his hands on her hips and gave her a boost, and she saw bowls on the top shelf, and inside them, a box of condoms. She grabbed it out. There was a note attached:

Nikolai! I put these for you in a safer place. Hope you had to look for them before you used the bowls. Ha! Ha! Jakub

"We have got to trade him," Nick said. "Note to self: never give your teammates access to your stuff."

Alyssa grabbed the condoms from the box and ran in a circle through the living room, letting the strip trail like a kite. He caught her in two steps, grabbed the strip with his teeth, and picked her up. She squealed as he carried her to the sofa, shoved her pants off, and grunted. "I think we were here," he said, running his thumb over her clitoris. She didn't try to answer.

They knew each other's bodies a little now, and she relaxed into him, confident in this. In *them*. She knew the man, his body—his heart. And oh, did he know her. He used his hands and then his mouth on her, then raised his head to look at her from between her legs. "More?" His voice was husky. She shook her head and grabbed him by the hair to guide him gently up. He grinned, then cupped her breasts and sucked at her nipples. She feather-stroked his abdomen, raising a growl from him, then ran her hands lightly over his body, giving him goose bumps before she bent to lick his cock. He groaned and shut his eyes, then tangled his hand in her hair and made deep throaty noises. She loved feeling so safe with a man who made such a feral sound.

Finally he stopped her, ripped a condom off the strip that lay discarded by the sofa, and shoved it on himself. He wrapped his big hands around her shoulders and pushed her gently down, then settled, heavy, over her and plunged in, bringing her knees up. She moaned softly and gripped his shoulders. She was exactly where she wanted to be, enveloping him, moving with him. No more misunderstandings. Moving together in every sense. He thrust hard, rhythmically, and when he nipped at her neck, just once, she was there, spasming around him. He came with her, shuddering with a low moan.

After, she lay with her head against his chest, hair splayed. "So that was unexpected," she murmured into his neck.

"Really? Because we seem to do this pretty often for people who've never gone out on an actual date." She leaned her head back and smiled up at him. He pushed her hair back. "There's a lot of this stuff," he said, wrapping her hair into a ponytail in his fist and leaning down to kiss her.

"I was never mad at you for sending flowers," she whispered. "I didn't blame you that I got fired."

He smiled at her, and it brought a warmth and light into his eyes. "I'm going to ask you again to let me take you to dinner." He flipped her hair back and forth and caught sight of his watch while he did it. "Oh, crap. I have a team meeting." He stood, dumping her gently on the sofa and chuckling at the look on her face. "Sorry, babe."

She dropped her head. Oh god. What had she done? She'd made the phone call when she hadn't thought he was speaking to her.

"Nick." She scrambled for her bra and panties, not sure which to put on first, and finally opted for the panties—Wedgewood blue with lace panels on the sides and not much coverage at all, really, but at least she wasn't technically naked now. She grabbed her blouse from under the sofa and held it, balled, in front of her chest. "I can't go out with you."

CHAPTER FORTY

"What?" he said, clearly confused. And maybe a little hurt. "Why not?"

Alyssa scrambled into her clothes, hopping on one foot to shove her foot into her shoe. She had a coat somewhere and didn't know where it was, and Nick was still standing there, somehow taking up more space than he had before. Like he was one of those shape-shifting toys that started off as a sexy hockey player and ended up . . . as an angry sexy hockey player.

"Alyssa."

She hopped into her other shoe. His shoulders were wider. How did he do that? And his hands looked bigger. Stronger. "Did you know that when Michelangelo sculpted *David*, he said he gave him the hands of a killer? Because you always think of David as the underdog, right? Because of Goliath. But David killed him." Was that babble? She was babbling.

"I'm not sure I want to talk about Michelangelo with you right now."

She gave him a tight smile, too bright, and caught sight of her coat beyond the sofa. "I need to go."

"Damn it, Alyssa." He caught her arm, his fingers holding tight. "What's going on? Is this some sort of game to you?"

He was right there, the bulk, the spicy scent, the stubble, his eyes searching hers. How could she hurt this man? But she already had, and there was no way to stop it.

"I was trying to do the right thing," she whispered. "I meant to help."

"The hell?"

"I made a phone call. It may have been inappropriate." She didn't know how to explain beyond that. "You'll see," she said. "At the team meeting."

"The meeting?"

"I sort of called it."

He leveled a stare at her, and she understood for the first time the intensity he must bring on the ice. What it would be like to see those eyes burning through his facemask, hurtling toward a goalkeeper. It was a little terrifying. "I was trying to help," she repeated, then said, "I'll drive separately." She snagged her coat and fled.

The drive to the rink was miserable, and not just because she'd had one final chance with Nick Sorensen, who was essentially perfect. He was a man who would shove water lilies in a bowl to help her get a wedding reception ready in time. He had grooves in his shoulder muscles that begged her fingers to explore. He could discuss art. He could do that thing with his tongue.

But he also was parked closer to the building and therefore pulled away first, which resulted in her following him through the city, turn after turn, while he stared into the rearview mirror. A taco truck pulled between them at one point and she relaxed, but then it peeled off after a few blocks. Nick pulled into player parking, and she couldn't follow, which was actually a relief. His hard stare in the rearview mirror, wondering what she'd done, what she'd brought to his workplace, had unsettled her.

Alyssa pulled into visitor parking, grabbed the box in her back seat, and thought about Pandora. She'd already unleashed chaos into the world—at least, into her world. And she hadn't even opened the box yet. A security guard expected her and let her in, then escorted her through corridors, bright with red paint and oversized action photos, to a lower corridor and into a room with a ping pong table and massive, sweatproof sofas. It wasn't a conference room; it was an area off the locker room where players were likely to be gross and smelly.

The entire team was already there when the guard walked her in and nodded to her, then stepped back into the hallway, the sound of his retreat echoing. She was acutely aware that she would never have seen this inner sanctum in ordinary circumstances. Nick stood near the ping pong table, rubbing a thumb along its edge. The players were in street clothes except for five of the guys who were already in practice uniforms, including skates. They just walked around in here on blades—she'd have to find out what the floors were treated with.

Devin was one of the guys already dressed. The captain stepped forward. "You may be wondering why I called this meeting," he said. "But only if you're Nick." Nick frowned and glanced around. "Everybody else knows what this is about." Nick shot Alyssa a hostile look, and she tightened her grip on the box she held in front of her chest. "Alyssa came to me a few days ago with some information she got from Dr. Simone Lavigne in the Art Department at Boston College." Nick looked confused. "You want to take it from here, Alyssa?"

She nodded to him and stepped forward, her fingers digging into the box. "I . . ." Her voice squeaked. Good god, she'd squeaked in front of an entire hockey team. She didn't know a lot about hockey, but she was pretty confident there was no squeaking in the NHL. She cleared her throat. "Nick almost finished degrees in art and art history. He actually has enough credits to get the art history degree if he'd just file the paperwork." She pulled a sheet off the box, stepped forward, and shoved it at him, then retreated a couple of steps.

"He said he had one project left to do for the art degree and that he wasn't going to finish it. So I called Boston College and talked to Dr. Lavigne." She didn't look at Nick, but the hairs on the back of her neck responded to the way he lowered his head. He was standing with his feet apart, balanced. An athlete ready to react to whatever was coming his way. And right now, she was the one hurling it at him. "Dr. Lavigne said the last assignment was to create a large-scale painting, at least four feet by eight feet, of a group of at least five people." She looked out at the Red Wheels, standing silently. "Nick was painting some of his teammates in Boston: Dragan, Tyler, Eric, Luka. And Sammy."

The guys looked at one another, mouths tight. *He'd been painting his best friends. The guys he'd lost.* They shifted. This was uncomfortable territory.

"I talked to Devin about the project," Alyssa said. Nick's head swung fast, and he gave the captain a hard stare. He was clearly not enjoying the team meeting. "And I bought a new canvas."

"We'll never replace those guys," Devin said softly. "But you've got friends."

Alyssa walked to the center of the room, brushing past Nick's strong and hostile shoulder. She wasn't sure where the guys had stashed the canvas, but Leif and Jakub stepped into the trainer's room and emerged with it. It was huge, and Alyssa had draped it in a white tablecloth. That seemed dumb now—a reveal of nothing. Devin found the easels she'd dropped by his house earlier, and set them up—two because the canvas was so long. "You have people, Nick," she said, pulling the cloth off. The canvas was incredibly empty. So was Nick's face. This was a bad idea.

The five guys on skates clomped forward. "Where do you want us?" Jakub, the Czech left wing, said. He swiveled his head back and forth. "Both my sides are my good side."

André turned his back. "I think my ass is probably my good side."

Someone called, "Considering what your face looks like, that's true!"

The guys fell in, jostling, resting elbows on one another's shoulders, lining up. "The team decided you should paint us because we're the best-looking!" Devin called. He was answered with hoots and a barrage of friendly abuse.

Alyssa walked forward with the box and opened it. "Paint!" she said with a false brightness that even she could hear.

Nick reached in and took out a brush. He rubbed the bristles with his thumb. "Did you consider asking me if I wanted to paint the last piece? If I even cared about the degree?"

"It crossed my mind," Alyssa admitted. "And I'm so sorry if this isn't the best way. But I thought you needed a little shove."

"I needed a little shove." His voice was flat.

"Just like you thought I did, with starting the business," she admitted quietly. "I was pissed at first too. But then I realized—that push you gave me, it was a gift. And I wanted to do the same for you."

"She's tougher than Moose McFarland, man!" someone called. "Don't mess with her."

"If I'd wanted to discuss this with the guys, I'd have discussed this with the guys," Nick said, his gaze steady on her. He did not look friendly.

"It's a good thing we found out," the backup goalie called. "We didn't know we were hanging out with a guy who hadn't finished at least two college degrees."

"Yeah, you're bringing down our educational average," someone called, then dissolved in laughter.

"We can talk about your loss," Devin said, moving out of the line of guys in uniform to put a hand on Nick's shoulder. "Or how you're feeling. We're your team."

"Yeah," Leif called. "I mean, if we can talk about the boil on Filip's ass . . ."

"How's your ass doing anyway, Filip?" someone shouted.

"Better. Thanks for asking."

"An unfinished painting isn't something we can't talk about here," Devin said gently. "Come on, Nick. Grab your brush and get to work." He stepped back into the line with other guys, expecting to be immortalized in oil.

Nick stood there, then dropped the brush back in the box.

CHAPTER FORTY-ONE

"You should have asked me," he said again.

Alyssa squeezed her eyes shut. "Yes, I should have. I'm sorry. But what about your monologue about how everybody needs a team?"

"My monologue?"

"You said nobody can go it alone. But that's what you're trying to do."

He leaned forward and hissed. "I've asked you out three times, and you keep saying no. And then slept with me anyway."

Jakub howled in glee. One of the guys shoved his face into the chest of the guy next to him to muffle him.

Alyssa flushed furiously. "Because you didn't *really* want to go out with me."

He stared at her and threw his arms out in a what-the-hell gesture. "I really did."

"Well . . . I know that now," she said weakly. "I thought you were mad at me. Anyway, you have to let people help."

"I have to?" His voice was still wooden.

"Yes. Because of Gretzky."

He cocked his head.

"Because he scored a lot of points. I don't know how many . . ." Here the whole team gasped. "Sorry to shock you," she muttered.

"My god, Nick. You sure you want to go out with her?" Devin called. Alyssa gave him mean squinty eyes.

"There's a reason they give a point for an assist," she said. "That's the player who helps set up the goal."

"I'm aware," Nick said. There was a faint smile in his eyes. Finally.

"Because people need help. Even what's-his-face Gretzky."

"This is killing me," André moaned.

Alyssa pushed on. "How many goals do you think he would have scored if he'd been out there by himself?"

"About the same number," someone muttered.

"You are not helping," Alyssa said crisply. "Nick, you'd understand more about life if you understood more about hockey." And now he was smiling, recognizing his own speech to her when she'd been angry about the ad he'd placed without asking her.

She thought for a moment, then took a deep breath. "I'll have a launch party if you'll paint these guys and file for your degree." She stuck her hand out.

The corner of his mouth quirked up. "Will there be pink cookies?"

"Oh, you know it."

He looked at her, then shook her hand. When they let go, she slapped a brush across his palm.

"Can you explain later about the rejecting me thing?" he asked.

"Oh, that was me being stupid." She waved a hand. "I'm over that."

"You're not stupid anymore?"

"Well, realistically there will be bumps. But if you wanted to ask me out sometime, I'd say yes."

"Huh." He reached into the box and pulled out the palette and the tubes of paint. He turned one over in his hand. "This is a good brand."

"Don't leave her hanging, man," Devin called.

"She really, really deserves it," Nick said.

"That's kind of true," Alyssa said.

Nick set up his palette, starting with white in the center. He clearly knew exactly what he was doing. He fiddled with the easels, lowering them, and then called, "Be handsomer. You're gonna ruin my art." The guys grinned. "Did you bring a beret?" he said to Alyssa. "I can't paint without a beret."

"Oh! I didn't know. I . . ." And then Alyssa realized that he was kidding, and gave him a gentle shove.

"She is worse than Moose McFarland," he called to no one in particular. "You guys were right."

Nick grabbed a pencil and sketched in the outline of the five players in uniform in front of him. Before he was done, the other guys had dressed in uniform and filtered over, one by one, to stand with the initial five. Every guy on the team. "You're just making more work," Nick grumbled, but his eyes were wet. He sketched them in, filling the canvas to the edge, as though it were a photograph taken too close. It gave the composition energy and immediacy.

"Hey, Schlicky!" Devin called to the equipment manager. "We need some sticks over here."

Schlicky understood and grabbed a handful of the nearest sticks, not bothering to make sure each player got the length and curvature he would have used while playing. The entire Detroit team tapped their sticks on the floor, the way they would on the ice during a game. The clatter was a show of support—what they would do when an injured player finally stood up. Which was more or less what Nick had just done, Alyssa thought.

"You know," he said, turning his head to talk to her, but keeping his eyes on the canvas, "I enjoy eating."

"Um . . ."

"It's a thing I do every night. Have dinner," he clarified.

"Oh."

"Sometimes it's nice to have company." The team tapped their sticks on the floor again, encouraging him. "Would you guys knock it off? This is embarrassing enough." They grinned and tapped harder. "You see what I put up with?"

"Yes," Alyssa said.

"Yes, you understand what knuckleheads they are? Or yes, you'll go to dinner with me?"

She grinned. "Both."

"Whoo-hoo!" Jakub shouted. "Finally."

Nick grinned back. "It may be a while before I get out of here, though," he said. He mixed a little blue on his brush, and Alyssa wondered at that—there was nothing blue in front of him. But then he painted a shadow under André's cheekbone, and it was perfect. He was using primary colors and bold strokes, and the team was coming to life in front of him. "Although Frank doesn't have his bridge in. That'll save painting a whole bunch of teeth." The guys laughed and bantered, and Nick painted. When Alyssa edged closer, he draped an arm around her.

"Too bad we don't have an octopus," one of the guys said. "That would look cool." There was a general murmur of agreement.

"An *octopus*?" Alyssa said.

"Yeah, the fans throw them on the ice sometimes, especially during the playoffs," Nick said.

"Oh, I am not falling for that! There isn't a chicken, but there's an *octopus*?" She snorted.

"Stay still!" Nick grumbled as the guys collapsed on one another with laughter. He looked sideways at Alyssa. "You should probably talk to your stepdad again."

Eventually she pulled up a folding chair and sat to watch while he worked. The team joked but stood still.

Alyssa texted Emma: *I need flowers for my launch party.*

Emma responded immediately: 😍 😍 *For your business?*

Alyssa: *Yes.*

Emma: *What kind of flowers do you want?*

Alyssa: *Fanciest thing you've got. I want fancy flowers.*

Emma: *Have you thought about color yet?*

Alyssa: *HAVE WE MET?*

Alyssa: *I have a whole folder.*

Alyssa: *We should meet to discuss.*

Emma: *I can be wherever you are in ten minutes.*

Emma: *Realistically that's a lie, but you get the idea.*

Emma: *Dinner?*

Alyssa: *I'll check in tomorrow. I'm having dinner with Nick tonight.*

Alyssa: *It's an actual date.*

Then she dropped her phone in her bag and ignored Emma's urgent buzzing. When Nick had done enough for the day and the room was heady with the stink of paint, they cleaned the brushes together in the trainer's room, their hands bumping each other's under the stream of water.

"Maybe I did need a push," Nick admitted.

"Maybe I did too," Alyssa said.

"Buuck!" Nick clucked. Alyssa pulled back and stared at him. "Hey, I think I hear the chicken."

She opened her mouth to tell him what she thought about that, but he stepped into her, wrapping her in his arms and sliding his tongue into her mouth, hot and hungry. The brush in his hand tangled in her hair, and she dug her fingers into his shoulders and moaned. "I have to practice." His voice was husky.

"No, you're already very good."

He laughed and lifted her hair out of his way with one hand and nibbled on the side of her neck. She moaned again. Someone cleared his throat in the doorway—Schlicky, the equipment manager.

"Can you stall them ten minutes?" Nick said, rubbing his thumb across the hairs at the back of her neck without touching the skin. Alyssa shivered.

"Nope," Schlicky called cheerfully. "Better get out on the ice."

"I'm not dressed yet," Nick said. "I have to get out of my street clothes."

"I could help," Alyssa whispered.

"None of that now," the equipment manager called. She flushed, realizing he'd heard. Although it probably wasn't any worse than the position he'd found them in, locked in an embrace by the sink. "There'll be plenty of time for your dinner and romance," he shouted over his shoulder, and from somewhere in the locker room a couple of sticks tapped their encouragement.

Alyssa sank her forehead against Nick's chest in embarrassment. She'd done so many *inappropriate* things. And everything had worked out anyway.

"Later I want to paint you," Nick murmured into her hair. "Nude. And I'll need to take breaks."

"To study Michelangelo?"

"Yeah. You've made me appreciate my art education again."

"Mmm. That's a really good plan." She stroked Nick's rough jaw-line and kissed him. Schlicky was right—there would be time. She and Nick were finally on the same team.

EPILOGUE

The next Thursday, Alyssa left Party Barn at four o'clock. Janet had given her blessing to the early departure and refused Alyssa's offer to make the time up later. As she left, Janet threw her arms over her head and shouted, "The future is now!"

A kid looking at Batman paper plates with his mom grinned and gave Janet a thumbs up. Alyssa rolled her eyes, but she smiled.

She drove to the bakery with the marble floor and old-fashioned curved display cases, because charming things should be encouraged. Its window boxes were filled with pine boughs studded with candy-striped lollipops and when she opened the door a warm rush of gingerbread and vanilla and nutmeg hit her. No candle in the world could, well, hold a candle to the real smell of a bakery.

There were three people ahead of her. Two were high school students who bought a single cookie each—the after-school crowd was here. Then a man with a white beard bought a red velvet cake and two dog cookies. The woman at the counter said, "You tell Waggsy and Ernie that I said woof!" A repeat customer, then. That was always a good sign.

Alyssa pulled the folder of launch party plans from her bag and took a deep breath as she stepped to the counter. "I'd like to order a cake and some cookies for an event after the holidays."

The woman gave her a bright smile that turned radiant when she saw the sketch Alyssa held out of cookies shaped like Persian rugs, exquisitely decorated with three different designs in the same colorway. She "oohed" appreciatively. "You want the cookies to look like this?"

"Yes. And I'll need pink macarons, and I've seen your pressed shortbread—can I get some with the heart design?" The woman pulled out a large order book and began making notes.

A woman moved into line behind her. Alyssa turned. "I'm sorry to hold you up."

"Oh, no, this is fun to eavesdrop on," the woman said with a genuine smile. "Everything is so elegant! Did you design those cookies yourself?"

Alyssa nodded. "I'm an interior designer." The woman sighed, as though that were something to aspire to. She was in her twenties and wore sensible pants that would survive a hundred washes and a turtleneck sprinkled with a holly design. It had a small mustard stain on the sleeve. Her whole outfit probably cost what Alyssa was going to pay for three cookies. Young, just starting out—possibly in need of a designer. Alyssa pulled a business card out of a box in her bag. She had to pry it apart from the one behind it—she'd picked them up at the printer's that morning. "Here's my card, if you ever need it," she said.

"Oh." The woman held it with two fingers, as though she wanted to return it, then decided that wouldn't be courteous. She flashed that smile again and tucked the card into her wallet without looking at it. "I don't think my life is quite as stylish as yours." There was no sting in the way she said it. "Although I do have quite a jewelry collection, if you count all the macaroni necklaces."

Alyssa laughed. "You're a teacher?"

"Second grade."

The clerk had a question then, and Alyssa turned her attention back to her order. When it was all logged in and she had a credit card out to pay the deposit, she pointed to a tall two-serving cheesecake drizzled with caramel. "And one of those please," she said. Then, to the woman behind her: "My boyfriend is coming over for dinner tonight." She enjoyed that word in her mouth. *Boyfriend*.

The teacher smiled and eyed the cheesecake as the clerk boxed it. "It has your elegant flair."

Alyssa laughed. "What about you? Big plans for the weekend?"

"I'm buying my own birthday cake, so no. I've given up on romance." Alyssa winced. "But I haven't given up on chocolate."

"Chocolate is definitely more reliable than men," Alyssa said, taking the cheesecake box the clerk held out. "But you never know. Maybe someday the right guy will drop down out of the clear blue sky." They exchanged a smile and Alyssa left the bakery. The December air was crisp. She blew out, just to see her breath rise in front of her. Everything felt right. She was having a launch party. She had ordered pink cookies, and they were going to be spectacular.

Nick had just settled into a black vinyl chair at the arrivals lounge when the airport address system announced that the flight from JFK had landed. Early? Unbelievable.

But sure enough, mere minutes later, there the guy was, outlined against the late afternoon sun so that his shadow fell halfway across the airport. Huge, as advertised. Somebody from the front office had planned to pick him up, but the team had heard a lot about this guy and wanted to get a look at him, so Nick had volunteered.

He stood and slipped his phone back into his pocket. The guy must have recognized him because he lifted a hand.

"Hey, I'm Nick Sorensen," Nick said when they reached each other.

The guy grabbed his hand and shook. "Angus MacGillivray."

Nick smiled at the brogue. "We don't get a lot of players from Scotland," he said.

"You know, Murrayfield has a stadium that holds sixty-seven thousand people."

"Really?" Nick said, surprised. That was three times the size of Detroit's rink.

Angus grinned at him. "Of course, they use it for rugby. The hockey team plays across town at a rink that seats three thousand."

Nick laughed and clapped him on the back. "Well, welcome to the NHL. I understand you're going to shore up our defense."

"That I am," Angus said. The guy didn't lack for confidence. Nick liked him immediately.

Alyssa buzzed Nick in and lit the candles while he was walking up. He came through the door holding a bottle of wine by the neck, his other arm cradling a profusion of white ranunculus, red roses, and evergreen sprigs with pinecones. Her heart leapt. This felt like *home*—the chicken smell wafting from the oven, the flicker of candlelight, and Nick's open face as he held the flowers out to her. This. This was everything. She took the flowers from him and they kissed.

"Everything go okay at the airport?" she asked as she grabbed a vase from a cabinet.

"Yeah. The guys will be texting me all night."

"What did you think?"

"We should just position him on the runway and keep opposing teams from landing. Be an easy way to win a game."

Alyssa laughed. "That big?"

Nick grunted and opened her fridge. "Oh, cheesecake!" She smiled and, out of nowhere, her eyes dampened. "Hey," he said. "Everything okay?" He shoved the fridge door shut and peered at her, a look of alarm on his face.

Alyssa nodded. "I'm just happy."

"Yeah, cheesecake does that for me, too." She swatted his arm with the back of her fingers and he laughed.

"I called you my boyfriend today."

"Yeah?" His voice was husky.

"Yeah. It was the first time I said it."

"Do it again."

"Huh?"

He stepped forward, the bulk and warmth of him a breath away. "Call me your boyfriend."

"What if I won't?" She gave him a flirtatious smile.

He grabbed her by the rib cage and wriggled his fingers in her armpits. "Then I'll tickle it out of you," he shouted over her squealing.

"Stop it, boyfriend!" she said, then squealed again as he gave her one final tickle.

"I liked that," he said. He stroked her hair, smoothing a stray strand. "Hey, girlfriend?"

"Yes, boyfriend?"

"You want to eat later?" He waved a hand toward the oven. "We could let it cool. You know, so we don't burn our tongues."

She adopted a mock serious tone. "I see. We should wait to eat for safety reasons."

"Yeah. Tongues are useful. You don't want to injure them."

"Because you need them to talk, right?" She flipped the oven off, then opened the door to check the chicken. It was done, and would be fine to sit there for a bit.

Nick stepped forward and wrapped his arms around her, then kissed her collarbone. "Exactly."

"What shall we discuss?" she asked. "Perhaps… art?"

"I like that idea." He kissed his way up her neck.

"Anyone in particular?" she murmured. "Caravaggio? Vermeer? Picasso?"

He kissed the tender skin behind her ear. "Not Picasso." His voice was raspy with need. "He got parts in the wrong places. I like to get them in the right place."

"Oh." Her voice was almost a moan. "Maybe Titian then? Or Cassatt?"

He picked her up and set her on the counter, stepped between her knees, and tangled his hand in her hair. "I thought we could concentrate on Michelangelo."

She wrapped her arms around him, pulling him even closer, and found her home there.

ACKNOWLEDGMENTS

So many people have helped in the production of this book. Thanks to Tracy Paulsen for walking me through the world of interior design and to Carmella McNeill for putting us in touch; to legendary sportswriter Bob Hammel for answering questions about professional sports team flights. Thanks also to Adam Ryan, MD; Dan McMahon, MD; and all my friends who've had serious leg injuries for sharing their recovery stories. Ouch, you guys! Please be more careful on the stairs.

Marissa Doyle, Jenna Estes, Larissa Hardesty, Ena Jones, Robin Lemke, Cyndi Marko, Deena Viviani, and Holly Westlund—you're the people I trust to bring the bail money, and why I need it in the first place. Calla Devlin, thanks for listening to me talk about plane crashes all the way through dinner. People who have supported me and made me a better writer include Liz Bedia, Anne Bingham, Jan Blazanin, Eileen Boggess, Linda Egenes, Jill Esbaum, Sarah Gilbert, Amy Grimm, Wendy Henrichs, Marcia Hoehne, Delia Howard, Becky Janni, Cheryl Fusco Johnson, Carolyn Lieberg, Mary Beth McFarland, Janet McNally, Rachel Martin, Sharelle Byars Moranville, Sarah

Acknowledgments

Prineas, Karen Schulz, Cynthia Weishapple, and everybody in the Iowa region of the Society of Children's Book Writers and Illustrators (SCBWI), and on the Discussion Board. Doug Cole, Brian Kenny, and Andrew Ryan should have been thanked before.

I'm throwing roses at the feet of my agent, Kate McKean, who's an astonishingly good sport and sometimes needs to be. The team at Alcove was phenomenal: editor Jess Verdi, who made this book so much better and also laughed at my rum ball story; Thai Fantauzzi-Perez, Rebecca Nelson, Dulce Bortello, Mikaela Bender, Mia Bertrand, Megan Matti, Stephanie Manova, Doug White, Matt Martz; and copy editor Jill Pellarin, with whom I had a lengthy discussion about what pirates sound like. No pirates were hurt in the making of this book. Ana Hard created the cover. Thanks to all of you.

My cousin Kira Vermond and I challenge each other to include something specific in each book, and our editors never know what it will be until they see the acknowledgments. Kira asked for a gerbil this time. Mrs. Gilroy was written in as an homage to her and in memory of Georgia, who left her cage whenever she felt like it and was Mrs. Gilroy's hero. Wait until you get my challenge for your next book, Kira. Game on!

My nemesis, Jerry Schlick, aggravated me on the day after Thanksgiving for years. RIP, Schlicky. And to Steve Reser, who turns out to have done half the things I blamed on Schlicky—here's your three-step head start.

My sister and I grew up in a home filled with stories, good food, a white cat, and a black dog. Thanks, Mom and Dad. Patrick, you're my happily ever after. And Brigid and Joe, I love you more than hockey.